T0328746

"Where's your sense of mystery, Bunk?"

"Don't have any. It's all as plain as your face. These've gotta be love letters, if you ask me."

Eamon shook his head in wonderment at his friend's lack of curiosity, then proceeded to rip one open.

Dearest lover it began in the most beautiful handwriting he had ever seen.

"Look at the flow, will you," Bunko said with new interest. "Jesus Christ. Nice, high uprights. Philosophical bent. Forward slope. Nice. Very nice. But the e's are blotted. There are tight and powerful secrets here. No question. And then you throw in those repressed, vivid understrokes. Sexual dynamo who isn't getting any. But that's just my opinion. Now let's take a look at that old signature . . ."

They had both taken the standard graphology course at Quantico, and though the class was taught primarily for purposes of spotting check forgery they covered the psychological basics as well. The remarkable fluidity ran several pages, both sides, and culminated in an emotionally-shrunken *Netti.*

"What I tell you?" Bunko barked with satisfaction. "Emily Dickinson with a vibrator. Now let's get the hell out of here."

Eamon Wearie didn't even debate pocketing the letter, even if it was a direct violation of postal code. For in that regard he was like most people, liking nothing better than a good mystery . . .

DEAD LETTERS

SEAN McGRADY

POCKET BOOKS

New York   London   Toronto   Sydney   Tokyo   Singapore

An *Original* Publication of POCKET BOOKS

POCKET BOOKS, a division of Simon & Schuster Inc.
1230 Avenue of the Americas, New York, NY 10020

ISBN: 978-1-5011-2378-8

First Pocket Books printing July 1992

10 9 8 7 6 5 4 3 2 1

POCKET and colophon are registered trademarks of
Simon & Schuster Inc.

Cover art by Simon Galkin

Printed in the U.S.A.

*For the faithful—especially
Mike, Corinne, and Ingebjorg*

. . . It was a nothing that he knew too well. It was all a nothing and a man was nothing too. It was only that and light was all it needed and a certain cleanness and order. Some lived it and never felt it but he knew it all was nada y pues nada y nada y pues nada. Our nada who art in nada, nada be thy name thy kingdom nada thy will be nada in nada as it is in nada . . .

   —Hemingway, *"A Clean, Well-Lighted Place"*

DEAD LETTERS

1

Lieutenant Eamon Wearie was at his desk, under sputtering fluorescent tubing, appearing washed-out and pallid in the empty brightness of the Command Post. It did not help that he had been out drinking with Bunko again last night and that he had not bothered, or had not really been able, to shave this morning. The amazing thing was that Bunko looked just fine, all rosy and newborn, just like he did every day, as if a bottle of Jameson were just milk in his coffee. If it wasn't for the classic honker, a nose like a topographical map of the moon, cratered and broken, the ungodly color just as livid, one might never guess.

Eamon popped another Tylenol and swiveled his chair to face the terminal, its greenish field flickering with out-of-date information, old addresses from the Super Removal Book that had been checked and rechecked, post office boxes that had been rented out under assumed names, which were long dormant and practically untraceable. Still, it was worth a look. Too many times the answer was just staring back at you in that electronic limbo. The Bureau had done their job, all right. They'd staked out Box 446 at Los Angeles General Delivery with a video camera for three months—and nothing. No one showed. The last occupant was listed as one Fred Roy of 1237 Myrtle Avenue in Del Ray, which, of course, turned out to be a load of manure. No such address. And the name sounded made-up as hell. The things that had been gathering in the box were all of the same ugly suit: kiddie porn in spades. The usual garbage. Homemade newsletters and magazines. Published in the basement or the garage, or perhaps even in the family rec room. Most of it done on desktop computers, that newest, most fabulous rage among the nation's pederasts. There was the slick stuff too, twenty-dollar picture books in living color, airbrushed into *Playboy* shape, from all over, but most often from Bangkok and Manila and that marvelous capital of commerce, Hong Kong. And let's not forget about the Polaroids. From his sick little pen pals. Everything wrapped in brown shopping bag paper. Without return addresses. From all over the fruited plain. Some fucking world, all right.

The problem was, this photo didn't fit in.

This guy wasn't a molester. He was a raging psychopath.

The Bureau had taken the whole business seriously enough, putting in a few hundred man-hours, but they'd finally given up, classifying it as a dead case. So Tony Montrez, their chief liaison at the Bureau, had just shipped the whole thing back to them with a little note: "Lotsa luck, guys. It's all yours now. Sorry we hurt your feelings." The last part referred to the way the Bureau wrangled the case away from them in the first place. The official FBI file on the Executioner must have been two hundred pages, mostly log-ons, unreturned phone calls, paper treading. All because of one photograph. It just wasn't the kind of photo you easily forgot, even if you dealt with these sickos all the time. Bunko had it now, and he was shaking his head in disgust. The Bureau had blown it up many times, enlarging particular areas, and Bunko was thumbing through the glossies at his metal desk, making thoroughly Bunko-like sounds:

"Jesus. Jesus Christ. Jesus Fuckin' Christ. Wouldja look at that? Where do these wormy pukeheads come from? Ugh. Fuckin' Christ. Makes you just want to sob, for the love of Christ. Just like that fuckin' Gacy thing in Chicago. Remem-

2

ber? John Wayne Gacy. The Killer Clown. There's no understanding this kinda thing. Fuck. We're in over our head, pal."

"I'd have to agree with you there," his partner replied.

The eight-point characters were blurring into no use, blinking back from the IBM screen like just so many matrix dots. Lieutenant Eamon Wearie got up, still feeling hung over and vaguely miserable, to walk over to the long slat of Plexiglas on the opposite side of the room. The opaque and incredibly streaky plastic, double-paned and mercifully soundproof, provided a window on a strange, antlike world of bureaucracy and menial tasks.

Below, three stories down, the United States Postal Service's Eastern Seaboard Mid-Regional Bulk Management Depot, Postal Depot 349 in Permanent Sector 4D, known simply as the Depot to the confederate blue-gray jackets roaming the myriad aisles below, was in Phase Green, which meant that it was a full-throttle Wednesday, that in fact the Depot was fully operational, with 258 of the 263 A-shift employees reporting for duty. This greatly pleased the Depot's supervisor-in-command, Captain Marcus Brown, whose affinity for numbers and on-time charts was a source of much private disgruntlement among the troops. The captain, though, was not the sort of man who paid much heed to the nuances of the human condition; in fact, he rarely acknowledged the frequent "Good morning, sir!" that punctuated his appointed rounds, rounds he made with a military bearing, as if he were some German field marshal on the lookout for scuffed shoes or missing buttons. This priggish, fifty-five-year-old lifelong bachelor, his perplexing toupee the color of ripe tangerines, forever shifting out of place, was given the moniker Captain Anal Retentive by Bunko several years ago—in a ferocious and legendary squaring off—and it was just one of those things that stuck. The many men and women Marcus Brown had suspended or docked pay from or merely demerited for what he always succinctly termed "slacking" immediately took to the shortened Captain Anal, and it was not long before they used this lowly beginning to develop a most elaborate nomenclature, referring to two of Captain Anal's assistant supervisors—Arthur Marlens and Arthur Lyon—as Big Pucker and Little Pucker. Ferdie Jenks, another of the assistants, was known simply as the Donkey, and poor Ada Frompner, Marcus Brown's long-suffering executive secretary, was cruelly nick-named the Enema. From there it did not take a great leap of imagination to inflict a name change on the Command Post itself: Assholes Incorporated won wide, happy approval.

Eamon Wearie looked out the dirty glass and saw what he always saw: a mess of confusion. The Depot was not like any other place on earth. Its very vastness was seemingly infinite, never to be fully held by the eye, sprawling out in every direction, at least the size of four or five football fields, perhaps the largest single-structure warehouse in the world, though that was only speculation. But surely it was ugly as hell, from the tar paper roof to the cement walls to the hospital ward paint job, dark and absolutely unwieldy, never having been touched by the sun's warmth, not a window to the outside in the entire place, as sick and grim as the workhouses in Dickens, as Byzantine as the catacombs, lit by naked, dangling bulbs, half of them burnt-out on any given day, just plain dark and unforgiving, man. This was not even to mention the constant roar—earplugs were standard issue—of the huge old sorting machines in Docket C 14, *chunk-chunk-chunk-chunk*ing away, or the groaning of the big diesels pulling into the loading docks with their twenty million pieces of mail a day, or the sound of the jets a mile away, at Patton Field, big army cargo numbers that touched down alongside the stripped-down DC-8s the Service used. And that was not to mention the letters and parcels themselves, mailbags in great heaping clumps, stacked to the ceiling, awaiting removal and processing, not to mention the boxes, every size and weight, mostly wrapped in ordinary brown paper, thousands of them crammed on rumbling conveyor belts—as intricate a network as the lattice of roadway running outside the Depot—ready to be weighed and shipped out, just waiting for the worker ants, for those beefy young men on their electric dollies to swing by.

It was just too much. With four main shifts, with over a

thousand people employed, the noise and commotion never died down. Twenty-four hours a day. Every single day, including Christmas and the Fourth of July.

You never got used to it. Eamon looked down to see one of the drug-sniffing canines pawing and yapping at one of the packages on one of the belts. Nothing so unusual. They made small finds all the time, an ounce here, sometimes more, sometimes a pound or two, marijuana usually, sometimes coke, not much else. There were ten of them, sleek black animals, roaming freely, through the dark aisles, around the cosmic clutter, in packs or alone, mostly unattended, at play in a strange universe. Their trainer, Special Agent Friedberg, took care of them. Friedberg was very, very weird. No one else was allowed to go near *his* dogs. At all hours you could see him down there in the pit, two in the afternoon, four in the morning, it didn't matter. Dishing out food. Talking to them. Even kissing them. Eamon thought Bunko was right about Friedberg. Bunko said, look at his eyes. He's cashing in, Bunko said. *He's cashing in.* And when Eamon started looking into Friedberg's eyes, he saw it, too; it's a funny color and it's a funny little swirl, and there ain't no other way you get it. But what was the sense in reporting it? What was the sense in doing Anal any favors? None that he could think of.

All too, too fucking much. The dogs. They were always stepping in to their old, hard doo-doo. It was all over the Depot, even though they had a twenty-man janitorial unit. Those guys always looked buzzed-out as they rode the motorized mops—gadgets that resembled John Deer lawnmowers—down the narrow passageways, usually plugged in to their Walkmans, their eyes just as often hidden behind a pair of menacing Ray Bans. The whole stinking place smelled heavily of the ammonia and Lysol; giant drums of the stuff were piled up in A Quadron, rusting and leaking, frightening with their Danger warnings and crossbones, as if it were one of those nuclear waste sites you were always reading about.

And the ceiling leaked. Big time. Men were always on the roof with hot tar and even plastic tarpaulins. But it didn't matter. The Depot had been built in 1923 in the heady months following Coolidge's inauguration, but Eamon Wearie could not, in all the nine years he had spent in this gray netherworld, recall a time when fiscal restraint wasn't the watchword. They were inundated with official memos from everyone from the postmaster general to the Postal Rate Commission to Anal's own rather tedious use of the office Xerox; always the call for swift Draconian measures, as if a reduction in paper clips and staples was going to wipe out a yearly two-billion-dollar deficit. *Yeah, right.* There never was going to be a new roof, and so the water dripped down, in hundreds of spots, like some kind of mad Chinese water torture, *drip-drip-drip,* plopping down into the makeshift buckets and garbage cans, spilling over onto the floors and Formica tables, onto the counters and onto the mail. That is why the only serious requisition Eamon could remember was the Maytag dryer. It was Bunko's idea, and wouldn't you know it, the damn thing did the trick. Some thought that the wet and moldy letters might combust if they were left in too long, but so far that had never happened.

Trish never used to believe him when he'd tell her the stories. Sure, she'd seen the building from the outside, like an out of control shopping mall, why even the parking lot was something to look at, but he could never get her the security clearance to see the shit, the real shit, and so she had remained skeptical. She loved the part about the dead letters best of all, the whole fucking idea of a letters' graveyard, where the Service had buried every postcard, letter, Manila envelope, box, crate, and object stamped **UNDELIVERABLE** and **NOT FORWARDABLE** since the Pony Express days. He'd tell her about the steel capsules in Quadrons B and C, the most authentic and spooky time capsules in the world, holding the older stuff, going all the way back to the 1840s when they first started saving derelict mail. The sheer numbers—numbers he knew by heart—boggled Trish's mind: He told her that the volume in the good ol' U.S. of A. averaged out to 525 million pieces a day, working out to an unbelievable 160 billion a year, and that out of that, two hundred thousand would become classified as "lost" in a single day. The problem was that they all managed, every single blessed one of them, roughly seventy million of them per year, not including the magazines and junk mail, to find their way to Postal Depot 349, known simply as Dead Letters to the rest of the country's mailmen, and there just wasn't enough space and time. Sure, they routinely incinerated the periodicals and advertising crap, and after a given time, 180 days to be exact, they even disposed of postcards and Christmas cards and other fairly obvious refuse.

But Trish wasn't all that interested in methodology, or the very exacting problems of inventorying and tagging. She wanted to know more about the stories. He had to admit there were great stories about Dead Letters. Stories about gold and unclaimed jewels. And Trish was always interested in those things that glittered. There were other things as well that intrigued her, that set the violet eyes aflame with greedy wonder, that had her asking questions with unusual vigor. For example, she couldn't believe it when he told her the stuff about the cars. The Mercedes sedans had come over on the *Queen Mary* in 1957, five of them, long, dark gangster-looking things, and somehow—who can figure it?—went unclaimed at New York customs. Winding up at Dead Letters for keeps two years later, to be covered with sheets, their odometers—set back in those gorgeous walnut dashboards—sharing the same odd mileage: 000008. Trish was anxious to know how long it might take to notice their disappearance. And Eamon had to tell his wife the weird truth, which was that he had no idea.

He didn't bother to tell her about the deterioration. Such a waste. The water damage. Rust rotting out the bottoms. Their engines would probably just fall out if they ever tried to move them. And then to tell about what happened to their beautiful leather interiors. Those king-sized rats gnawed through anything. What could you do? After the poisons and traps, totally useless, they tried cats, but that turned out to be one humongous blunder. The Labrador patrol had a field day.

Yeah, Trish. It's too bad she couldn't see the beauty of Dead Letters. She was just like most people in that regard. Always wanting to know about the Treasury money and uncashed IRS checks and lost credit cards. She loved the stuff about the Ring Room. Just couldn't get herself to believe in those tables of diamond rings. Glowing ever so darkly. It was a strange thing, all right, but it was a screwy world and there were a lot of screwy babes in it. And all too often when an engagement went sour and the oaf demanded his ring back, they just stuck the rock in an envelope—almost always licking on enough postage—and conveniently forgot to put an address on it. Just send it off into the void. **RETURN TO SENDER. RETURN TO SENDER.** Then they could always tell the poor sap: *Hey, what can I tell you? I mailed it a week ago. I guess the darn post office lost it.* Eamon had heard it all.

Yeah, Trish was just like everyone else. No wonder she ran off with a scumbag lawyer. Her big violet eyes were always browsing through expensive catalogs, pausing over expensive things, things they weren't likely to buy on the salary of a federal postal inspector. Not that he made bad money, no, not at all. It was just she wanted to live like something out of "Lifestyles of the Rich and Famous." At the end, when she asked him to steal, he understood, without passing too much judgment, that something had gone out of her soul, and it saddened him, that's all. He had been telling her about some of the more lucrative freight, the big-screen TVs and crates of porcelain that sometimes landed like beached whales at Dead Letters, and she just said maybe he wasn't looking at things right, that maybe he should reexamine the situation a bit. Think smart, those were her words. It really didn't surprise him. Nobody really seemed immune to it. Even some of the blue-gray boys had taken. Only a few cases of French champagne. And those Havana cigars, he almost forgot about them. Still, it wasn't his deal. He slept better not touching.

Besides, it wasn't the obvious riches that interested him. He liked the intangibles, the very weirdness of the joint. Here he was thinking of the Unpublished Novelists' Hall of

Fame. Bunko came up with that one; it was the kind of thing Bunko was good at. The Hall, the size of a small high school gymnasium, shelved thousands of battered manuscripts, cramped one on top of the other, collecting dust and rotting away, as if they were housed in some library time forgot. Usually the books had postage due, or else the publishing houses had just refused to accept them, refused even to open them. From the looks of things, there must have been millions of people writing potboilers in their attics, with half-baked dreams of bestsellerdom and immortality. Sometimes, when Eamon had nothing better to do, or he just wanted to escape Anal's microscopic scrutiny, he'd go back there, into that cobwebby old sector, and pick out a book, any old one. He had to admit they usually weren't much good. Although, on one occasion, he did find a terrific spy novel, a real Cold War number, brilliantly plotted, the whole cat-and-mouse thing, that had him heading back to the Hall for days.

To Trish it was just a mountain of decaying paper that could be recycled, for all she cared. She had absolutely no sense of wonder. He tried to tell her about the coffins they'd found on a routine seizure in the back of Q F, but she thought it was disgusting—wouldn't hear a word of it. The only time she came close to getting it was when they came out of that Indiana Jones movie. The last scene took place in this huge government warehouse—an amazing structure, he had to admit—brimming with crates and barrels and all kinds of interesting shit, tempting Trish to ask if the Depot looked anything like that. He spread out his hands and told her to imagine for a moment, to imagine a place at least a hundred times more vast, at least a hundred times more beautiful. She just shook her head like he was so full of shit, it wasn't even worth bothering with. Well, that was her problem. Wherever the hell she was these days.

Captain Brown didn't want Red Team wasting time with that damn case. The field agents had not had a very good month, their Twin K efficiency was lagging far behind the March numbers from last year, and it was paramount that

Depot 349 not stand out in any way from the seven other BAG A-1 priority processing plants in the country. In three months his transfer and promotion, subject to executive approval by the Board of Governors—but practically a done deal—would land him in the cushy confines of the D.C. Bunker. It had taken him thirty years to get in that enviable position, from his humble beginnings as a letter carrier—enduring the hazards of neighborhood dogs and inclement weather—moving up through the ranks with laborious slowness. He worked in the mail room and then the postage stamp windows in Eastfield and Rosedale Terrace—fifteen years of tedium, explaining the difference between first class and second class so many times that it was as if God Himself were personally tormenting him—until he was named assistant postmaster at Dundalk, only to catch a momentous break when Postmaster Higgens used a shotgun on his wife. It just proved that if you played it by the book, you were sure to be rewarded. Sometimes it just took time, that's all. He knew the men did not often like him—after all, he did not socialize with them, nor did he like to waste time talking about the Orioles or telling jokes about eating pussy or whatever. But it was much more important to be respected than to be liked. He thought, then, of Richard Milhous Nixon, someone he very much admired. They didn't like Dick either, that's what that Watergate nonsense was all about, by God, but history, the historical record, would show him to be a great president, you could be sure of that.

They had a job to do, and he wasn't running any damn Club Med. He believed that the measure of the man was in being held accountable. That was the key. Still, every once in a while, when the work didn't consume him, which wasn't very often, there stirred in the captain something very much like misgivings. In these brief, almost grievous, moments he would fill with the realization he had missed out on something important in his life. And then he would fill with shame. The men did not know he still lived with his mother.

"Attention, Red Team," he announced across the rows of steel gray desk in that nasal twang that further amused his detractors and had contributed to an earlier nickname. Elmer Fudd still enjoyed a small following.

Bunko was at Eamon's desk, going over that file, an exercise in futility. They had squat. The scrunched-up Marlboro butts, filling two Styrofoam coffee cups, attested to that, and the last thing they wanted was to deal with Anal. They each made a spontaneous grimace, such was their enthusiasm. At least they still talked to him. That was more than Blue Team would do.

"I really don't want you two wasting time on this Executioner business. We have much more important things to do. And besides, if the Federal Bureau of Investigation can't solve it, I don't think you two cockroaches are going to get anywhere."

Marcus Brown stood in front of the door to his office, waiting for Bunko and his inevitable thunder. Arthur Marlens and Arthur Lyon immediately came to his side to show solidarity. They were meek men—Lyon had suffered a heart attack only six months earlier and became upset at even the mildest hint of confrontation—known for their clipboard-toting ways and a certain unfounded hysteria they exuded over missed deadlines. Unfortunately, they also looked like an advertisement for low sperm counts: ingenious hairlines, seemingly originating at the base of their necks, which they swept up over their crowns with verve; eyeglasses, thick and myopic-looking, in styles and colors made popular by scientists of the 1950s; not to mention their sad little bodies, which, if nothing else, prompted their wives to lead inordinately rich fantasy lives.

Master of the dramatic effect, Bunko glared at the three Mouseketeers and slowly lifted himself up from his chair. He was six five, 250 pounds of unrestricted manhood.

"Captain," he said, not too loudly, "do you know the meaning of the word *glabrous?* That's right, glabrous. I'll give you a minute."

Eamon watched his partner with something like awe. Bunko was the best of the postal elite, and he had learned much from him over the years, but that didn't begin to tell it. Just bigger than life, that's what he was. A dinosaur in the

Age of Unisex. A whiskey-slurping, chain-smoking son of a bitch. Married three times. Even had his own detective agency before he somehow found his way onto the force. Saw action in Vietnam too, early on. Wounded. Decorated, all sorts of shit. Still kept his hair like he was in Saigon—just that the bristles were gray now. The man made his own fashion statement, that was for sure. Who the hell else wore white socks and black shoes these days? Those fucking bowling shirts. And unlike the other guys, who kept their guns safely tucked in their desk drawers or in the glove compartments of their unmarks, he always kept his .38 secured under that all-purpose checked sport coat. Just added to the effect.

"*Annnnnnt.* Time's up. What's your answer gonna be, Captain?"

"I'm not playing your silly stupid games, Bunko. What do you think this is?—'Jeopardy'?"

At that, Little Pucker and Big Pucker smiled like a couple of weasels. Bunko appraised them with equanimity. Man, he hated dealing with higher-ups. The only happy bastard was the one who didn't report to anyone. No boss. No wife. No nothing. Hell, if he hadn't gotten himself in all that financial trouble way back when—hell, he must have been the only private dick in history to file Chapter Eleven. All spilt milk now.

"Well, if you faggots must know, glabrous means, like, you know, smooth, very smooth. Like a baby. I woulda thought you faggots would know that. Knowing how you guys like to shave your legs and all."

Captain Brown thought he was doing a fairly admirable job of holding in his displeasure; Bunko deserved a formal reprimand, but he knew better than to do that.

"What's your point, Lieutenant?"

"My point, Marcus, is that turds like the Executioner always seemed to get their whole bodies waxed. Not a hair on the pervert. Not a hair. Did you notice that?"

"I can't say I have, Lieutenant. And I really don't care anyway. I want you and Wearie doing other things. There must be thirty other worthwhile cases on your desks. Ones that are solvable. Unlike this one. Look at the excellent job Yellow Team did on that pyramid scheme in Jersey. That's the kind of thing I like to see—"

"Oh, Jesus Sweet Fuckin' Christ. Marcus, not another pyramid. Oh great. Just great. You just saved another lonely lady her last five dollars—"

"I'll have you know, Lieutenant, that this pyramid scheme was bilking citizens out of hundreds of dollars. Now that seems mighty impor—"

"Oh, give me a fuckin' break, Marcus. I got me here a real lunatic. A guy that's killing and mutilating little boys. That's what I call fuckin' important. In fact, I can't think of anything more important in this whole mighty universe. Can you?"

"Well, Lieutenant, we don't know if he's really done anything at all. It could be a gag for all we know."

"A gag? You got to be out of your fucking ever-living mind. This is the real thing. That photograph is as bad as it gets. And I want to have carte blanche on it, or else I'm going to write a nice little letter to the D.C. Bunker. And I'll just bet, if I'm not missing my guess, they'll sure want to know why we've lost interest in catching molesters and serial killers."

"Lieutenant, you're exaggerating. We have no idea if he's killed anyone. We have no identification of anyone in that photograph. We have a meaningless post office box in L.A. Rented out under a false name. I repeat, that's all we have."

"Marcus," Bunko said in a lower voice, perhaps more humbly, "give me a few days. That's all I ask."

Captain Brown never knew how to handle his field agents. They simply were not regulation. They hadn't come up the ranks the old-fashioned way, had no particular affinity for the business of mail—and at the moment, looking around the Command Post, it seemed to him that they were a rather offensive lot. How he dispised their lowly cigarette smoke, lingering there like so much yellow smog, and the way they kept at it, even though he had addressed memos to this very topic. He noted the small annoyances about, the doughnut boxes and cheeseburger wrappers, no better than a bunch of cops, no pride whatsoever. They were unkempt, untidy men in wrinkled two-bit suits. But he did not want to be too hasty here. He did not want to make a tragic mistake. He realized, however fractiously, that his inspectors had been schooled in ways that he had not. While he might know every inch of the mail delivery system—why, he had had a direct hand in the implementation of overnight delivery and the highly successful policy of first-class zoning—they were, on the other hand, students of criminology, either having gone through the Justice Department's rigorous BETA program or the Bureau's own demanding training at Quantico. He had to admit, however begrudgingly, Bunko knew his turf.

"Lieutenant, I'm going to go against my better judgment and grant you a little leeway on this one," he said, thereby surprising both Lyon and Marlens, who seemed to experience trouble suppressing their disappointment. "But let me just add, I expect you and Wearie to maximize your energies on the other pertinent matter constituting your caseload. I cannot emphasize the importance of improving your G-quota numbers. That is all."

What a color-coded moron, Bunko thought. "Thank you, sir. Yes, sir," he managed, his scorn very much evident.

Captain Brown made one last assessment before turning his attention to Blue Team: It's a shame really. Wearie's not such a bad lad. With the right partner . . .

"Now, Blue Team," the captain said as gently as possible, not wanting to trigger another episode with Lipsick. "That was excellent work on NELCO Bio-Tec Laboratories. We have a clear photo opportunity here. I was hoping to have the *Sun*'s Morty Yaphank in this afternoon. You know, a few poses with the haul. I just wanted to check on your availability."

Frank Shoe and Barry Lipsick, comprising Blue Team, had—quite by accident, really—discovered a big-league methamphetamine operation. What happened was simple enough: They were wandering about out front, by the loading docks, trying to cop a smoke out of Anal's sight, when Shoe—a very observant person in the first place—

14

noticed something odd about the shipment on the platform. Forty crates of orange-flavored vitamin C from NELCO, supposedly a generic drug firm working out of Wilmington, were awaiting transport. All Shoe said was, "Hey, do you smell anything?" And Lipsick immediately understood: All those fucking orange vitamins without a whiff of Sunkist was mighty peculiar. The next thing to get their antennas going was the labeling. These babies weren't en route to drugstores or supermarkets, as you would certainly expect, but to individuals with names like John Smith and Mary Doe. Having established "just cause," Shoe took out his lading blade and stripped one open. Rock Candy City.

Shoe was ready to give the captain Blue Team's answer. He directed Eamon, whose desk was located directly across from them, to inform Anal that they would not be taking part in today's media festivities. He said, "You might add, Wearie, if you're up to it, that we find the whole notion demeaning and foolish."

As silly and repetitive an exercise as this had become, Eamon repeated Shoe's instructions almost to the letter.

Before retreating back to his office, the captain replied, "Very well, then. Wearie, you might tell Blue Team for me that the photo opportunity will go ahead as scheduled. With or without them."

This awkward relay system had been going on for eight months, and Eamon was not at all keen about being put in the middle of their little contretemps. He glanced over at Lipsick, a gawky, strange-looking one who suffered from one of the nation's worst haircuts—a leftover mop from the Beatles' American Invasion that did nothing for the man in his midfifties—and decided, though he regretted thinking it, that Lipsick had lost it somewhere down the line. As Eamon thought about it a moment longer, Lipsick caught his gaze and returned it right back. Eamon immediately turned away, but Lipsick held his aim, the eyes white and unfriendly.

"So what can we tell from that photograph for sure?" Bunko asked.

"Not fuckin' much."

"Bullshit. We got plenty, look at them again. Here."

Bunko handed over the enlargements. The whole thing was making Eamon feel profoundly removed. He wanted to get in his business-as-usual mode, but that photo was bad news. It made him think about America. In a way that he knew to be unfair and misleading. After all, America was a gigantic, unfathomable place really, a country so large that one could never imagine, let alone realize, the extent of those millions of individual lives. Although he knew this, knew it to be true in his heart, for most people were good and truly decent—how could it not be so?—he couldn't help but think of all the monsters living in America's basement. The bright green and pink suburbia of dreams, picket fences and neat, perfect squares of Astroturf, spreading out in all her morning glory, always seemed to be the biggest lie to Eamon Wearie.

He had seen some nasty shit in his time, and over the years he had learned one hard and difficult-to-keep truth about the nature of evil. It never seemed to come in the expected ways. So he knew. So he knew that this guy's name was Herb or Len or Wayne or Chuck. Something real normal like that. If you lived next door to him, you'd say he's the best. Great guy. A-Number One. Why, Herb was probably the nicest, friendliest son of a gun on the block. Good ol' Herb. Always helping out. Driving the kids to Little League games. A scoutmaster in his spare time. And every Sunday, you can bet, you can just bet, this Rotarian of the Year slicks back his hair and splashes on plenty of Aqua Velva, then puts on a three-piece suit, making sure to pin Old Glory into the lapel, and goes off to church, happily, merrily, whistling some show tune from *Oklahoma,* singing Howdy-Do and Good Morning To You.

This was the kind of thing you ran into. All the time. All the fucking time.

But nothing had prepared him for this one. In the nine years he'd been working at the Depot, he'd thought he'd seen some things. But this was ugly, hard to look at. His dad and uncles had been city cops, had spent the better part of their lives patrolling the gutters of the human condition, so he'd heard stories, plenty of them. But at the moment he couldn't think of one that matched this.

Bunko was right, though. *Stick with what we know.* Don't waste time jumping to conclusions. Just look at the photograph.

As he examined it, looking for clues, he was aware that some of the Bureau's best-trained minds had already strained their eyes poring over it. What could he possibly find that they hadn't already? It was a feeling that you had to resist.

You began with the fact that it was real.

An eight-by-twelve. Black and white. The Executioner most probably developed it himself. A closet darkroom. In all likelihood he had taken the photo using a tripod and a timer. Which would mean he knew a little something about photography. But it would've been a mistake to totally discount the possibility of outside involvement. He remembered that case they broke three years ago. That sadomasochistic cult. The Devil's Helpers. Yeah, they hadn't wanted to believe that either. No, he best keep that in mind.

The torture chamber had to be in the basement. Had to be. Part of the oil burner appeared in the far right-hand corner. The Bureau was able to positively identify its make and model number. A Blue Marvel, JPA-66. Built in 1972 by the J.P. Edward's Heating Company of Reading, Pennsylvania. They sold fifty thousand units that year, spread out over the entire Northeast corridor. Computer blowups could not locate an individual serial number. It might not have helped anyway. The Edward's Company was unable to provide a master list of the purchasers' names. Either the new burner replaced an old one, or else the house was also built in '72. That could be valuable later on.

The Executioner himself was a dumpy, out-of-shape white male. His age and height could not be easily ascertained. His head was draped in a black leather hood. Otherwise, he was naked as Lady Godiva. His body did not have a hair on it, not even a pubic strand. *Glabrous.* He glistened, as if he had rubbed baby oil all over himself. He didn't show a tattoo or birthmark or any other unusual marking that might help in identification. His fingers were free of rings or traces. He was not even wearing a wristwatch. It was the Bureau's best guess that he lived alone, that it would otherwise be impossible to maintain secrecy. Taking into account the Bureau's own authoritative study *Sexual Homocide: Patterns and Motives,* it remained their assumption that he was a bachelor, having never married, between thirty and fifty years of age. That was a difficult and unhelpful span.

The naked boy, twelve or thirteen years old was the Bureau's best estimate, was shackled to the cement wall. He was gagged and blindfolded. His hair appeared bright blond; one speculation had it that the Executioner dyed it. The boy's emaciated rib cage showed, displaying the effects of malnutrition. There were slash marks across the chest, as if he had been whipped. On the floor next to him: a U.S. Army surplus blanket and a doggie bowl filled with what looked to be water.

As gruesome as it was, it was still not the sickest part.

There was also a single shelf holding three large pickle jars. Forensics had paid particular attention to those jars and had concluded with "reasonable bearing" that each one contained the sex organs of a male Homo sapiens. It would be impossible to establish anything else without actual physical evidence. Though it was only reasonable to conject that they were packed in formalin.

Other details were worth noting:

A neatly stacked pile of porno magazines. They were able to bring into focus the top issue: *Boy Love,* volume 22, September. That tied in nicely with the chemical analysis of the photo paper, which indicated it had been developed in late September or early October. Today was March 27. Elapsed time: six months.

A beer can. In the far left-hand corner of the photo, on the edge of a large plywood table—which held an elaborate model train set and which can only partially be seen—was a can of Old Mallory. The Old Mallory Brewing Company was relatively small, serving only eastern Pennsylvania and the state of Delaware. It confirmed, or at least seemed to limit, their geographical radius. Especially when you considered the postmark.

The plain brown envelope was processed October 13. At Philadelphia's main post office. Either the Executioner lived in Philly, or he worked there, or he played it extremely safe. There was no telling.

The typewritten address—P.O. Box 446/L.A. General Delivery/CA 90005—matched the typing on the back of the photo. The cryptic phrasing was in caps: JOHNNY'S BEEN A VERY, VERY NAUGHTY BOY AND NOW HE MUST BE PUNISHED. There was no telling if Johnny was a real name or just part of the game. The Bureau determined that a Royal 500 had been used. They also made a note that Royal 500s were standard issue in many school districts. *Perhaps he's a junior high school typing teacher?* one of their investigators jotted alongside.

Of course, the photo was brushed for fingerprints. They came up with several, but the National Crime Information computer could not make a match.

The National Center for Missing and Exploited Children, a federal agency under the Department of Justice, listed ten thousand Johnny possibilities in the investigation's official radius. Which seemed unbelievable to Eamon. Ten thousand boys, between the ages of eight and sixteen, who were missing. Ten thousand boys missing in just one little square block of the country. Even knowing that a large percentage of them had been taken in domestic disputes, or had simply run away on their own, did not make it go down any easier.

The Violent Criminal Apprehension Program sent details of the photo to police departments in parts of Pennsylvania, Ohio, New Jersey, and Delaware. You never knew. Shared information was often the key.

Then there was a ton of analysis.

The FBI Behavioral Science Unit offered their usual theories and interpretations. They provided the standard profile of a serial killer. There was nothing new here. The whole unhappy childhood deal. Heavy doses of neglect. Sexual abuse. Physical violence. Single-parent homes. Absence of male authority figures. Raised by women. Mothers, aunts, grandmothers. Plenty of disturbing signs early on. Fascination with death, pornography, weapons. The usual antisocial patterns. Inability to relate and to care about others. Chronic, compulsive masturbators. In and out of jobs. Living alone. Drinking problems. On and on.

The whole file was fat with frustration. It seemed as if the Bureau hadn't left a stone unturned. There was even one section by a forensic psychiatrist—whatever the hell that was—devoted to "examining the motive and strange rationale behind castration." It was titled "Inside the Deviant Mind."

Ever so surely it began to dawn on Eamon that he and Bunko were not going to come close on this one. This was just way out of their league. Serial killers. Torture chambers. Castration. This just wasn't typical mailman territory. Even if you were a federal inspector. They'd done a lot of work, good work, in the past tracing the kiddie porn trail. There was a lot of it. A lot of scum out there. So he'd seen some pictures that were none too pretty. He thought of that one little four-year-old girl. Lizzie Schlosser. Jesus. And they were lucky on that one. Bunko never gave up the scent, and they nailed the son of a bitch to the wall. A pediatrician in Rockville. Ten to twenty. Hell, he's probably out by now. God knows how many kids he messed with. God knows how many of them went on to do the same thing. The whole thing was just too fucked up. All those haunted kids out there. No way to reconcile that.

But hell, the last big case they broke was almost embarrassing to admit. It had been a slow month, and Anal had them on print detail. It was simple enough. They scoured the magazines in search of fraud. The ads they were interested in were always in the back, easy to spot, full of loud exclamation marks and money-back guarantees, with touched-up before-and-after photos and the usual suspect testimonials, accepting of every credit card under the sun, with marvelous, lawyerly disclaimers in print so small, it threatened to disappear. He wasn't so sure what they did in the rest of the world, but in America all you had to do was take a little pill. It was easy. It was so simple. You want a mind-blowing Riviera suntan? Take a red one. You want to lose fifty pounds that first day? Without feeling hungry? Two green Weightomatics. Feel tired? Not enough energy? You needed a bottle of InstoPep.

Sometimes it was more difficult. Sometimes a simple pill just wouldn't do. Sometimes you had to work at it. Doubling your current breast size took at least six to eight days. But it would be worth it. That extra effort. One simple-to-follow exercise. Send in your buck. Now. Today. Don't wait. Penis growth was even more difficult. And dangerous. It took a special set of weights and pulleys. It took a fearless dedication.

This was the kind of moronic crap they had been working on. It was embarrassing. You couldn't very well blame the attorneys at Justice—having plenty of better things to do—for not wanting anything to do with it. Anal actually thought it was a major coup breaking open the Spanish fly operation. It was easily the dumbest thing Eamon and Bunko had ever participated in. Bunko was right. If those idiots were dumb enough to send in their money for "the ultimate in sexual performance–enhancing pills"—well, that was their problem. As it was, they were prosecuting through the Food and Drug Administration.

Now that they had a real case, he felt up against it. Out of practice. Going from the Big Spanish Fly Caper to the Executioner—a fella who liked to pickle cocks in his spare time, just lovely—was moving it up a notch, that was for damn sure.

"So whudda we got?" Bunko asked.

"We got dork."

"Yeah, me, too," he said a bit tiredly. Then: "Let's take a break. Whattayasay? Let's improve our Twin K efficiency rating. Yeah, that's the ticket."

A nasty little glint came into Bunko's eyes. It was an old gag, but it never failed to amuse. He knew Eamon thought it was running a little thin. But it made him so stupendously and momentously happy that he couldn't resist.

They rode the freight elevator down. On the ground floor they grabbed one of the electric go-carts and scooted away.

Even with the earplugs, the noise was maddening, making any kind of talk impossible. It was always strange to maneuver through the cardboard jungle in that eerie drone. It took them ten minutes—even with Bunko Andretti driving—to reach the heart of Dead Letters. They passed the Unpublished Novelists' Hall of Fame and the huge safes from the old First National. They waved to Yellow Team as they passed the North Pole. Poor bastards. The Christmas decorations—a sorry white tree and strings of tutti-frutti color—were forever blinking. Yellow Team's sole job was handling Santa's mail. It arrived every day of the year—addressed to Mr. Kringle or Mrs. Claus, or to Rudolph and the elves—and it was their responsibility to weed out the truly needy and deserving. These were then forwarded to the many charities that specialized in making Christmas wishes come true.

Eamon knew Bunko was looking for a good year. Not too far back. Didn't want the recipients to be dead or anything. Bunko chose 1962 as his golden oldie. He liked the early sixties. Probably because he was still young then and there was everything to look forward to, Eamon thought. Yeah. Kennedy hadn't been wasted yet. Vietnam was just some foreign-sounding place on a map. And Bunko hadn't even proposed to anyone yet. Yeah. He was still getting laid in his Chevy.

Eamon just watched Bunko go about his business. It was all pretty straightforward. Bunko just looked for about five or six letters that had been detained for some easy-to-figure reason, something like insufficient postage, or maybe just the result of a sloppy, unsteady hand. Bunko then made the necessary corrections and mailed them on their way.

Of course, you could pretty much guess the outcome. The local papers would do a cute little story about the letter that took thirty years to reach its destination. Then the wire services would pick it up and send it out across the country with some headline like EXPRESS MAIL or SPECIAL DELIVERY. Whatever.

It was a dumb gag. But it drove Anal insane.

2

The Blue Marlin was busy late on a Friday afternoon. There wasn't any netting strung up on the ceiling, no rotting foam buoys, not even a stuffed marlin to splash up over the gin bottles. It was a nice long mahogany bar that went the distance, miragelike. He was smoking a cigarette and staring, unabashedly. She was deeply beautiful, young and blond and greatly aware of it, and she stood in the sweet pale light of the juke, like all the great beauties before her, slotting her quarters. He took another long draft off his Oxford. The work week was fading behind him and he was where he most wanted to be. In the small life, surrounded by his old friends and his new ones, in beery contemplation.

He didn't know it, but he had a chance, a good one. The girl, whose name was Patty Hegel, had been checking him out for the better half of an hour. Eamon Wearie never fully realized the extent of his good Gaelic looks. He had been slight and slender from day one, but it was the abundance of curly, good-natured hair that gave him a boyish, tender look at thirty-three. It didn't matter. He was happy. He was always happy in Friday's twilight, doing the slow fade, burning down.

He shouted down to Boxcar Bertha for another round.

She was pulling the spigots and falling behind and therefore a little irritable. She yelled back, "Fuck you, Eamon! Wait your turn like everybody else!"

At this point Bunko came to life: "Do you know who you're talking to in that wholly unacceptable tone? Why, Lieutenant Wearie is one of the few. One of the proud. One of the brave. The United States Postal Inspector Corps, ma'am."

"Fuck you too, why don't you, Bunko!"

"That's what I love about this shithole," Bunko shot back. "Its charming informality."

"Well, then you'd be alone in that regard," Eamon said with a smile.

They were in their usual corner, waiting to play winners. They had already been up once, but Bunko—usually a dead eye—was off his game. They always came down on Fridays for the cricket and free buffet. The Marlin was just one of many neighborhood bars dotting the tiny side streets of Fells Point—not far from the Depot, which did its sprawling by the Canton docks. It certainly wasn't much to look at, beer mirrors and old pennants fighting for wall space, its hardwood floor littered with peanut shells, but they made a good charred burger, and it was easy to like their happy hour, two for one and merry with regulars. It was an egalitarian little crowd—power ties and hard hats, secretaries and assembly line gals—that had no trouble melding together amidst all that congenial noise and smoky warmth.

They were definitely in luck today; the metal bins were brimming with hot steamed shrimp—not the usual sticky chicken wings—and the girls somehow outnumbered the boys. Patty Hegel was still at the juke, moving her hips to Madonna's bouncy beat, a boy-toy lost to the world, dreamy-looking and all alone in the tainted light. He'd decided he'd better make his move soon, before she left, or else before one of the other yo-yos gave it a wing.

"Why don't you just go for it?" Bunko said, all touchy-sounding. "They always go for you. So what's your problem, huh?"

"What's with you?"

24

"Ah," he said, catching himself. "Nothin'. Just the drink, you know. Ah. If you must know, I haven't been laid in a while. Christ, I'm sorry, Eamon. And that stupid case. Anal's right. We're never going to solve that baby."

"No kidding. Tell me something I don't know."

"All right. I will. That girl is hot. And I wish I was younger. Isn't that a hoot? But that's what I wish. I'd like something like that to look twice at me once, you know. Me, I just get Mrs. Taglianno. You ever see Mrs. Taglianno? Green hair, my friend. No kidding. Supposed to be blond."

Then Bunko called down to Boxcar for shots all around. His time-honored way of smoothing over any remotely inhospitable situation.

Eamon hadn't even bothered to notice Gena at her waitressing station. He had dumped her over a month ago—with the dreaded "Let's be friends" speech—but Gena was having a lot of trouble letting go. She saw the way his eyes kept flitting to the little bimbet by the jukebox— and it hurt. She felt herself flinching inside, knocked for quick little loops by the sight. Everything seemed slightly out of control, and she felt capable of most anything. In an instant she saw herself storming out, quitting her stupid job all at once, and throwing a drink in Eamon's ridiculously smug face. Then she would pause to think, and she would remember how badly she needed the money. That bastard. Only a few short weeks ago he had been inside of her.

He didn't know what he was going to say; it would just come out, somehow. He entered into the juke light, and she said, "Hi, I was wondering when you were going to cruise over."

"Yeah, I'd been thinking about it. Name's Eamon. Want something to drink?"

"Yeah, yeah I do. White Russian, okay?"

Patty Hegel watched him order the drink. She was eighteen years old and trying to figure things out. She had to find something to do. Everybody else was going to school or some shit, and she was still stuck at home. So she figured she had to find a place of her own soon. Real soon. She worked part time in a jewelry store. But it was only temporary. That was Patty Hegel's life story.

They touched glasses. He noticed right off that she'd overdone it with the blue eye shadow, and that got him wondering about her age. But she was in this black mini thing—might just as well have been naked the way his eyes roamed over her—along with these sexy lacy gloves. They drank together and lit each other's cigarettes, and when the platters changed, she'd ask his opinion. She liked his blue eyes, clear and true, and that's probably why Madonna's "True Blue" kept singing inside her head. She already decided she would sleep with him, as long as he had his own place and all.

He didn't know that Patty Hegel had slept with six men—old young single married what's the difference—over the last thirteen days and that she was drifting through the bars and the lies men told. There was an emptiness in the very core of Patty Hegel that no amount of sex, or even love, could ever fill. She herself was only dimly aware that she had been abused as a child. It remained a vague, floating feeling that never seemed to catch the light. And the other night, offering not even the slightest amount of resistance, she let a man she only knew as Deeves take those kinds of pictures of her. She was not ashamed, though. No, that did not enter into it at all.

"Is she your girlfriend?" she asked, pointing to Gena at the service bar. "'Cause her eyes keep following you. You're not married to her or anything, are you?"

"No, no way. We used to go out, if you really want to know."

Gena Davio was a nice person, and they'd had some good times, getting pizza and going to the movies, but at the end, especially when they were in bed together, a kind of despair settled over him. He felt too responsible for her, as if she were losing herself in him, losing her identity, that thing that had made her so attractive to him in the first place. It was raining badly the night he gave the speech about it not going to work out. They were in his car, parked somewhere. It didn't really matter, at least not to him, but Gena was a little homely, flat-chested and lanky and real self-conscious about it. It just made him feel particularly cruel telling her, as if she would never find another to care about in the world. She just started to scream and then she just ran out into it, into the night and the bad rain.

Even though Gena was watching, he slipped his arm around Patty. He didn't do it to hurt her; just thought it would make things more final, that's all. He was slugging back beers with determination. He let it wash over him, as he did every day now, let it take him there, to that deep and sorry place which he knew as the red malaise. The Marlin was just a hot swirl of color and wild laughter, all foam and fizz, a vast spilling-over. In the red malaise everything tasted strongly of yeast. He liked the feel of the girl's waist, whoever the hell she was.

Bunko called over for the darts, and he tried to just shake him off, but Bunko wouldn't hear of it. "C'mon, we're up," he demanded, as he gave Patty the once-over.

"No, I don't feel like it. We're about to leave and all, you know."

"Jesus, what was I waiting around for then?"

"God," he answered, strangely.

"Sometimes you don't make any fucking sense, Wearie. I mean that sincerely. So who's your friend? You didn't have the decency to introduce me."

"Patty," she said, clearly bored and distracted.

"I bet you didn't even know that. Did you know that, Eamon? Did you know that this nice girl's name was Patty? Christ. Life is always like that. You're as bad as that case we're working on—"

"What the fuck are you talking about, man?"

"People fuck and they get fucked. That's what I'm talking about, my friend."

"Now you ain't making sense, my friend."

"It's a terrible drive, that's what it is," Bunko said finally, before turning away.

The girl, who'd been slouching against the juke, scarcely there, just waiting for them to finish up their bullshit, came to life over that little exchange. That whole *case* thing stuck in her mind, and now she was wondering if they were undercover cops or some shit.

"So like, what do you, like, do, you know?" she was careful to phrase.

"I don't do anything," Eamon insisted.

"No, really. Like what do you do for a living?"

"I read porno magazines for a living, if you really want to know."

"Then you'd be interested in what I was doing the other night," she said suddenly, mischievously.

Nobody was making any sense tonight, he thought, and let it go at that.

It took no more than a few minutes to walk to his brick row house on Sycamore, a quiet residential stretch that seemed mercifully removed from the bars. They saw the Friday drunks staggering into alleyways, and turned from the convulsive sounds. They also heard a foghorn in the distance, one of the tugs on the thick, dirty water. If you listened hard, you could hear it slap against the pilings at the pier. It was almost April—and though the day had been mild and sweet with the possibility of spring, the night was a reminder of February frost, cold and disdainful of the human heart. Car windshields were covered with rime, and the cherry blossoms, only weeks from bloom, were just gnarled and featureless.

He had lived in Baltimore for an even decade, and though he liked it well enough, he often felt misplaced. He grew up on Long Island, in a nice little split-level in Northport, had even gone to school at the state U at Stony Brook, and he still made it a point to go home every Christmas, even if there wasn't much left of the old gang. He talked to his folks on the phone once a week, usually Sunday morning; listless, unmarked conversations that somehow tugged at him. Nothing had been the same since Trish left two years ago. He harbored no bitterness, and had even come to see it for the best, but he knew there had been a moment, and it had only been a flash, but there had been this moment when he could see it happening, the whole thing unfolding cleanly.

Kids, the mortgage, the dog, growing old, the rocker on the front porch, grandchildren, dying. As it turned out, he only wound up with the mortgage.

Thirty-five Sycamore was a renovated two-story, two-bedroom, two-bath number with Norwegian wood and skylights that Trish fell in love with on first sight. He had to admit it had been a steal at fifty-three, but he never quite got over the fact that Trish left the day before they were supposed to move in. She didn't even leave a note. He just thought something happened to her, something bad. They didn't let him fill out the missing persons report until the third day—but she finally called, a day or so later, just like Sergeant Welsh had assured him. The call had the snap-crackle of long distance, and she didn't bother to explain: *It's a bitch, baby, but I think you should have seen it coming, I really do.* At least we'll always have Paris, he thought in the AT&T droning.

That's what happened when you met people in bars. He'd met Trish at Frankie's, where she was cocktail-waitressing, and they used to close up the place, doing shots together. Then maybe they'd go to some twenty-four-hour diner for coffee and eggs. Yeah, they used to like to pal around in the old days, and it wasn't any great big deal to become lovers on a lonely snowy night.

"How come the lights are on?" Patty asked as they climbed the steps.

"Oh yeah. I forgot to tell you. I have this boarder. He's real odd. Pay no attention."

Daniel P. Pinkus was more like mondo bizarro. Eamon kept meaning to give him notice, but in his favor, he paid the rent on time and remembered to feed Trish's cats, Pacino and Brando. But he never left the house. Not even to go to class. Pinkus looked to be in his late thirties—a strange nomadic figure, whose long, flowing hair and beard compounded the Jesus thing—and he had spent his life wandering from graduate school to graduate school. Last year he supposedly studied theology at Yale, and now he was supposedly enrolled at the Maryland Institute of Art. Eamon had agreed to let him hang his canvases throughout the tiny place, which turned out to be a mistake since he hadn't known Pinkus painted modern crucifixions. The big oils of lawyers and car salesmen nailed to the cross were in miserable shades of blue, and they distilled gloom in the otherwise sunny house.

At the sound of the key in the latch, Pinkus flicked off Eamon Wearie's big Zenith and darted into the safety of his own bedroom. Pinkus was afraid of everything. He was convinced he was going to die from a most terrible and horrible disease. In the mornings he checked his body for spots and rashes and other telltale signs. It was taking longer than he expected, and he prayed to God for forgiveness constantly. He would repent, he would repent. He prayed to all the dead people he could think of. He asked his dead grandparents and the dead friends of his parents to watch over him, to help protect him. These prayers took up most of the day. Daniel P. Pinkus did not drink or use drugs, and he had not had sex in over eight years. He was in great tormenting pain and so he prayed.

Eamon led Patty by the hand up the stairs to his bedroom. He excused himself for the bathroom. Patty Hegel wasted no time undressing and positioned herself on the bed. Just as she'd done countless times before, she waited in the darkness for the inevitable, ghostly touch.

3

It made sense that it was raining on Sunday. The Block was Baltimore's answer to Times Square: go-go bars and strip joints, X-rated movies and all-night smut stands, video arcades and dollar peep shows. Even in the rain, a cold wet drip, even at eleven in the morning, the neon sparked and the hawkers called out their dreary specials. It looked right in the rain, that's all. You were supposed to wear a raincoat in the rain.

Though he knew that was a bad misconception. The perverts and exhibitionists were just the smallest fraction in the equation. Jumbo's Zoo bore this out. The Zoo was an extremely well-lit porno supermarket, aisle after aisle of magazines and cassettes, most of them carefully sealed in cellophane wrappers. There were strategic ceiling mirrors and hidden cameras and two armed guards at the entrance; he had seen banks with less security. At eleven in the morning on a Sunday, it was standing room only.

Many of the men had just come from church, their dark suits sure giveaways, and Eamon took a place with them at the huge center rack. The only women at the Zoo were on the glossy pages that the men thumbed through with apparent distraction. It was deathly quiet. As was the code, each man kept to himself, taking care not to stare or notice another's selection.

Just as he had assumed. What he was looking for was nowhere to be found. He would have to ask at the register, which was no problem. The cashiers knew better than to raise an eyebrow; it was their job to appear disinterested.

The sins of the flesh were everywhere. Every magazine cover a small explosion of boobs and ass. Every one of them a splashy promise of participation without risk, of the joy of distance. Just a bunch of damn pictures, after all. He suddenly felt bad for the grim-faced men around him, even for himself. Life was such a long and terrible series of compromises.

All those disconnected body parts made him think of Patty. She was like some bad blue memory. A series of midnight Polaroids. It was anything but exhilarating. In the emptiness of morning's half-light she had finally turned over and gone to sleep. He had trouble. Her slumbrous form was practically angelic, totally removed from experience. Before fading to black, he glimpsed her panties, turned inside out on the rug, some sad crumpled reminder of the real.

At breakfast she asked if she could stay on a few days, and he told her that wasn't a good idea. Then she asked if he wanted to take a few pictures to remember her by. He asked her what she meant. And she told him about some sleezoid named Jeeves or something. It seemed Jeeves talked Patty into doing some close-ups of her asshole. He was evidently very proud of this coup, and he was going to send them off to the amateur photo competition of his fave porno mag.

Still, it got Eamon to thinking.

It was just the kind of oversight the Bureau might make. They were so thorough that it was almost outrageous, and though their report contained pages of raw empirical data on violent sex offenders, though it contained numerous psychological profiles of homosexual and heterosexual molesters, though it provided extensive and exhaustive detail on the manufacturer of an oil burner, though they had investigated the origins of a can of beer with excruciating exactingness, though they had blown up the original photograph a thousand times in the search for minutiae, they had overlooked one singular detail. Nowhere in the report was there an analysis of the contents of the September issue of *Boy Love*. They had been able to identify it at the top of that pile, and yet no one seized upon the obvious. Tony Montrez, a stickler, would be pissed that his men let that one go.

It was just a hunch, after all. But what else did they have to go on? Nothing from nothing was nothing. He went up to the three-hundred-pound cashier in the Elvis Lives T-shirt and asked where he could find back issues of *Boy Love*. "That would be in next to *All-Star Gay* and *Cycle Queens*," he said with nothing there. "Back of aisle four."

Eamon found their display rack just where he advised, but was unhappy to see that they were individually sealed. He methodically went about the business of collecting, finding the last ten issues—which was as far back as they went— including the all-important September extravaganza. Arthur Marlens, in charge of expenditures, was sure to give him a hard time, but who the hell cared. He paid for them with his American Express card, making sure to get a receipt.

He dumped the stuff in the trunk of his Pontiac. He should have just gone home, but instead he found himself wandering across the street to Troy's Famous Girl Bar. Most of the neon lettering was burnt-out, but it continued to wink every few seconds, oblivious. Empty pint bottles showed up on the sidewalk every few yards, and so did the sorry human clumps on the steam grates and in the doorways. The smell of urine was pervasive.

It was an ugly day. He fought back the urge to call Gena. Go see some movie on a rainy Sunday. Eating popcorn with his arm around her in the darkness. Sounded nice.

He stepped inside, into the velvety darkness. "Made the right decision, John," the bouncer said. "Lucy's on." The wide bar circled an elevated stage. About seven or eight people were sitting on the red vinyl stools. Eamon took a seat next to a tall, ugly black woman in a yellow wig.

A topless waitress—who couldn't have been more than

seventeen—came for his drink order. It was damp and cold inside, and goose pimples emerged on her breasts. He ordered a whiskey, which wasn't his usual drink, but then again, this hadn't been a usual day. "Enjoy the show," she said in a little voice. "Remember we're here to serve you."

Lucy was a big-boobed brunette with a body made of cellulite, and she danced in a gold G-string to ancient Donna Summer hits.

The woman in the yellow wig started talking. "I got what you want, little sugar darlin'," she said in such a husky, masculine way that Eamon couldn't help but realize she was a he.

"You probably think it's expensive, but it's not," the man in the yellow wig continued. "I guarantee it's not. Trust me, sugar darlin'."

He wasn't exactly sure how he wound up at Troy's Famous Girl Bar in his raincoat, in the throes of one of the world's worst strip shows, sipping an unfamiliar drink as an ugly male hooker propositioned him. But Eamon Wearie suddenly understood that these things could happen with a relative and awful ease.

4

There was excitement of all things in the Command Post on Monday. Captain Brown did a complete turnabout on the Executioner case. He was so pleased with Lieutenant Wearie's find that he assigned additional men to help. Yellow Team didn't care what they had to do, so thankful were they to be off Christmas duty, even if it was just for a day or two.

Strange things were happening. Arthur Lyon and Arthur Marlens even offered to pitch in. The captain was quick to inform Tony Montrez at the Bureau, but when Montrez tried to finagle the case right back, the captain would have none of it. Seldom did anything of magnitude land on Marcus Brown's desk, and he certainly wasn't going to give it away on some silver platter. Why, a successful resolve would put him in the catbird seat. He would have his pick of posts in the D.C. Bunker. There really was no telling. This was the kind of thing that made someone. By God, there'd be books written about it, people would become famous, there'd be television movies, all sorts of things. Just no telling. Marcus Brown was no dummy, no sir.

If anyone had chanced to visit the Post that day, he or she

would have been treated to a rich governmental sight: a bunch of middle-aged bureaucrats sitting around with their feet kicked up, flipping through the latest issues of *Boy Love*.

So far they'd found five pertinent photos.

The "Meet Your Neighbor Contest" was obviously a very popular feature in every month's issue, to judge by the sheer number of entries. The winning photo was given the center-fold and twenty-five dollars. Contest rules clearly stipulated:

"First and foremost, all contestants must be over twenty-one years of age to participate. Now then. We are looking for that certain someone who arouses in us a certain special curiosity. We are looking for a certain boyish quality that ignites our attraction. In short, we are constantly looking . . ."

Most of the bleeding Polaroids, six pages worth in each issue, were shots of nude men jacking off or bending over. Indeed, most of the men did appear to be over twenty-one, although many shaved their bodies and displayed a bold expertise with the makeup brush. Underneath the photos were personal captions, either typewritten or in the contestants' own handwriting, which tended to sound alike. One fairly standard introduction went: "I live to spread my sunshine and joy to you. I enjoy meeting new people and am an avid collector. Love and kisses, Bert. Rockford, MA (photo by Frank)."

Bunko, usually raucaus and unconcerned, was uncomfortable with the blatant homosexual element. It was not that he was homophobic per se, since he believed that heterosexual love could be pretty darn spooky, too—just check out the swingers' sections in the hetero mags—but he had to admit he carried an unhealthy amount of ambivalence. To relieve his own tension, Bunko called over to Arthur Marlens: "Hey, Art, you faggot. I see you gettin' sexually excited over there. Take it into the washroom, buddy boy."

Marlens was tense enough without Bunko's kidding. In fact, though he had been married thirty-two years, though he had never had a homosexual experience, Arthur Marlens believed himself to be gay. He had never uttered this terrible truth to another living human being, not even his psychologist, and because of it, because it colored everything, his life remained a great and shaky lie, an unbearable house of cards. Too often he thought of putting his service revolver into his mouth.

"Fuck you, Bunko," he returned. "You big sick homo."

Eamon, for once, was all business, and he wished they'd just cut out the clowning and get to work. He had provided the first new leads in a dead-end investigation, and he was proud of his detective work. It had been some time since he felt like this. This was a dream case. You waited your whole lifetime for something like this. He just didn't want to blow it. He wanted to be careful, to be detached. He had learned a great deal over the years, and now he was going to get a chance to put some of it to use.

When he started out, he had dreamed of a whole slew of cases like this one. After he had completed his studies in criminology, he'd opted for the FBI's training program at Quantico. Though he really didn't have a vision of himself as a stiff, by-the-book G-man, he was fascinated by modern technique and science, the whole genius behind catching criminals; what he hadn't counted on was finishing in the middle of his class in a lean recruitment year and being scooped up by the Postal Department. Who the fuck ever even heard of the Postal Department's Office of Instruction and Mail Depredation? No one, that's who. And it wasn't that he didn't like his job, he did basically, but working for the post office made you a plain old mailman to most people. Even his own father had difficulty understanding his role in the scheme of things. No matter how many times he explained that the whole deal had been established in 1830 to deal with all the stagecoach robberies, his dad would say something smart like, "Yeah, those stagecoach robberies, yeah, they're really messing up the fabric of the nation." What could you do?

Actually, the Office of Instruction and Mail Depredation —later changed to the Office of Inspection, the first of many name changes—had quite an illustrious history. Eamon could see the beauty in it now, where as a young cadet, it seemed he'd drawn the shortest straw. Over the years he had become greatly interested in the lore of the special agents. In the early days they had been accorded almost celebrity status: brave, lone figures who rode into the dirt towns with a six-shooter and a federal badge. It was the special agents who were responsible for guarding the stagecoaches and trains and post offices, responsible for tracing the missing letters which often carried people's life's savings, responsible for bringing the mail depredators to justice. Of course, with the advent of the money-order system in 1864, which finally made it possible to put money in the mail without actually sending it, their duties changed.

Still, Eamon liked the image of these rough riders who brought law and order to the West. And now he finally had a case worthy of his pedigree.

Here's what he knew so far.

Boy Love had only been in existence two years. It was published out of Ocean City, Maryland. The publisher, Rube Fuchs, had, as they suspected, a criminal record. He had served five years for molesting his own son, and he was now out on probation. He was not cooperative over the phone. They would need to look at his files, no question, even if it took a warrant.

They had found five different entries, each new one appearing after a two-month interval, from the "Meet Your Neighbor Contest," that they believed to be the work of the Executioner. Each time he used exactly the same pose. Each boy—and they were quite sure that, unlike the other "contestants," these were minors—was photographed lying on a king-sized bed, as if asleep, clad only in his underwear. They would need the original negatives, but it seemed clear, even from these reproductions, that the boys had been physically abused, were in fact covered head to toe in bruises. It was, further, Bunko's contention that the boys were not sleeping but dead; or why weren't they cuffed or tied down?

Each boy appeared to have bright blond hair, as if dyed.

Each boy's face was half-hidden by a black sleeping mask. Making identification this side of impossible.

Each boy wore plain white Jockey shorts, whose only

identifying mark was a single stripe running through the elastic.

Then it got strange.

The boys all had what looked to be the outline of a lipstick kiss on their left cheeks. The trace was clear and dark, meant to be seen.

The size of the bodies varied tremendously. It would be difficult to judge age, but the youngest might have been nine, and the oldest might have been seventeen. There was some kind of progression at work.

Each boy clutched a different object. These objects were without doubt a key to something. The smallest boy hugged a teddy bear, while the largest one gripped an old-fashioned brassiere. In between: a Little Richie Rich comic book, a catcher's mit, and the Beatles' *Abbey Road* album.

The typed caption under each of the photos was exactly the same: "Johnny's been a very, very naughty boy. And now he's in dreamland. Howie M., Bear County, PA."

That caption iced matters.

The Executioner was alive and well and perhaps living somewhere in Bear County. Eamon had already talked to Tony Montrez at the Bureau. He was acutely aware that the captain wanted this baby for himself, but there was no way in hell they were going to get anywhere without the Bureau's help. Besides, Montrez was a pro; years ago, Eamon had been in his document identification class. They would need people to go through phone book listings in search of the elusive and perhaps all too fictional Howie M. They would need to know the names of those customers who routinely bought *Boy Love* and other hard-core homo mags at the porno emporiums in the county. There was a good chance that the Executioner traveled to parts unknown to make his purchases; still, they would have to check everything. They would need lists of all known sex offenders living in Bear. They would need to comb through Rube Fuchs's subscription lists. They would need to seize the original photos—to have them combed for prints. They would need blowups. One of them revealed a nightstand with a couple of books on it; they'd want to try to identify them.

Bear was a small county in the northern reaches of central Pennsylvania, near the New York border, that tallied up 34,793 residents in the last census. Its largest town was Ashland, the county seat, listing in at 17,658. Calls would have to be made to their police department. How many missing children cases could they possibly be working on? In the big cities you had your sexual exploitation task forces, but surely this kind of thing was uncommon as hell up there. Had to be.

He was making a mental note to stop off at Record World after work—who knew what strange clue *Abbey Road* held?—when Tony Montrez called.

"Wearie, Montrez. Listen, talk some sense to Brown. This is amateurville. You've done some good work—I expect nothing less of one of my former cadets—but I think we should take it from here."

"All due respect, sir, but I think we should work together on this one. I don't think we should be cut out, sir."

There was silence. Eamon had no trouble envisioning Montrez in his green leather chair, sucking on his pipe. He was a tall man with a ridiculously distinguished head of silver hair who always looked freshly shaved. He was also absolutely humorless. The only human thing Eamon knew about him was that he collected duck decoys.

"If you're worried about credit," he said finally, "then don't."

"No, sir, that's not it. We want to participate."

"At the moment I don't have a choice. Officially it's been turned over. Not that I like it. When were you planning to go to Ocean City?"

"Tomorrow."

"Do you need assistance? I think you're making a mistake. Very well. I'll want your report and tapes. One last thing, Wearie: Why do you think he dyed the boys' hair?"

"It could be to mar the indentification process, but I don't think that's the only reason. He probably wants them to all look like someone. Someone from his past. At least that's what I think."

"That's good, Wearie. We probably shouldn't have shipped you off to Postal. That's what our people think, too. Think it has to do with sexual rejection. There's a lot of precedent for this sort of thing. It could be he's killing a former lover or something over and over. Just speculation, of course. We'll be talking."

Eamon was used to Montrez's abrupt exits, but as he held the receiver in his hand, he had a sudden reckless urge to call him back. To turn the case back over to Montrez. He and Bunko were being bona fide assholes. Not only were they in way over their heads, they were probably even jeopardizing the case itself. Then he consoled himself with the knowledge that Montrez was no dummy: Surely he had already assigned some of his own men to it, officially or unofficially. And it was this thought that got his competitive juices flowing.

He had one more hunch to act on before the day was through. It was the long shot of long shots, but he wasn't about to discount luck and instinct, two old and favorite horses. Bunko thought he was wasting his time. "Jesus H. Christ. You might just as well buy a lottery ticket, Wearie. I ain't kidding," he was grumbling as they got on the elevator.

The heart of Dead Letters was the Holding Station. It was here that the mail was put through Intermediate Delay and Recovery, a woeful, tedious process of trying to procure the destination of the lost letters. The lost letters were simply divided by postmark: placed into the appropriate state of origin and shelved by town. Lost letters were almost always without return address—otherwise they were just sent back **RETURN TO SENDER** with **ADDRESSEE UNKNOWN** or **FORWARDING TIME EXPIRED**—and they almost always wound up at Holding by way of the simple, small mistake. Too often people simply forgot to even address the envelope. Blank. Nada. Or they just didn't use a ZIP. The letter would be addressed to someone in, say, Johnstown— and the state would have three Johnstowns. Or they just didn't know how to spell. Berry Lane became Bury Road, and cities like Decatur and Biloxi and Schenectady came out dozens of interesting ways. Lots of times the addresses were just unreadable. The Son of Sam School of Penmanship, or else it was just another case of a felt-tip pen not weathering raindrops. Whatever, the problems were unvarying, and the solution was just as unbeguiling: The lost letters were kept at Holding for two years before being duly classified as dead, at which time they are cordoned off in their very own climate-controlled vault.

Eamon Wearie had learned all this the hard way, having had to spend his first nine months—just as every new recruit was required—sorting through the island of the lost, and it had saddened him to find that with all those piles of possibility, the letters themselves provided scant evidence of life's mystery. In point of fact, the job had been an absolute fucking bore. More often than not he was called upon to trace a particular piece—usually something with a check in it, a misplaced IRS refund or a Social Security blunder—and this usually took the form of furrowing through the chaotic mounds of Washingtonian excess. Why, the IRS alone took up a square acre of the Holding Station every year with nearly seventy thousand undeliverable refund checks. Eamon had found that the cause was usually a failure to leave a forwarding address, although it was not uncommon to find that the unclaimed refunds belonged to taxpayers who died shortly after filing. Unless someone made an effort to claim the checks—or anything else in Dead Letters for that matter—little was done to speed them on their rightful way. They were simply undermanned— and it was generally accepted by the Service, though this was far from being spelled out, that there would always be a tiny fraction of mail that somehow managed to fall through the cracks, that this had to be expected, since a certain amount of loss and mismanagement was part of any business.

Nothing less than an act of Congress, in the hectic postal year of 1873, in accordance with the new Comstock Law, which forbade the use of the mails for obscene and indecent material, had given the special agents the right to open the mail. Even so, it was not their modus operandi to tear into the public's private correspondence without reason. It was highly unusual to slit even one letter open; if and when it was done, it was on the off chance of finding an inside address. Well, Eamon had to admit, that wasn't really true. Early on he'd opened plenty of letters, with no real intention of solving the riddle of ownership, just for the hell of it, just for the read. But after a while, after going through a bunch of them, he found to his utter discouragement and annoyance that most were boring as hell. Where he thought he'd eavesdrop on his fellow citizens—as surreptitiously as a mother sneaking through her daughter's diary—where he thought he'd be let in on terrible, terrible secrets, where there should have been aching, burning life, he found dreary pedantic exercises in forced expression. A million thankless thank you notes. For unappreciated birthday checks. For wedding gifts that were no doubt gathering attic dust. For your concern and your condolences. Too many seemed bound by familial duty. Wives wrote sleep-provoking small talk to mothers-in-law. Fathers wrote sons in college with sanctimonious advice about the time for bearing down. Grandchildren sent totally unsatisfactory Hallmark cards. A line or two, no more. Get well soon! We love you and miss you! So few wanted to write. So few wanted to connect. So many merely wanted to sign their names. Eamon had sorely wished that more of them could have been revealing, could have told something essential about the letter writer, could have confided that something human. Instead there were stale anecdotes, dull impressions, vague references, sad attempts at self-deprecating humor, unfortunate political observations, false chumminess, phony sentiment, forced wit, large excesses of ego, an abundance of white space.

Anyway, the public didn't seem to care about lost mail unless there was money involved. He could remember only a few—a very few—instances where that wasn't the case. There had been that old couple who made such a big deal about finding that photo-packet containing pictures from their fiftieth wedding anniversary. And there was that lady who wouldn't let up about those bronzed baby booties, her firstborn and all; and they actually wound up unearthing them in Lost and Found. The Lost and Found was last stop for many of the larger objects picked up by the metal detectors, a veritable mail-order catalog of consumer goods, tables of golf clubs and alarm clocks, wristwatches and china, all carefully tagged and dated. In fact, thinking about it, Eamon realized that the most important find they'd ever made had been an ordinary green canvas sack in one of the musty, forgotten corners of the Holding Station. A U.S. Army mail bag. From 1969. By way of Saigon. Many of the letters had been written by kids who hadn't made it through the war—and no one can imagine what that's like, getting a letter from your dead son or dead fiancé, twenty years after the fact, to hear words from beyond the grave. Now, that had been important. Had meant something.

"Ah, we're wasting our fuckin' time," Bunko growled again. "Might just as well go to Pimlico—as long as we're playing hunches and all."

As they entered the domain of Pennsylvania, Eamon knew that his partner had a point. It was a total waste of time, and he wasn't sure why he was dragging them back into that paper forest. It might have been that he just liked it back there, that's all. He really didn't know; it was like many things we did, led by invisible and contradictory forces, sleepwalking through so much of any given day. He started with Ashland—at least the towns were in alphabetical order, even if they weren't done by county—and worked his way through Great River Falls and Hill City. There really wasn't much to it. It was a million-to-one shot. But it was true that the kiddie porn, more than most other things, often found its way to the Holding Station; of course, this was due to the fact that people seldom put a return address on their dirt and sludge, and it was also due to the fact that they mostly sent their surprise packages to other short-lived post office boxes. Why, that's how they came across the Executioner's original blowup in the first place. You just never knew.

Except today he knew. They were going to crap out. The

dice just felt cold. After he sorted through North Platte and Rosie's Range, he came to Sandstone, the last on his short list of the towns of Bear County.

"Sweet Jesus," he exclaimed, sighting the stack of letters. Whereas he had only come across a few odds and ends in the other slots, Sandstone must have had close to fifty lost letters, which was highly unusual for such a jerkwater place. "Hey, Bunk, take a look at this, will ya."

"What? Don't tell me you actually found something to do with our A-Number-One sicko pervert?"

"Naah. Much more weird, buddy. Check it out."

All of the letters had been stamped and addressed to the same person. Just a first name. *James.* No address, coming or going. Bunko took a handful and riffled through them. "Mailed out of Sandstone at weekly intervals, my friend," he said with some finality. "Now let's get the hell out of here."

"Where's your sense of mystery, Bunk?"

"Don't have any. It's all as plain as your face. Gotta be love letters, if you ask me."

Eamon shook his head in wonderment at his friend's lack of curiosity, then proceeded to rip one open.

Dearest lover, it began in the most beautiful handwriting he had ever seen.

"Look at the flow, will you," Bunko said with new interest. "Jesus Fuckin' Christ. Nice, high uprights. Philosophical bent. Forward slope. Nice. Very nice. But the *e*'s are blotted. There are tight and powerful secrets here. No question. And then you throw in those repressed, vivid understrokes. Sexual dynamo who isn't getting any. But that's just my opinion. Now let's take a look at that old signature . . ."

They had both, even if it was years apart, taken the standard graphology course at Quantico, and though the class was taught primarily for purposes of spotting check forgery, they covered the psychological basics as well. The remarkable fluidity ran several pages, both sides, and culminated in an emotionally shrunken *Netti.*

"What I tell you?" Bunko barked with satisfaction. "Emily Dickinson with a vibrator. Now let's get the hell out of here."

Eamon Wearie didn't even debate pocketing the letter, even if it was a direct violation of postal code. For in that regard he was like most people, liking nothing better than a good mystery.

5

Daniel P. Pinkus was distressed to find, while examining himself in the privacy of his bedroom, in front of the full-length mirror he bought expressly for these purposes, a pimple in his pubic region. He immediately jumped to severe conclusions. Now, he was sure that this was the onset of herpes simplex something or other. He had read all about it. It was in the papers. Every day. Constantly. On the news. There was no escaping it. We were inundated with millions of bits of unpleasant factoid every horrible waking moment. The world was suffering and dying, and he had been reading about it, and so he had always known that no one, no matter what precautions one took, would be immune from this rash of wrath. God was going to punish him, just like He punished everybody else. There was no telling with these sexual diseases. They could just sit there in waiting for years, years and years of anxiety, in what they called an incubation period, and then all of a sudden, for no particular reason, perhaps stress, perhaps not, maybe hot and spicy food, they became operative. There was no justice. This is what happened to people who indulged in wanton sex, sex with strangers, with people you didn't even know. It had been eight years, but he had dreaded and expected this. He had fucked people for no better reason than for his own personal orgasm. And now he was paying.

Daniel P. Pinkus sobbed into his pillow. He prayed to his grandfathers to ease his pain. But the dead people were tormenting him, and he knew it would not be long before he would have to join them in that gaseous nowhere place. He wanted to live so badly. He loved every single God-given moment, no matter how truly frightening it was. Actually, he didn't really think he had herpes: He knew it was far, far worse. But he would not even think it, let alone utter that word aloud. It was the most horrible word he ever heard, and he wished he never had to hear it again. They just have to find the fucking cure, he thought deliriously, so that humanity can find the room to love again.

Daniel P. Pinkus knew exactly why it had happened today of all days. He had been watching TV when Eamon had come home unexpectedly, and so he had not had time to turn off the set the usual way. It was important to flick it off on a good, upbeat phrase. It didn't matter if it was a commercial or anything, but the words had to bode well, not have anything to do with disease or injury or death or in any other way be misconstrued. And since he did not have the time to flick through the channels for that telling phrase, the last thing he heard was Dan Rather droning, "And now with that outpatient story . . ."

Eamon could hear his boarder's anguished cries underneath, and it worried him. Something was definitely wrong with Pinkus. He hadn't actually seen him in weeks, and from what he could tell of the pots and pans in the kitchen, he'd been living on macaroni and Velveeta. A steady diet of that shit might do that to anyone. If this kept up, though, he would have no choice but to ask him to leave.

He went over to the Hitachi and turned the volume up on Elvis Costello, with the profound hope of drowning out the Pinkster. In what was becoming a standard evening ritual, he'd brought up a six-pack of Old Bohemian, the cheapest beer he could tolerate. It was the old get-sad-and-feel-sorry-for-yourself deal. He looked over his bedroom with remote eyes, as if he didn't sleep there every night. There was a cheerless team poster of the Orioles on one wall, and on another he'd recently tacked up a beaut of Michelle Pfeiffer lying seductively across a piano. She was in this sparkly red dress, and her eyes had this great come-hither look. He wasn't into that celebrity bullshit, just thought it brightened the place up a bit, that's all. The Hitachi, one of those expensive miniature jobs, along with the compact discs— one of the few luxuries he allowed himself—was set up on the bookshelves, above the Stephen King collection and those imitation Chandler detective novels he craved on rainy forlorn nights. The highlight of his room was the great old fireplace, center stage, with the exquisite moldings, a fireplace that had not seen a roaring fire in some while, which just stared back like a cold, empty reminder.

He kept the pictures on the mantel. His dad and his Uncle Paddy, ever somber in their dress blue. Graduation Day at the Academy. There was that one of the brothers—his brothers—on that fishing trip up at Lake George. Shea and Brian were each holding a string of healthy-sized fish in front of a cooler packed with Budweiser. They looked plastered to hell. He hadn't heard from them in a while. Shea—Sergeant Shea Wearie of the Sixty-fourth Precinct, sir, yes sir—was there with his well-disciplined family at Christmas. Jesus, couldn't the guy ever give it a rest? No sir, sir. But Brian—well, Brian was another story. Eamon didn't want to know. For Christ's sake, Brian was up to dangerous things in the south of Florida. Every family must've had one. Then he fixed on the one of Trish and him. Inside that tiny Vegas chapel. Leona's Jackpot House of Marriage. Their smiles had that evanescent quality, as if the happy moment was already busy receding. There was a picture of Jenny, too. Prom Night, 1975. He was in a gaudy baby blue tux, ruffles galore, but she looked good, even with that huge corsage covering half her bosom. Jenny creeped into his thoughts too often, he knew that, and it was no secret he felt like calling her many times, on many nights like this, with a can of beer in his hand and a drunken feeling on his brain. The last time he had seen her had been bad news anyway. It had been a mistake to go to his tenth reunion—and then it had been all kind of sad and everything to meet Jenny's husband, this Rick bozo. The guy corners him and tells him all about the spine-tingling excitement of the retail pet food business, and all Eamon could think was, Jesus, Jen, were you that lonely?

There were many kinds of loneliness. There was being lonely for other people. There was wanting a woman. But these were not the worst kinds of loneliness. The older you got, the more you learned what a bleak and unfriendly terrain it was. You got older and you survived and you paid your dues, just like the next guy. You learned not to expect too much. You learned not to set yourself up for disappointment. The things you wanted when you were younger—the things that seem to glisten and beckon, the girl goddesses that look to be the soft, warm answer, the answer to all loneliness and all the hollow space in a man's heart—never really changed, and you never quite let go of the urgency. But as time went on, Eamon had discovered that even the old, sweetly held dreams could lose their vibrancy, that they too could become drab and hopeless in their own way.

He slipped in a John Lennon disc. "Imagine" was the first song, and it was hard to reconcile the beautiful cracking voice with Lennon's life trickling away on a bloody sidewalk. It was just a bad old world. Just the way things were. No one had to tell Eamon about mean streets. To live in Baltimore, to live in any city really, was to know the grim realities. Crack deals went down a block away, in front of the Laundromat, twenty-four hours a day, right in front of that squalid brightness. You often heard gunshots in the night, and the hellish sirens never abated. Helicopters, the newest rage in law enforcement, flared searchlights into the windows at all hours, looking for God knows what. The homeless wandered the streets like out of some kind of Romero movie; the walking dead scavenged from garbage pails and accosted everyone for change. In the mornings when he went to get the car out of the garage, he'd find that people had been there in the night, that perhaps they even lived there, and then he would set about the task of removing the lugubrious clues, which included condoms and needles, porno mags and pizza boxes.

He had slugged back four of the Old Bohs and could feel himself fading into the night. The moon, full and opalescent, hung outside his barred windows. He could hear an argument out somewhere in the street, an ugly, loud skirmish between a man and a woman, and then he heard glass breaking, followed by the woman's expletives. There was no reason for remembering the mysterious letters of Sandstone then, but it came to him like a soft afterthought to the harsh city sounds. It was still in his jacket pocket, just where he left it. He settled back into bed with the last of the Old Bohs and began to read:

Dearest lover,

I decided to go to our pond, as still as ever behind Savor's farm, just the lily pads and the croaking of frogs. It is far away from all that moves and all that bustles. We go here often, you and I. Your face reflects back off the green water in prisms of Renoir's golden light. I thought of all the things that are good in this world, all the things that can matter and lift us to whatever better places there are. We always liked the smell of the coffee and bacon in the Starlight diner. It is a delicious smell that never smells as good at home, and you need to hear the clatter of the cups and the conversation wafting up like so much steam. And we always like to go to baseball games, and it never matters who wins or who loses when the Hens play. But Bucky Hatchet is the best and you know that, and it doesn't really matter if he strikes out more than he hits the long ball because when he gets into one it is like a golfer's drive, hit for distance and God. That is what is good about the bush leagues, 'cause we can just get drunk on that bad old beer and eat barbecued corn on the cob. I like that, I really do.

The movies are always good in Great River, even if they're always months late and sometimes on videotape already. It's our Last Picture Show, rich with dankness and stale popcorn and the perfume of age. It seems like nobody but us goes there anymore. I hope they never close it, that would be way too sad. I think the high school kids still go there on Friday night, and I'll bet they take their girls up to the balcony. I always like it when you kiss me up there. It makes me young and it makes me think of Donnie Filbert trying to squeeze me through my pink angora sweater years ago now.

I like the cows. The spotted black ones best of all. They swing their tails and it makes me drowse.

There are so many things, you know. The grass is wet with dew and I like that. The autumn is the best time, and September is the best month, warm and hot in the day, but at night cool with premonition. And you always tell me that they should start the year in September, because it is the time of beginnings. But you know, this September hasn't been the same and if we're rating them I'd have to put it at the very bottom.

I go to sleep these nights by reading. I've stopped reading the new books and now I only read the old ones because they're the only ones that are any good anyway. Scott Fitgerald and John Cheever belong to the same good school and I always go back to the short stories. But you know that. And the old Russians are always very good too. Because they lived strongly and wrote truly.

I like the way Frank Sinatra sings a love song. I know I'm supposed to go for rock and roll like the rest of my generation, but it all sounds so brutish these days. I want to hear clarinets and saxophones and I want the words to have Cole Porter's sultry elegance.

Chocolate is a good sin and beer is good anytime and cigarettes were meant for smoking and everyone should go to bed with a snifter of cognac so they can wake up in a better mood.

I always like sneaking away. We're good at that, you and I. The best place is that lounge on the turnpike with the blinking martini glass whose name I always forget. Their jukebox has Patsy Cline and Peggy Lee and all the slow ones. And Rita is the best bartender because she buys every other one and has the best laugh. And she never minds it when we're drunk and kissing.

You're the funniest, though. You make me laugh and no one else does and that is our great conspiracy.

And I need my Sunday papers. A ton of them. And I always want pancakes and real maple syrup on Sundays.

Pepperoni pizza from Mama's is another thing worth noting.

But love is the only thing that shakes the lonely feeling. I need a lover to sit next to me on the train so that I can talk about the scenery. Talking is the only hobby worth having. And when I drink I need you there so that I can get really wonderfully drunk. Now James I've really thought about it and I'll tell you why people have affairs. It's not for the sex and not for the thrill of another, like everyone always says. No, it's not that. It's to discover—now James pay close attention here—other sides of ourselves. It's to find what's lost and what has been long buried, tenderness and humor and the wickedness of touching.

Netti

6

Eamon had never been to Ocean City in April. He and Trish had gone there summers, but he'd never been crazy about that overwrought mile of Holiday Inn–America. The modern hotels were grim monolithic presences, casting large shadows over the desultory brown sand. Ocean City was just another one of those Virginia and Myrtle Beach deals: a sparking, blinking tourist attraction, featuring thousands of holes of miniature golf and a Denny's every block or so. It was not his thing. He preferred the quieter reaches of shore to the north, Bethany and Rehoboth, which made him long for the Long Island of his youth, for those great stretches of pristine beach in the Hamptons and Fire Island. His dad used to take them on the all-day fishing boats, out of Greenport or Montauk, and he always liked the color of the water once you got out there. It was bright as emerald miles from shore, and all you could smell was the rotting bait and the beer, and believe it or not, these were the very best smells. The memory filled Eamon with a sudden warmth, putting him on the very verge of tears.

It was a dull, even miserable, three-and-a-half-hour drive. They'd crossed the Bay Bridge at eight and stopped at

Hemingway's restaurant, the Eastern Shore's first landmark, for a hearty breakfast of scrambled eggs and sausage. Eamon drank more coffee than usual, trying to keep up with Bunko, and as a result, he felt a little more jangled than usual, too. The rain made for difficult driving, even if it was only intermittent. It would splatter down like crazy on the unmarked Aries but then suddenly lift for a few minutes, leaving them lost in the foggy grayness. Then that jackhammer rain would start all over again. The radio was out, but that didn't really matter when Bunko was in such an expansive mood:

"This is just great. Really. Out of the fuckin' office for once. I mean it. A little adventure. Course, it's all a waste of time. We stand an ice cube's chance in hell on this one. And those are my good odds. I mean, don't get me wrong or anything, I think we can give input on this sucker and even do a little good today, but it's up to Mister Tony at the Bureau. But he knows that. He must know that. Doesn't he know that? Sure he knows that. The man's a pro, for Christ's sake . . ."

Bunko, master of the rhetorical question, lit up another cigarette, which didn't get in the way of his driving, since he only kept a finger or two on the steering wheel anyway.

"So anyway, my point is that it's a nice respite from routine. At least we're not on magazine duty. Jesus Fuckin' Christ. Where was our dignity? Which reminds me. Anal has not been his protozoan self lately. I mean, why does he suddenly give a shit about the Executioner? It's like the guy actually wants us to solve it, which seems mighty hard to believe and all. Which reminds me of something else. Now, that was strange what Mister Tony's men dug up from the Ashland police. Now, three boys under sixteen missing may not seem like a big deal unless you bring into it the fact that they all came from stable family situations and all. It's not the ol' nasty divorce bullshit where one partner hightails it outa there with the kids. But the sheriff there in Ashland is voted in, you know. Doesn't know a damn thing about police procedure. The sheriff—a man of limited brain cells—classifies all the cases as runaways, which is right up there with classifying a steak as a vegetable, if you get my meaning."

"Bunk, I think we oughta go up and talk to the parents of those kids."

"Mister Tony and his boys are already up there, believe me."

"Yeah, I know it. But I think we oughta take another ride. Get us out of Assholes Incorporated for a couple more days. Besides, I haven't seen that part of the country. Probably nice up there. We could do some fly-fishing. How's that sound?"

"Sounds beautiful. That's how it sounds. You know the thing that complicates shit—is those boys are real spread out, couple towns away from each other. Gets rid of the usual spectrum. I thought it might be a teacher or something. Someone the kids all knew. Maybe a bus driver or something. You know, I was reading a couple books about these serial kooks last couple nights—"

"Fuck, Bunk, you read a book. I'm mighty proud. What's next? Season tickets to the ballet? A gourmet cooking course? Japanese gardening?"

"Yeah, yeah, yeah. You oughta go on 'Star Search' as a stand-up comedian, Wearie. Really, I ain't kidding. You have that something special. I just get chills whenever you launch into one of your rousing routines. Hell, fuck 'Star Search'—you oughta go on 'Letterman' and do stupid pet tricks. Now, as I was saying, I'd been reading about—"

"Make sure to get those ballet tickets right down the third-base line. Mezzanine level."

"It's a gift, Wearie. Like gonorrhea. Now, listen up, you might learn something: It's a mother thing. That's what it is with these eunuchs. Their mothers are whores, real prostitutes or very, very slutty. Or another scenario is that they're way too mothering, you know. Giving them baths when they're teenagers. Sleeping with them. The whole fruitcake. Totally fucks them up. Either they become impotent or they start killing whores that look like dear old Mom, or sometimes they go the homo route 'cause they don't want nothing to remind them of her. All sorts of derivative shit here."

"Bunk, you know what the problem for me is? Can't make it real. I try and I draw a blank, man. I picture the Executioner in his hood, and it just doesn't ring up."

"Yeah, me too, buddy."

"What else you learn from that book?"

"If they don't know their victims, they usually have some gimmick. Pretend to be cops. Using false badges and other paraphernalia. Or maybe they'll act like they're hurt, crutches and casts, the whole fake vulnerability route. And oh yeah, they often drive vans or campers. Easier to snatch up their prey."

"Jesus, I wonder if any of it's real. This whole thing got started because of a lousy picture. All we got is a bunch of lousy pictures."

"Don't I know it, buddy. Listen, I got another theory: I think that first one with the torture chamber was a mistake. I think the Executioner just put the wrong photo in his little envelope, that's what I think. Ah, who fuckin' knows. On another front, I heard from Allie last night. Not so good, pal, not so good. Of course, I'm sending her money, but that ain't going to save her. She needs to find something she cares about in this life. I worry about her, I do . . . ."

He went on about his daughter, the one who'd been in and out of hospitals. Allie heard voices, and the voices told her to do things that a sane person could not begin to try and understand. Eamon closed his eyes, thinking about Bunko's little girl, in some vomit-colored room somewhere, which seemed as distant and unreal as anything else in this world.

They checked in to the Sheraton, a huge, towering structure on the boardwalk, which was practically deserted on a dark, rainy Wednesday in April. The hundred-dollar-a-night rooms went for bargain-basement prices, affording them adjoining suites on one of the upper floors. Their view turned out to be just a smear of fog and some phosphorescent light from the glassed-in pool and atrium below. They could hear the breakers, only a few yards off, a repetition that soon became solidly depressing.

The antiseptic suite, in unfamiliar shades of pink, with its wrapped toilet and bolted-in TV, had Eamon feeling anonymous, as if he were a permanent stranger in the world. He looked around at the barren, immaculate setup and suddenly missed his unremarkable home a great deal.

Bunko was singing his own version of "Melancholy Baby." The sunken, heart-shaped tub got him to thinking about his second honeymoon. They'd gone to Ocean City fifteen years back and tied the knot on a drunken whim. Tenita was a young nurse he hadn't taken the time to get to know, and it had been in a luxurious high-rise much like this one that his life had begun to come apart.

"We shoulda gone to Atlantic City," Bunko said. "Jesus, let's get outa here. Let's shake that fuckin' porn king down."

They had to drive. The El Meridian was located a hundred blocks farther down. It took forever. The traffic lights were all on the blink, flashing yellow, forcing them to brake at every intersection. The wide thoroughfare bisected the narrow peninsula and ran through a ruined American landscape. While the colossal hotels trampled the oceanfront, the bay side was a mad pastiche of corporate trademark. It was a fast-food Toontown: Plastic milk shakes and hamburgers revolved on their axes like giant illuminated globes; fifty-foot-tall cartoon characters, off the Disney and Warner Brothers' lots, helped hawk pizza and snow cones; fish and chips were served up on Spanish galleons, and all your hot dog needs were met by a fabulous Day-Glo frankfurter; the bright pop art colors streaked together into a Hanna-Barbera rainbow, in the full spectrum of the cash register, all of it as soulless as ordering fries at the drive-through window.

The El Meridian turned out to be a modern glass office building, not the kind of place they were expecting at all. The ground-floor directory listed him under the all-encompassing Silver Star Management. Sixth floor. The other occupants were mostly dentists and doctors. In the elevator Bunko said, "I'll play bad cop if it comes to that."

Besides *Boy Love*, they'd discovered that Rube Fuchs published three other magazines of dubious charm. He was also doing a burgeoning little side business in cassettes and telephone entertainment. Bunko pictured the guy as a sleazoid with an open shirt and a bunch of gold chains. Eamon had more trouble imagining the appearance of the man who'd molested his own son.

Nothing was turning out the way they expected. The receptionist, a young man in tortoiseshell glasses, was smartly outfitted in a camel's hair jacket and paisley tie. He asked if they wouldn't mind taking a seat while he checked to see if Mr. Fuchs was in. They fell back into one of the expensive-looking leather couches. Copies of *Fortune* and *Money* had been set on the chrome coffee table. The walls were painted a dusky rose, and the rich carpeting seemed a perfect match. If it wasn't for one little detail, they might have been in the reception area for *Time* magazine. The carefully framed photographs, placed about so unobtrusively, were part of a series devoted to the rise and fall of a man's penis.

"I'm sorry, what were your names again?" the receptionist politely inquired.

"Just tell them we're federal agents. Postal. He'll know what this is about."

"His secretary will be with you in a moment."

Shortly thereafter another young man appeared. Eamon couldn't help noticing his sartorial elegance, the gray flannel suit and tasseled shoes, and was beginning to wonder if they'd made some kind of mistake. "This way, gentlemen," he said. They followed as he led them through a maze of partitions, past several other well-dressed young men at their desks, past the pitter-patter of word processors, until they arrived at Fuchs's office in the very back. "You may enter," the gray flannel suit said.

They were surprised to find a salon out of Louis XIV's France. It was inordinately dark, as yards of red and gold drapery took care of the windows. Fuchs was on the phone, with his wing tips kicked up on a magnificent mahogany desk. He waved them into antique high-backed chairs. Eamon and Bunko didn't know what to make of it. The ceiling was this unbelievable Sistine Chapel number, and there were huge gilt mirrors and ornate vases and rugs. Eamon couldn't take his eyes off the paintings, which looked as if they weighed a ton. Naked boys frolicked in rich pastoral scenes, under golden apple trees, with mountains and verdant hills in the background. But it was the dark blue skies that told the story, as angry and foreboding as anything.

"Jay, you're just so insouciant," Fuchs kept saying into the phone. A grandfather clock ticked off the time.

He was an ugly little man who dressed wonderfully. He was in a shiny double-breasted Italian suit, but his jowly pink face was not nearly as fashionable. A bullfrog waiting for a passing fly, Bunko decided.

"Later, dove," he signed off sweetly. Then he turned to them and snarled, "So what the hell do you cocksuckers want? I thought I was through with you guys for the time being."

Bunko spoke very evenly: "I think you should listen closely, Mr. Yves Saint-Fuckin'-Laurent: I'm Lieutenant Ryan, and this is Lieutenant Wearie. Special agents from Postal. And if you don't make a very significant attitude adjustment, I'm going to have you indicted on some very old and very quaint laws. I've seen your *insouciant* magazine, and though this is only a subjective point of view, I considered it marvelously obscene. Did you know that it's a crime to use the mails for the transport of lewd and lascivious materials?"

"There's no need for intimidation, gentlemen. I think I've already been most cooperative today. There's no reason to think that I won't continue to—"

"I don't know what you're talking about. But we're here to gather evidence on a federal case. We'll be needing—"

"Everything and anything that might have to do with one Howie M.," Fuchs answered, clearly tired with the whole thing. "They were here only about two hours ago. Don't you people ever talk to each other?"

"What the fuck?"

"An Agent Dupar and someone not nearly so good-looking. FBI. Helicoptered in, as I understand it."

"Christ." Agent Dupar was one of Montrez's chief deputies. "What did you give them?"

"Everything. They used an approach that was amazingly similar to your own. All the pictures. We had them on file. We even had a letter he wrote. Very enchanting. Dupar and the other fellow didn't give me a clue to what it was all about. But I gather Howie did something dreadful."

"Jesus, what a waste of time," Bunko snorted. "And I can't even tell you it was a pleasure to meet you. I can't even extend my hand to crud like you. I should add, however incidentally, that if it turns out that your little magazine printed pictures of minors, if you knowingly or otherwise promoted the exploitation of said kids, I will nail you, you insouciant son of a bitch."

As they got up to leave, Fuchs turned his attention to Eamon. He offered a kindly smile and said, "We never did get a chance to talk, but I was wondering if you by chance had done any modeling?"

They were drinking Irish coffees in the Sheraton lounge, a losing proposition all the way around. It was a disco called Bandanna's, a lonely little place that reeked of ammonia and old one-night stands. There were six or seven people listening to a girl singer in spandex belt out the hits of the Eagles under an assault of multicolored light. Welcome to a weeknight in hell.

A sour-faced waitress in a Playboy bunny getup stood at the service bar chatting to the bartender, a muscular narcissist who ignored his customers. Bunko was coming on to a horrible, blowsy blonde. She was drunk as a skunk and made sitting on a stool look like a giant adventure. Eamon was losing respect for the man by the minute. They sloshed around like a couple of cubes melting down in their whiskey glasses. Their conversation was impossible to follow:

"Iss too long . . . a . . . story," she slurred. "Thas wha happens when a person . . . uh . . . makes decizz . . . ins."

"God is a big ugly bitch," Bunko said.

"Iss Betty. Oh. Did . . . I . . . tell . . . you that?"

It was also painful to watch. She was rubbing his leg while he slurped on her ear. Fortunately it wasn't long before they paid their tab.

"Good night, sport," Bunko said, giving Eamon a hearty slap on the back. "We'll leave bright and early."

"Don't wait up," she shouted, just before falling off her stool.

He was glad to see them leave and didn't hurt for company. He stared out past the empty cocktail tables, past the empty circle of dance floor, to the spandex singer in a field of flashing hot light. She was all alone out there. No backup musicians or anything. She sang and danced to one of those all-purpose music boxes. She wasn't any good, there wasn't any question about that, but Eamon admired the fact that she gave it all she had on every song. He felt like clapping when she finished with "Lyin' Eyes," but that would have only embarrassed her. He was in full stare, his eyes ablaze with her, as she shimmied in the moving prisms of light, when some guy interrupted his reverie.

"Do you mind if I sit here?" he asked, pointing to the one next to him. Eamon looked down the bar at the long line of unoccupied stools and simply shrugged his shoulders, as if to say, it's your nickel, pal.

"Would you like another drink?" the same guy asked, pointing to Eamon's glass, long empty, crusted with whipped cream.

He wondered what the guy was after. "Naah, it's okay," he said. "I'm going soon."

The bartender took a slow walk down, as if another customer was all he needed. "Yeah?" he asked, almost threateningly.

"I'd like some champagne," the guy said. "A bottle of your best."

The bartender looked at him skeptically. "That be the

Don. Hundred bucks a bottle. How do I know you can pay for it?"

"You don't. Life's full of doubt," the guy said. "Now, get me that bottle."

Eamon liked the guy better already. That Neanderthal of a bartender didn't force the issue and went to get it out of the ice chest.

"What, celebrating?" Eamon asked, good-naturedly.

"Yeah, it's a wake," the guy said, grimly.

It was dark at the bar, but on closer inspection Eamon could see that the guy didn't look so well. He was thin and gaunt, and he had purple splotches on his face. He looked as if he could have been in his fifties, but Eamon was starting to think he was younger, much younger.

"You see, I'm dying," the guy said. "Won't be long now."

Eamon stayed quiet, because he couldn't think of anything to say.

The bartender came back with the champagne, and the guy told him, "Make sure to get yourself one. And anyone else who wants it."

"Thanks," the galoot went.

The guy downed a glass of the bubbly, then another. "Are you sure you don't want any? It's the best hangover there is. Tomorrow I won't remember any of it. But hell, life's one big hangover. Isn't that right?"

"Sure, sure," Eamon said. He wanted to get up and leave now. The guy was spooking him.

"And that's all she wrote," he said into his glass, as if he were all alone in the bar. "Just because I fucked around a little. Just because I needed something—and was stupid enough to go looking for it. But that shit's all so out of control. In washrooms, in fucking public toilets. Doing all kinds of things with all kinds of strange people. Like someone else's bad dream, man."

Eamon wanted to get the hell out of there. He said, "Yeah, well, it's been nice talking to you, but I've got to turn in. Have an early start tomorrow. Take care of yourself."

"Fuck you," the guy said.

7

At moments like this Captain Marcus Brown thought of his hero Richard Milhous Nixon, the thirty-seventh president of the greatest country on earth. Now, Dick had been kicked in the pants a few times himself. Montrez was just like that Harvard Romeo. Montrez had gone to some Ivy League school, and he was full of his own fancy excuses. Marcus Brown thought now of that first television debate. Why, there was Dick full of good sense and practical advice—but did anyone listen? No, of course not. All the women were just staring at JFK with his magic tan and his fancy hair. Montrez even had Kennedy hair. Well, if he thought Captain Marcus Brown was going to just lie down and play dead, he had another think coming.

The captain was furious. Montrez had sent his own men down to Ocean City with the cunning of a fox. It did not matter that Montrez had already called in his apologies. Crossed wires, he explained; promised it wouldn't happen again. Oh, that Montrez was cagey. Had an answer for everything. Well, he would learn—like so many others—not to fuck with Marcus Brown.

The captain thought of his hero again. He saw Richard Milhous Nixon getting onto that chopper, departing for the last time. Dick turned to face the loyal men and women of his staff, collected on the White House lawn, on that most terrible and tragic day, many with tears in their eyes, and he saluted them. The epitome of grace under pressure.

Bunko realized they were being cut out. He didn't have much problem with that. He was amazed that Anal was taking it so hard. After all, Montrez's people were more experienced in these kinds of things. He suspected Anal was pissed most of all by the way the Bureau sent over their little care package. It contained photocopies of all the materials they'd seized from Fuchs yesterday, up to and including the envelopes Howie had used, and they'd rushed over this all-important package Federal Express. They hadn't had the good sense to make use of the Service's own overnight delivery. Anal was incensed.

Bunko was trying hard to keep his attention on matters at hand, but he was tired from last night and the morning's drive. Betty had been more than he bargained for, and the two of them had engaged in one of the longest, most prolonged, and unsatisfactory fucks in the history of drunken mistakes. It was all very tragic, really, and the whole thing had given him pause, just as it always did. The whole idea of a one-night stand. There he was, in some damned hotel room, grunting over some woman-beast he'd just met. What the hell was he doing with his life? It was a terrible need that always seemed to control him, not the other way around, and he had regretted it the second after he came. The worse part was that Betty wasn't a bad person; just another horny, whacked-out divorced woman wandering the lunar landscape. Christ. All he knew about her was that she was Polish and that she worked for the phone company or something, and then she said the usual tripe about not being that kind of girl and not normally doing that kind of thing. But just the same, he thought she did that kind of thing often enough, and just thinking about it triggered that whole terrible sad and poignant feeling, feeling bad for her and for himself and everyone else who woke up to the flush of toilets and the brutal face of a stranger. Betty couldn't find a pen or a piece of paper, so she tore out a blank check that had her address and phone number. Now, either Betty was one of the world's most trusting innocents or this was someone with truly limited resources. Either way, it didn't say too much about her. Jesus, the whole thing pained him. Made him see her vulnerability; filled him with tenderness, yet repulsed him at the same time.

He had to concentrate on the work. That was the ticket. There wasn't much there, and God knows Wearie hadn't been much help. They'd had a long, quiet ride back, and in the gloom Bunko detected hostility. Probably because he didn't get any, Bunko thought. Or maybe they'd kept him up with the noise. Who knew. It wasn't his problem. His problem was to piece together some kind of profile of the Executioner based on the Bureau's limited findings. He slipped on his reading glasses, a recent unhappy addition. He was forty-eight. Fuck that. He glanced over at Wearie, who was hip-deep in those stupid love letters from Sandstone. He'd gone down into Dead Letters and scooped up the whole bunch of them. Bunko, you wouldn't understand, the kid said. Like he couldn't understand. Sometimes the world was full of ugly shit and you just wanted to get away from it for a little while. Find a nice shady tree to sit under for a spell. Who couldn't understand that? Fuck it. It was time to get down to business.

The short, perfunctory note, in the Executioner's own handwriting, was the most important clue:

Dear Sirs:

I would be most pleased if you would consider my latest entry for your "Meet Your Neighbor Contest."

Thank you for all due consideration and your valuable time.

Respectfully submitted,
Howie M.

P.S. Mother and I greatly admire your quality magazine. Keep up the good work.

DEAD LETTERS

It was hard to believe that the Executioner had a mother. Hell, it was hard to believe the son of a bitch was even conceived in this world. Maybe it was a sick joke. Maybe she was an invalid or something. Maybe she was already dead. Maybe it was one of those Bates Motel deals. He figured she was dead. It was just a feeling, something that stuck in the guts. Wearie had been right about one thing: The three- and four-cent stamps were unusual and pointed to the involvement of an older person. Probably killed his ma for her stamps. Who the fuck knew?

The three recovered envelopes, standard yellow nine-by-twelves, were plastered with the commemorative stamps, which were no longer sold. Three different ones were in use, a three-center from that golden oldie 1957, and two four-centers from 1960, that all-time favorite chart topper. Hell, that was a great year, kind they don't make anymore. Jesus Christ, he was still a senior in high school, captain of the football team, would you believe, Big Man on Campus (shit, you never even heard that phrase anymore), dating Bunny Ann Lyons, the prettiest cheerleader in the forty-eight continental. Different world, you bet. Guys talking about going all the way. Girls dreaming about wedding nights and setting up house. Suddenly he remembered all those Sunday afternoons with his dad in the garage, working under the Chevy, changing oil pans and adjusting hoses, tinkering for tinkering's sake. His dad would bring out a couple of cold Blue Ribbons and they'd just stand around in that awkward father-son way, talking Johnny Unitas and Brooksie Robinson, Colts and O's, just those things that counted. Everything seemed to go on between the lines, nothing wrong with that, damn straight. Hell, he had to concentrate. Get down to it. Stop thinking about such nostalgic bullshit.

You could tell that the stamps held some clue to all of this. That monster was screwing with their heads. Had to be. The three-center was an old-fashioned one "Honoring the Teachers of America," with this prim and proper schoolmarm holding some book, and these two lily white all-American kids standing respectfully in front of a globe. The eager-beaver boy was even wearing a tie, for Christ's sake, and the cherubic schoolgirl was all blond curls in this pink dress. Jesus, he could just imagine them making that stamp today; how different it would have to be. There'd be no more of that Wonder Bread shit, that's for damn sure. The new kids would be black and Hispanic and Indian, the whole Jesse Jackson rainbow deal. Which probably wasn't such a bad thing, if you asked him.

He wondered then, for the umpteenth time, because they kept coming back to it, if the Executioner was a teacher. But it was such an obvious thing, like the turd was leading them around by the goddamn hand. He knew it would be a mistake to let that take hold, locking out so many other possibilities. Once you got something cemented in your head, it tended to work against you, tended to shut down the process. And the process was everything. No one had to tell him that. The process was what got results. They came no other way. You had to keep all the fucking doors open. Ask questions. Disregard nothing. Throw it back and forth until you couldn't stand it anymore. God, he wished Wearie would snap out of it. He could've used a little help about now. But shit, there he was, all dreamy and psychotic-looking, lost in a bunch of weirdo letters, useless to the world.

The two four-centers were also throwbacks: One was a tribute to "The American Woman," featuring a rather creepy-looking mother-daughter combo. They were just staring straight ahead with these dark, absolutely humorless expressions. The other, "Employ the Handicapped," showed a middle-aged fellow in a wheelchair operating a drill press. Was it possible that the Executioner had suffered some disabling injury? Except they had that picture of him, buck-naked and standing up besides. Maybe he was a machinist or something. Or maybe it all meant absolutely dork. Just more wild geese to chase. Another thing was bothering him: Why was it the turd's slapping these thirty-year-old stamps down in the first place? If they're not clues and all? It wasn't like these particular stamps were worth much, ten cents a pop maybe, not even—but Jesus, they weren't exactly commonplace either. He could've been a collector, except these babies weren't really worth the trouble. Christ, he had to move on. Come back to it later.

The postmarks proved that everything had been mailed out of Ashland. That was one definite. And one big plus. The Bureau confirmed that a Royal 500 had been used to type the naughty-boy captions on the backs of the pictures. Several sets of fingerprints were found. But the crime computer could not make a match.

The handwritten note came on dippy, flowery Hallmark stationary. Not the kind of thing a man would likely buy.

But Bunko was most struck by Howie's handwriting. He had never seen anything like his *i*-dots. Now, he knew teenage girls often drew little ditzy circles above the *i*, displaying a small dollop of adolescent vanity, but he had never seen them dotted with a complete happy face. Howie the Executioner had taken the trouble to fill in each one with crude eye-slashes and smile. Yeah, have a nice day. The small sample definitely showed signs of severe metal disturbance. Although the spacing was orderly, and obvious care had been taken in the phrasing—as if it had been copied from some fucking etiquette book—the writing itself was extremely loopy, full of dangerous and unwanted extensions. Especially disconcerting were his missing *t*-strokes, which was doubly weird when you considered the elaborate *i*-dots. That was definitely fucked up. On the one hand, he's got too much of something. On the other, he suffers from inadequacy, incompleteness. Jesus. This was some weird shit.

Bunko tried to remember some of the other things he'd learned. Now, he knew that very uneven writing, a wildly fluctuating flow, lettering that dipped and leaned in all sorts of directions, as if the writer were incapable of walking a straight line, was a clear indication of being fucked up. That wasn't the case here at all. The size and flow of Howie's writing, even on unlined stationary, was rigidly maintained. But his uprights showed a clear leftward pull, which could have been a sign of self-loathing, or perhaps he was really burdened by the past. All of the above, most likely. After all, they were dealing with a total sicko.

He tried to make sense of it. What could he learn from it? *Who was this guy?* He was definitely full of contrasts. Okay. Now what? Well, the son of a bitch was capable of violence. Like they fucking didn't already know that. The writing was dark and forceful, imposing. But those crazy loops, sweet and affected, indicated something feminine, something far and apart from the muscle of his pen. The signature was different from the rest of the sample. The lettering was printed, not connected, and much more spaced out. Probably because it wasn't his real name. Jesus, he just didn't know enough about this shit. If Wearie would only snap out of it. He needed to slam this back and forth with someone. Fuck, the day was almost over anyway.

At ten minutes to five on the plain school clock, located above portraits of the current postmaster general and Richard Nixon (Captain Brown refused to update the presidency), which for some reason was caged in mesh, as if the Command Post were overrun by juvenile delinquents, the captain, accompanied as usual by the two Arthurs, marched over to Bunko and Eamon's little corner of the world.

"Attention Red Team," he said. "After much thought, I have determined that our needs can best be served by putting additional men on the case. As of right now you will be working closely with Blue Team. They have already been informed of my decision."

Jesus Christ, was all Bunko could think. Frank Shoe and Barry Lipsick were models of depression. Lipsick was nuts. The guy didn't even speak to half the people in the Post. And Frank—well, Frank was a walking dirge. He was a year away from retirement and solidly convinced that he was going to die before he collected a single pension check. Heart attack, cancer, something. When anyone mentioned any kind of future event, Frank would just say, It doesn't concern me, I'll be dead anyway. Believe me, he would say, I know how this works. This guy—the fucking life of the party.

"I think we're doing fine on our own," Bunko said matter-of-factly.

"My decision has already been made," the captain said. "Further, we've made arrangements to send you and Wearie to Ashland tomorrow. I want you interviewing the families of those missing boys. Blue Team will take it from this end."

"Marcus," Bunko said, "the Bureau has already covered that angle. We'd just be retracing their steps."

"Just do it. Just do what you're told for once. I want this. *You understand me?* Do you have any problems with that, Lieutenant?"

Eamon, who was intently reading one of Netti's letters, trying hard to ignore Anal's anxiety attack, looked up in amazement.

"There's no need in reminding you men that we're on the trail of a genuine psychotic. I want to leave no stone unturned. And we will get our man, I assure you—"

"Save it for the fucking newspapers," Bunko said.

"Well let me tell you something, Lieutenant. I'm thinking very seriously of bringing the gentlemen of the press into this. I've been thinking that a little publicity might help our cause. Help root out our man. See what I mean?"

"Marcus, you've got to be fuckin' out of your mind. Montrez will blow a gasket. It's the exact opposite of what we need—"

"Montrez can go jerk off," the captain said. "The little prick does not even have the decency to share his findings. Well, he will find out what many others have found out before him . . ." His words trailed off. Then, in a newly composed voice: "The Bureau has simply not been cooperative. We must take the bull by the horns. In fact, to that end I had a very *illuminating* talk with Sheriff Marvis Smitty, a fine man. Very instructive."

"That retard from Ashland? The man's as sharp as pumpkin squash."

As if he didn't hear: "Well, he was most helpful. Indeed. Still thinks it's a problem with runaways, though. Anyway, those are your marching orders. Good luck, men."

"Jesus Christ. You must have been practicing this show of

resolve for a week, Marcus. Can anyone tell me what the hell is going on around this joint?"

The captain did not bother to turn around. Arthur Marlens, in charge of expenditures, handed Bunko their tickets and ran down their itinerary.

"Allegheny out of BWI. Eight A.M. sharp. That'll take you as far as Williamsport. One of those commuter jobs. Stops in between. There'll be a car waiting for you at the Hertz counter. The drive up to Ashland will take you a few hours. I couldn't find a Holiday Inn in the area, so you'll have to check yourself into something. Something moderate, I might add. Let's not go about wasting the taxpayers' money. Also, I don't see why you and Wearie can't share a room. What was all this business about separate suites in Ocean City?"

"Arty, you just wouldn't understand," Bunko said. "Eamon and I are a couple of good-lookin' bachelors. Understandably, we get laid a lot."

Marlens was glad to see them going. Just to have Bunko out of the office for a few days would be a great relief.

The Command Post was practically deserted. There were only a dozen special agents to begin with—half of them out on assignment at any given time—and nobody ever stayed past quitting time. For the most part they worked regular hours, nine to five, very cushy. Besides them, the only other agent in the place was Santos. He was at his metal desk, in the glow of his VTD, writing a letter to his mother. Bunko wished there were a window to the outside. He wondered what it was like out there. Was it still raining? Or had it finally stopped, leaving one of those nice dewy-perfumed evenings on tap?

"I was thinking about going over to the Marlin," he said, putting on his coat.

"No, thanks, Bunk. I need the sleep tonight," Eamon said. He was still reading the letters from Sandstone.

"You know now, we're going to miss opening day," Bunko said wistfully. He hadn't missed one in twenty years. The O's were something to live for.

"Yeah, it crossed my mind. Give the tickets to Boxcar. If she doesn't use them, she'll sell them."

"Pick you up at seven, all right?" Bunko said. "Hey, our Netti have anything interesting to say?"

"Yeah, yeah, she does. She's a nice lady, Bunk. Got some poetry in her soul. Know what I mean?"

"Naah. You know I only go out with real pigs. Know what I mean?"

That night Eamon went to the multiplex at Harbor Place. Pinkus had been crying, and a movie didn't seem like such a bad idea. He bought a jumbo order of popcorn and walked into the sequel of a sequel. The movie was one that featured massive car pileups and a hero who carried around a rocket launcher for a gun. Eamon hardly ever went to the movies alone. Men who went to the movies alone always made him think of Travis Bickle in *Taxi Driver*. Jobless. Friendless. Societal rejects who were most likely planning a semiautomatic assault on a nearby shopping mall or a popular political candidate. And the women who went to movies stag always had that desperate, haggard look, like they'd spent the better part of their lives rummaging through the personal ads. Tonight he felt like he belonged with those misfits. He was that alone.

The popcorn was salty and smothered in fake butter. He started wanting for a cold beer. He lost interest in the movie and found himself staring at the backs of heads and the occasional lip-locked couple. He was not jealous and he did not long for someone. Attraction was the way of the world, round and round. Love was the impossible. No one had to tell him. He wondered, in the flickering darkness, if anyone cared enough to think of him at that moment, besides his parents. If out there, anyone was longing for and imagining Eamon Wearie. He supposed Trish might've thought of him from time to time. With the tiniest bit of affection. Why not?

He thought of the woman from Sandstone now. Netti loved James in the impossible way. She would've given anything for James. Now, that was intriguing.

8

So I finally did it, James. I know you thought the day would never come, but it has come and gone and I've done that most American thing. She stared back at me through the glass of Monty Irwin's showroom—you know the one, up by the old Sinclair station—with her homely headlights, like some sad and unwanted puppy in the pet store window. No, she is not a great and lusty beauty, not something that sparkles and accelerates, but she goes at a steady trotter's pace, just my style. I've named her Elouise, after your mom, whom I see from time to time. She baked me a blueberry pie last May and I may have told you this but she had the decency to come by with it and I think she may have cried a little. She loves you so.

It's just a little Honda Civic but she's my first new car in my entire long-winded life, James. You always made fun of my old Dart with her battered red interior, her stuffing falling out, but old Janey always got me there or died trying. But we always have fun just riding around, you and I. Now you, you have a smart car, and I always like it when you pick me up after classes, even though sometimes it's embarrassing when my students catch us

74

in the act. But what do they know? Someday they'll get older too, and they'll also have to steal their little moments. That will take the smirk out of their young faces, living does that, in so many terrible ways. I see them every day and they have clear-bright eyes—that is the difference.

Don't mind me. It is cold today, and the leaves have mostly fallen, and I took my new Elouise up Spruce Road to the river, up to where the trout are, in your favorite pool, but I didn't bother to bring my boots and gear. I took a flask, though. The stupid one you gave me in the shape of binoculars. James, you know it, I'm drinking too much but I love the taste of the Jack in the cold, nearing twilight, in that battered blue, rabbits everywhere, the sound of the white rushing, the wind picking up, in the bitter twilight. It feels hot going down, God. There is nothing better and I have so many people to miss.

I should have done so many things. I should have been a writer like you always tell me. But I never want to write about stories, you know James. I like writing about the way the Jack tastes in the early winter at my trout stream. The way that midnight-blue has got a streak of blood in it tonight. I think writing must be hard work and that's the part I don't like. I just want to have drinks with charming dressy people in the Paris of the '20s. Ski the winters away in Austria and return for the Riviera sun. And every once in a while, when the urge struck to be famous and talked about, I'd write something just to stay on top.

At least you did good work. That is something they can never take away. Never, not ever. I like watching you work. I like the way you never pay any mind to me. Your big red barn is the greatest and your dog Monty is a saint and you're the best painter, for sure. It is all in the small things. Watching you mix the colors. It takes time. Stretching the canvas. Hammering the frame. The radio on to that damn farm report you always love to listen to.

I'm way too sad tonight to keep on writing. But don't let it interfere with your painting.
Do you remember when we were kids? And you wouldn't talk to me when I'd come over on my bicycle. I do. I remember all of it. It is truly a curse.

"Bunk? You know what's strange?"

Bunko wasn't feeling the greatest. They were ten thousand feet up on a creaky old propeller job that wobbled and dipped with every tiny shift in the wind current. They were on the wing—the no-frills hull only held about fifteen passengers—in the middle of a howling, sputtering racket. They'd already bounced down in Lancaster and skidded into Harrisburg, and Bunko had never liked flying to begin with.

"You know what's strange? She writes these letters to this guy she's supposedly in love with and all, right?"

"Kid, I follow you so far." Bunko swallowed down another aspirin with his Rolling Rock. He'd had four beers, even though it was only a little after nine in the morning.

"Bunk, you all right?"

"Fine, kid. What's your fuckin' point?" he said rather testily.

"No big point. Except she buys this new car, right, and she's writing to him about it, and I'm thinking, why doesn't he know that already? I mean, if they see each other and all on a regular basis."

"Jesus. Who knows. Maybe it's all in her fuckin' mind, kid. Maybe she's just another weirdo with delusions and shit. Maybe she don't have no boyfriend at all and she's locked up in some fucking home, for all you know. Christ, just give me a break with that crap."

"I think you're wrong, Bunk. It's not like that. This woman is the real thing. At least I found out she's a schoolteacher. I'm betting English because she mentioned wanting to be a writer. The thought of an intelligent woman—"

"Oh, c'mon, already. Don't tell me you're falling for the wench now. Jesus, what next?"

"Not like that at all, Bunk. I just find it all rather interesting, that's all. I wouldn't mind unlocking it. In fact, I was thinking about going over to Sandstone—since we're going to be up that way and all—and having a little chat with their postmaster. Maybe he's seen—"

"The hell you are. We're not going to waste any time with that shit at all. We have a job to do. Now, let me shut my eyes for a minute, all right with you?"

Eamon knew Bunko was scared to death of flying, so he just let it go. He had no such fears himself. He had a philosophy that kept him in good stead—and that was that when your number was up, it was up. You didn't have much say in that kind of thing. What in the hell was the sense of worrying about it? Tell him that.

There were only a couple of other passengers left. Small-potatoes businessmen reeking of Aqua Velva and carrying old Samsonites loaded down with samples. They were served by America's oldest stewardess, a trembling-handed senior citizen who managed to spill coffee on most of their wrinkled gabardine suits. It was the minor leagues of air travel. Even the captain didn't seem that reassuring. Eamon was used to those cool, silky voices that told you all was swell with the world, even as you were plummeting to a fiery death. "Nothing to worry about, folks. Just a tad bit of turbulence." But Captain Eddie did not instill confidence with his folksy pilot patter: "Okey-dokey. Coming on down. Say a little prayer, boys and girls."

It did not matter. Eamon looked out his octagon portal, buoyed by the sight of patchwork countryside, that beautiful green and gold quilt of farmland that put him close to God.

Bunko's mood improved dramatically once they were on the road out of Williamsport. Arthur Marlens had arranged for a putzy Ford Escort at the Hertz counter, but Bunko quickly upgraded them to a brand-new Cadillac Eldorado.

"American engineering," Bunko said. "Can't even feel the fuckin' road. It just goes by, silently, like glass, baby."

Somehow, Eamon thought, Bunk looked right behind the wheel of a Caddy. It was the only car that gave dignity to his bulk. She was mighty sweet, though. He liked that walnut dash and the tinted blue windshield. It was much colder than they'd expected—at least a thirty-degree drop from Charm City—but it was warm and snug in that crushed red interior. Bunko had the heater purring and the radio tuned to some all-Elvis station. They passed dairy farms and old, run-down gas stations as the King crooned down the slow ones.

It was a bleak, ashen day, interrupted by the occasional flurry, perhaps on the verge of spring snow, but Eamon thought it was beautiful all the same. It did his heart good to be out in the country, cruising through dark hills and sad, dilapidated towns, away from the city, away from the hostile stares of strangers and that maddening claustrophobia, that feeling that you could never find a clean, open space of your own. They followed the road, and the tattered, pothole-riddled road took them past closed-up summer camp-grounds and mom-and-pop motels, past silver grain silos and vast sections of newly turned earth—the rich, permeating smell of manure—past giant peeling billboards and Russian Orthodox churches, past barnyard animals and their absolutely stupefying expressions. But as they traveled along, moving farther north, the scenery shifted, the valleys and farms receded behind them and the terrain grew rockier, meaner. Except for some mangy clusters of pine sticking out of the granite hills, it was a bald, unforgiving landscape. Snow began to fall. They passed through dead factory towns, towns built on a single paper mill or coal find, and it saddened them to see the boarded-up stores and weed-covered rail tracks, the remnants of yesterday. The big, wet flakes collected easily on Route 46, but the big Caddy showed no trouble and plowed on.

Just when it seemed hopeless, that their somber mood would never lift, they came around a long bend to find lush hills and mountains, thick with evergreens and blue spruce, dark and silent and deeply chilling.

"God," Bunko said. As religious a thing as Eamon had ever heard.

The White River ran alongside the road, its icy glint

disappearing and reappearing, under trestles, suddenly out from the brush, snaking back away, continuing to tinkle and burble out of sight. It was a wide, swiftly moving current, as sharp and clear as winter, whose shallow bottom lit up in a silver and copper mosaic. Trout water for sure, Eamon thought. The day was all blue and the snow continued to fall, sticking to the blue greenery, dissolving into the shining river, falling out of the midnight blue, even if it was just afternoon, ever so slowly falling, millions of parachuting flakes, filling a blue universe, blue blue blue.

"I used to go deer hunting in a place that wasn't nearly as pretty," Bunko said. Then he lit up another cigarette, opening the window a crack. Fragrant, cool air rushed in.

"We give up a lot in this life," he said after a while. The wipers were so quiet, they were hardly noticeable. "It makes you wonder, that's all."

Just outside of Ashland, they stopped for lunch. Ma's Old Kettle was at the bottom of Big Grizzly Mountain, which wasn't much of a mountain, just an old, dumpy hill that had been mowed down for skiing. Nobody was skiing, though—and the lift, with its rusty cables and dented cars, creaked in the wind. There was a decrepit, faded banner: WELCOME TO THE BIG GRIZZ '81 INVITATIONAL. At the bottom of Big Grizz, people had taken to discarding their unwanted tires and old, worn-out washing machines, an appliance graveyard in the snowy shadows.

Still, they were hungry, and the Kettle seemed a warm prospect, its chimney serenely smoking, its gravel lot filled with flatbed trucks. When they walked in, though, through a door strung with jingle bells, the locals stopped their talking, like in some kind of bad movie. Mostly they were big, hefty men, in plaid woolen shirts and spattered denim, with W. C. Fields faces, fleshy and red-veined. They sat around small tables, leaning back in their chairs a mite precariously, holding on to their Bud tall-necks. Eamon and Bunko proceeded to the Formica counter, where they were welcomed by the fatty smell of frying ground beef and a sour-faced waitress by the name of Myra. At least that's what was sewn into her bright pink uniform.

"I just hope you're not more FBI people, is all I gots to say," she said.

"Coffee for both of us," Bunko replied.

"Because," she said, "we've had about all we can take of you people, if your really want to know the truth."

"Coffee—and we're pretty hungry. Got some kind of stew and mashed potatoes?

"Got venison stew today. I'd recommend it as much as I'd recommend anything around here," she said, still feisty. "But I'll tell you something: I don't want you askin' my customers any more questions. You people have badgered everyone enough. Would you like soup with that? Got split pea. Won't kill you."

"Isn't it a bit late for snow?" Eamon said.

"No, it ain't. Sometimes snows as late as May. Often does, matter of fact. Still, I don't want you agents bothering my tips here. Understand?"

"How come you're so keen as to think we're G-men?" Bunko finally asked.

"You don't look like hunters. And you don't look like no traveling salesmen I've ever seen. And don't give me any of that beeswax about tourists or anything. That's been used. By that Agent Mathews."

At that she turned and called her order in through the galley window, to a man with tatooed arms. Gradually the others returned to their conversations.

"Ever see that movie *Deliverance?*" Bunko whispered to Eamon.

The stew turned out to be more than just hearty, a savory, spicy concoction that had more than a splash of burgundy to it. They dipped their bread into it and ate in wary silence.

Ashland's Main Street belonged to a thousand American towns. Leftover trolley tracks, from the age of electric, still ran down the center of the avenue, went the distance, past the tiny shops, the shoe repair, Jenk's Stationery, the barbershop with its candy striping, the new video store, past the impressive First National with her Greek pillars and the tiny brick post office, went all the way down to the well-kept town park, a grassy haven surrounded by massive oaks, whose bandstand stood in silhouette, bleak and forgotten this day. It reminded Eamon of the bandstand in Northport when he was growing up; they would smoke dope there in the winter, when no one else was around; he kissed a girl there once, for an hour or so, both of them high as kites, in the cold, some girl, he couldn't remember who now; it just went through him.

There were signs of decay everywhere. It made Bunko uneasy, made him think of *The Last Picture Show.* It was that kind of town to him. The big lollipop clock in front of the bank had a humongous crack in its glass casing. Her hands were lodged on the Roman numerals VII and III. Seven-fifteen forever. The movie theater was closed up—the coming attractions posters were for the very first *Star Wars*—and the big five-and-dime in the middle of Main was hammered up with plywood. The butcher shop and Sam's Family Restaurant had gone out of business only recently, guessing by the waxed-up windows. He noticed something else: Most of the parking meters were missing their heads or had their stems bent out of shape. Shit, he didn't like this place at all, not at all.

The police station was adjacent to the courthouse, both of them built like mausoleums. They hurried up the steps. It was just past two in the afternoon, right on time.

After making them wait for twenty or so minutes, in the stuffy, miasmic outer office, which consisted of wooden benches and a locked-up gun rack, Sheriff Marvis Smitty decided he would not be seeing any other visitors. His secretary, a hoary, Brillo-haired woman who chain-smoked Salems, continued with her two-fingered typing on the old manual.

"Marvis is way too busy," she said, not looking up. "I'm sure you boys understand that."

"Ma'am," Bunko began. "I'm not sure you understand—"

"I understand plenty. Marvis is busy. Why don't you boys

just leave him alone? FBI people already here. You got questions, why don't you ask them all about it? I don't understand the fuss. Marvis is plenty capable. If anything could have been solved by now, Marvis would have done it."

"Anybody else around I can talk to?" Bunko asked. "A deputy, perhaps."

"Jack's out on patrol. Now, can't you see I'm trying to type this?"

She was a real sweetheart, absolutely scintillating. He noticed her full ashtray, jammed with her ugly, lipstick-smeared butts. "Ma'am, you oughta give them up," he said politely. "I'd hate to see a fine young thing like you come down with cancer. Have you been in for a mammograph recently? Oughta take care of that, darling."

When they were back outside, Eamon said, "What the hell was that all about? We could wait ol' Marvis out, no problem."

"I already got what I want," Bunko said, cryptically.

He'd noticed the deputy's green-and-white out in front of Manero's Barbershop earlier. Bunko hadn't really thought he was going to get anything new out of Smitty. Everything had been complicated by the fact that Montrez and the Bureau were not sharing their information with Postal. After they'd handed them the Ocean City file, they'd closed them down. So he didn't have any fucking idea of what had transpired up in Ashland. Actually, Bunko thought Montrez was doing right. Postal had no business here anymore. But he had his orders, too. Even if they were doled out by a chickenshit like Anal.

Just as he had suspected, the deputy wasn't getting a haircut at all. He was just sitting in one of the lifts, like the other men there, thumbing through a *Playboy,* chatting away his shift in the warmth of the shop. An old barber was shaving somebody with a straight razor. Bunko stuck his head in and called, "Jack. Yeah, Jack. Marvis said you might give us a word out here."

The deputy didn't look too happy about it, but he came on out, without his coat. Evidently this wasn't going to take long. "Yeah?" he said, in the cold, the snow still falling slightly.

"Well, Marvis said—"

"Cut the bullshit," the young deputy said, blowing cold smoke. He was tall and broad-shouldered, with an all-American face. It was just too darn dimpled, too wide and trusting and plain dumb-looking. And it belied everything. "Everyone knows I think Marvis is a dickhead. What you men want? You FBI?"

"We're Postal," Bunko said. "We're special agents. Investigating the same case. I'm Lieutenant Ryan. This is Lieutenant Wearie."

They showed the deputy their blue and gold badges. He examined them closely. "Okay, shoot," he said, rubbing his hands together.

"First, FBI talk to you?" Bunko asked.

"Stupid fucks bypassed me. Did all their talking to Marvis Nitwit."

"Take it you don't think these boys are runaways either."

"Fuck no. Something shitty's happening around here. You talk to the families yet?"

"Just got here today. What can you tell me, Jack?"

"The Jakes are here in town. They might talk to you, might not. I think they're your best bet. The Hohenbergers, on the other hand—I'd be surprised if they gave you time of day. Don't want to believe the worse. They're going along with Marvis that Greg took off on his own. And then you got the Lauterbergs up in Rosie's Range. I don't know about them. FBI boys went over all these folk real good. They might all be talked out, for all I know. Except they probably got a glimmer of hope. There's always a glimmer, ain't there?"

"Yeah," Bunko said. "Tell me something I don't know."

"Okay," the deputy said, staring Bunko in the eyes. "You don't know that there was a girl murdered. Right here in ol' Ash. Not five months ago. Gertie Johnson. And we ain't close to solving it."

"Yeah?"

"Well, nobody else thinks so, but I think they're connected. We don't have murders up this way. The last one before this happened thirty-eight years ago, and that was some drunken bar thing. Now, Gertie here was fifteen years old. And she wasn't a particularly good-looking girl, I hate to say."

"So what are you getting at, Jack?" Bunko said quickly. It was cold, and all three of them were rubbing their hands and blowing smoke.

"Well, Lieutenant. Suddenly we got missing boys and a murder. In a place where none of these things happen. That's one thing. But I saw the body. It was bad, real bad. Gertie was a big fat girl, and she was raped and mutilated. And as I understand it, you people are investigating possible sex crimes or what have you. You think the boys were put in some dungeon or something. I'm not too clear on it. But anyways. This girl, Gertie, she was abused in a strange way. The killer stuffed carrots up her vagina. It was all pretty sick. As you might imagine."

Bunko was at a loss. This whole girl thing was too new; he couldn't absorb it yet. "Was an autopsy performed?" he thought to ask.

"You bet. Doc Viola up at the hospital. Took samples, everything."

"FBI know about this?"

"Probably not. If they're relying on ol' Marvis Moron."

"Why's Marvis suppressing evidence?"

"He just don't look at it that way. Unrelated cases, in his mind. 'Sides, he's got an upcoming election. Don't want people thinking that the place is overrun by maniacs. Even if it is run by Marvis Dipshit."

The deputy's face was turning an interesting sort of grayish-purplish color in the cold, and odd stuff was starting to dribble out of his nose. Bunko decided it was time to give him a break. "Jack, you've been a great help. We'll be talking to you."

"One other thing," the deputy said, with one hand on the barbershop door. "Might talk to Evan Lancaster, editor of the *Gazette*. He thinks like I do. Give it a whirl." Then, shaking his head: "Postal, huh? Now don't that beat all. The mailmen hit squad. What, those missing boys avid stamp collectors, or what?"

The deputy was still chuckling to himself inside. They heard that kind of shit all the time—and it never failed to rankle. The first thing Bunko decided to do was call Mister Tony at the Bureau. He didn't give a shit if they weren't playing ball. That didn't mean he wasn't going to do his part.

There was a phone booth in the middle of the desolate block, which stood out, appearing luminous, even ghostly. Somebody had busted out half the booth's paneling and scrawled four-letter words all over the metal seat. Eamon waited outside while Bunko told Montrez about Gertie Johnson. Working with Bunk often made him feel useless, like he wasn't contributing. Bunko asked all the questions, took center stage. That was the way they'd always done it. It was Eamon's job to listen, to piece it together. Sometimes it just made him feel less than whole.

The Jakes lived up on Holland Drive, a nice little slice of suburbia in the country. This, no doubt, was the good section of town. The comfortable homes, big new colonials with jockey lanterns and circular drives, were on professionally landscaped half-acre lots. Holland Drive was awash in that strange blue light, the apocalyptic glow of the television, spilling out of living room windows all down the street into a starless black night.

They were both uneasy about their chore, not knowing what to expect. The last thing they wanted to do was intrude on somebody's grief. They knew Christopher was thirteen years old and that he'd disappeared last fall. Robert Jake was a supervisor with Pennsylvania Bell. Mrs. Jake had sounded nice on the phone.

Number 10 was like the others, two stories of shingles and forest green shutters, with the basketball hoop attached to a two-car garage. The lights were on throughout the house, every room seemingly aglow. It was warm yellow light, the light of family and hearth, a light to come home to. It was just somehow unexpected, that's all. They rang the bell.

A pretty brunette in an old-fashioned white apron opened the door. "Hi, there," she said. "I'm Barb. You must be that special task force. We talked earlier. Well, don't be strangers, come on in."

Introductions were made. Robert was on the living room couch with the evening paper, in front of the family megaset. He got up and gave them a friendly smile and a firm shake. He was still in his tie and white shirt. "Bob," he said. "Let it be Bob." Peter Jennings described some Muslim holy war in the background. Bunko wondered if they had the right fuckin' house.

"Will you be joining us for dinner?" Barb asked. "I've prepared my special lamb chops. Bob just dies for them."

"Well, they sure are good," Bob said, beaming.

"Well, Mrs. Jake," Bunko said, "it's not that it isn't a tempting offer, but I'm afraid we're in quite a hurry. Would it be all right if we got right down to it? I know how unpleasant this must be—"

"Nonsense," she said. "And it's Barb. We don't have any formality around here."

She led them to the two big La-Z-Boy recliners, while she joined her husband on the bright floral couch. Everything looked brand-new, including the plush white carpeting, almost as if it were all bought that very day. Bunko noticed the beige walls, which were completely unadorned. There weren't any paintings or mementos or pictures or anything. There was just this great blankness. The place even smelled freshly painted.

"You keep a sparkling house, Barb," Bunko said. It was more a question than a compliment.

"Well, yes, we did just buy some new furnishings," she said.

"Barb thought that's just what we needed," her husband added. "And I couldn't agree more."

Eamon thought it was like out of the *Stepford Wives* or something. They hadn't even bothered to turn down the TV;

Peter Jennings droned on, unchecked, about the leading economic indicators.

"Let's talk about Chris," Bunko said.

"Yes, let's do," Barb said, almost perky.

Bunko said, "Well, I was curious if he was having any emotional problems, or if he was depressed, things like that."

"No, full of spunk and vinegar," Barb said.

"Loved life. Top of his class. Smart. Good-looking kid. Girls were already developing crushes on him and everything," Bob said with evident fatherly pride.

"Was anything missing from his room? Clothes? A diary? Favorite music tape? Anything at all?

When Bunko had been a private detective, in that other lifetime, he'd gone after runaways, lots of times. He knew this series of questions by heart; he knew what to look for. The thing of it was, those missing kids always turned up. Turned up alive. Always.

"We've been all through this," Bob said, a little irritated. "Lots of times. Don't you think we hired our own detective by now? Of course we did. Franklin Lipps. Out of Philadelphia. We went and got a good one, and we went all through this. We weren't going to trust this to that oaf of a sheriff."

"Yes, that's right," Barb said, looking a little more strained. "We gave him lists of all Chris's friends and his hobbies and interests and all that kind of thing."

"For Christ's sake," Bob said, clearly sick of it, "we've had a tape recorder on our phone for six months. Just in case the boy calls. Mr. Lipps went through the phone bills and talked to his friends. All that. He even checked with the bus depot and the trains and taxi company. In case anybody saw Chris going. And now the FBI has been here, and those fellows didn't miss a beat either. Don't you already have all that information?"

"Well, yes, of course we do," Bunko lied. "We're just going over it again. I'm very sorry to put you people through this."

"He's dead," Bob said, his voice suddenly very hollow.

Bunko and Eamon looked at him funny.

"Yes, he's dead. And the quicker we come to accept that, the quicker we'll recover from this. Chris would not want to see this family destroyed," he said with some finality.

"Chris loved us," Barb said. "Barry told us that he's in heaven. He's watching over all of us."

Eamon couldn't believe how vacant her face was. "Who's Barry?" he suddenly asked.

"Why, Famous Barry. He's a psychic, don't you know. Why, haven't you ever heard of him? He even has his own television show. In Philadelphia. WKRX. That's channel six. I never miss him."

"Well, I guess we'll be—" Bunko started to say in that voice he always used for leaving.

"Wait a minute," Eamon interrupted. "How does this Famous Barry know Chris is dead?"

"My, you really don't know anything," she said brightly, more than happy to explain. "Famous Barry talks to dead people. That's all he does. Talks to dead people. It's a gift. So if anybody would know Chris was dead, it would be Barry. And I got in to see him—which isn't easy, let me tell you, we had to wait a good two months, although the normal waiting time is close to a year—and so anyway Barry told me that Chris was with his Grandpa Buddy. They're together, and they're in the good place."

Bunko couldn't believe this shit. A real crazy lady. He saw the way her husband was looking at her, like she'd been through a lot, like this was a small thing to tolerate.

"But," Eamon said, still on the subject, "how do you know it's not a bunch of it?"

"With Barry you just know. Why, he even knew Chris's name before I said one word. He goes, 'I'm so, so sorry about Chris,' before I even sit down. Then he tells me things about Chris that there was no other way he could know."

"What kinds of things?" Eamon demanded.

"Oh, I don't know, just things. He knew Chris liked this one rock group. What is that group? Oh, my mind's a blank. And he knew about the baseball. Chris loves baseball. Or, he *loved* it. Because Barry told me that he wanted me to have his old mitt. Well, if you knew Chris, you'd know that was just about his most favorite possession in the whole wide world. Yes, it was."

"So how come he didn't tell you who the killer was if this Barry knew so much?" Bunko interjected, sarcastically.

"He couldn't talk about it. Not with me at least. He just couldn't. I gather it was very horrible. Because he let out this terrible, terrible scream—a scream that only Barry could hear—and wouldn't stop for the longest time. Barry told me that that had never happened before."

"Well, I think that's about enough of that," Bob said, clearly uncomfortable. "I'm sure these two gentlemen have more important things to concern themselves with right now."

Eamon surprised himself by saying, "Barb, would you mind too much if I took a look at Chris's room? It'd just take a second."

"Well, I don't see why not. Everybody else has already gone over it. It's upstairs. I'll take you."

They left the two nonbelievers behind in the living room. At the top of the stairs, Eamon noticed two little girls, identical twins, couldn't be older than three or four years old, playing quietly on the floor in one of the bedrooms. They were building things with those Lego blocks. Eamon couldn't remember two more quiet children in his entire life.

"Samantha and Allison," Barb said in a whisper, for some reason.

Chris's bedroom was what you might've expected. There were baseball pennants, the Phillies and Pirates, and a giant poster of the Buffalo Bills quarterback, Jim Kelly. There were also those psuedomenacing posters of heavy metal bands—all fire and smoke, leather and hair—in this case Mötley Crüe and Guns N' Roses. Nothing so unusual about any of it. The bookshelves housed a complete encyclopedia set, along with a bunch of sports bios—*The Joe Namath Story* and *Magic* among them. He lifted up one of the myriad trophies that competed for space on the top shelf and held it to the light. It was a glittery sapphire number with a golden figurine-catcher simply inscribed: '88 League

Champs. As well as the numerous Little League baubles, Chris had earned trophies in swimming and basketball. Eamon took note of the *The Far Side* calender, over the neatly made bed, still registering October. He walked over to take a closer look at the cartoon.

He wasn't at all sure what he was looking for. Barb stood in the doorway, pensive, perhaps hopeful—however remotely—that the lieutenant might somehow see something that all the others had missed.

Chris had made notations in the little date boxes, one-line reminders for basketball practice and track, nothing more. The only other thing was that October 20 was circled in red, for some reason.

"You probably want to know about the twentieth," Barb said, somehow anticipating his question. "That is odd. Because that was the last day anyone saw Chris. That Mr. Lipps did some investigating. But the only thing that he could come up with was that was also the day for his class pictures. Still, it wasn't like Chris to get excited about something like that."

"Barb, did Chris keep a diary?"

"Heavens no. He was a boy, after all, you know."

"This might sound odd, but did he have a pen pal or anything like that? Someone he wrote to on a regular basis."

"No, he was like most kids. Hated writing letters. We always had to make him write his grandmother to thank her for Christmas and birthday checks. You know how it is."

"I suppose you went through his loose-leaf notebooks and all?"

"The FBI took them a few days ago. But we'd been through them. There wasn't anything, just doodles and squibbles and doodads. That sort of thing."

He'd run out of questions and ideas. He stepped over to Chris's window and looked out. It was an ordinary view of an ordinary backyard. There was a deck and some patio furniture that had been left out over the winter, as if nobody cared enough. The Jakes had a swimming pool too, at the moment just a black tarp with some snow on it. Eamon thought about Chris doing laps in his yard, getting fast, getting better, and then he remembered the basketball hoop out front, had a picture of Chris driving for a lay-up on his garage door. And then he juxtaposed that with the picture of the Executioner, in his hood, in his little chamber of horrors. Suddenly Eamon realized why he'd wanted to come up and see the room in the first place. To make Chris real. To make it all real.

He heard Barb's voice—her Stepford Wife voice again—coming from behind him. "Have you found a place to stay yet?" she was saying. "If you haven't, allow me to recommend this perfectly quaint inn just right outside of town . . ."

9

. . . and death is all around us, James. We grow up living
but we do that living knowing that we will be dying. That
is truly the difference between man and the rest of the
animal kingdom. We know, not just sense or rely on
some vague hidden instinct, that we have a limited time
to act out the little drama of our lives. And yet you know
the funny terrible thing is that it hardly matters a wit,
that it makes no profound difference whatsoever. People
know that they will die but we can't do anything about it
so we live our fraudulent little lives, never doing the
things we dream about, never doing the work that feels
good in the soul, never making love to the people we
really want, never giving out enough love anyway, and of
course it's not news to anyone and believe me I know
that, James. Or should I say Richard. Because it is
Richard. Because it always will be Richard, even if I call
you James.

I know this letter is pointless and I know you must
hate me for boring you with my unhappy little tune. It
was our Rita, our favorite ol' bartender, and she never
told anybody that she was ailing, and she was ailing,
with a cancer in her ovaries, and well, she just didn't

make it. And so I'm brooding. Not that we really knew our little Rita but she always had a nice word for everybody and she made me laugh at her dirty jokes and she made sure our bar bill never got too high. Well, those are fine qualities, James. Hard qualities to find. I didn't know about it, out of touch as I am, never reading the papers anymore, and so I just passed that blinking martini glass on the turnpike and I thought I'd just get maudlin and think of good times with you and put a few quarters in the jukebox and so I just walked in and there was somebody new behind the bar. All I said was, Rita's day off? You always get the worst news when you ain't looking for it, when your back is turned. I was going to just have a beer, but then I asked for the old Irish whiskey, you know how it is, darling. You weren't around that day and so I drank like no one was watching me. It was syrup in my veins and strange men tried to pick me up, thinking I was an easy opportunity, but I called Paul, and he hurried over, gave me a ride home. I would've called you but like I said you weren't around, old friend of mine.

James, I'm sorry. Have you painted any good ones lately? Ones that give you the fervor and make you work late into the lamplight. I know how you are. You can't go to sleep without finishing the ones you like. Because you know, in the morning everything is different and we can never just start where we left off, can we darling.

Oh what's the use, what's the point of even trying. Can you believe I'm writing you from school. I gave them a terrible horrible test, as foul as my mood, and they keep looking up at the clock, nervous and tense, as if any of it matters, their pens racing with so much greedy young ambition. We put so much into a life, learn so many things, every tiny bit of trivia and knowledge, all the people and all the nice things we do that go unrewarded, all those things, all those cups of coffee and cigarettes, all those sweet kisses, all the memories, a lifetime of memories, remembering everyone who ever counted for anything, all the good true people who make you want to keep on trying and thinking and waking. Forgive me, James. Forgive me for doing my lousy Holden Caulfield imitation. People say to enjoy every God-given moment and to live every one like it's your last, not to take any of it for granted. But you know it can't be done that way. You can't live your life thinking about death and the great gloomy beyond. You have to put it out of your mind and do all the hard work of everyday living. Because if you really thought you could go at any time, who'd do anything? Who'd go to medical school? Who'd put in the long dreary years—if there wasn't going to be some kind of beautiful payoff? Who'd write a book for instance? Not me, James. Not me, that is for sure.

Heaven sounds like such a drag. It sounds so boring, all harps and trumpets and old angels with wings. Doesn't anybody get laid up there? All white fluffy clouds and azure skies—boy, I'd sure get tired of that in a hurry. The thing of it is, we probably just die, huh, James. It's over after that. No more of us. No more of anything. I think that's the way it is. It's one of those ashes to dust kind of things, where you're just a memory in the minds of the living. And that doesn't bode well for us. People forget so fast. That is the saddest thing. You're in the ground and people forget you the day after tomorrow.

But some of us are lucky and we carry God inside of ourselves. God is not in everyone because you can see certain people who have no God in them. You can see that. I swear you can. But I carry God inside of me, James, and I know you do, too. And Rita had God in her, no doubt about that. I'm sorry to be breaking such bad news to you. Now you say a little prayer for Rita; she might need it where she is.

So Richard, because I said I was going to start calling you that, James. So Richard, Richard Lonetree, might as well use the whole thing now, so—No, I never did like that name. It just doesn't work for me. Let's just go back to James, James. Isn't it funny the way I like to repeat

*your name to myself, like some kind of crazy mantra,
like it brings you close to me when I'm writing my
invisible letters. You keep painting, James. Don't let me
get in the way.*

Netti

Richard Lonetree, he mumbled to himself. He finally had
a name, not that he was necessarily going to do anything
with it. He was sitting up in the dumpy bed, a bed that had
cost him a good night's sleep, in one of the nautical-inspired
rooms of the Driftwood, a dingy, heartless motel hundreds
of miles from any ocean, with immortality on his mind.

Death was not something he liked to dwell on. Like Netti,
he supposed he saw the world in mostly finite terms. Some
bad day he wouldn't be around, and that would be that.
He'd been brought up a Catholic, even gone to Saint Mary's
early on, which had been a lot harder than any public
school, he could tell you, full of terminal black nuns and big,
dark, windowless classrooms. He'd gone through catechism,
sitting there in his little blue blazer, full of hot fear and guilt,
sure that God knew of the sinner in His presence. In his
dreams he repeatedly burned in hell, and he worried end-
lessly that God would take him with one dramatic, well-
chosen thunderbolt to the head. And when his next-door
neighbor, Dougie Weaver, a ten-year-old known for his
cursing and hard ways, got run over by a car sled-riding, he
became utterly convinced of God's ironclad policy of retri-
bution.

But as Eamon got older, he learned to put it aside. It
wasn't that he didn't believe in God, he believed in God, all
right, but it was more in the way of Netti, like something you
carried inside. His faith was a quiet thing, nobody's business but his own, and he didn't need to go to church on
Sundays to prove anything to anybody.

Still, he had some trouble imagining heaven.

He pulled open the nightstand drawer and found the Bear
County white pages under the Gideon Bible. He looked up
Richard Lonetree. To his surprise and satisfaction, he found

him. There it was: Lonetree R., 49 Reedy Hollow Rd., Sndstne—555-7233.

He could decide what to do with it later.

After western omelets at the Choo-Choo Diner, an old converted caboose, not far from the Driftwood, they headed over to the *Ashland Gazette*.

Evan Lancaster was not what they expected. He was not some old-timey editor with a folksy manner and ink on the hands from setting the type himself. Instead Lancaster looked to be in his midthirties, trim and fit as if he worked out on Nautilus machines, with a smug, unlikable exterior, dressed in stylish expensive clothes, clothes that seemed to be worn for the express purpose of usurping power. And to top it off, he had the kind of unpleasant face that all too often came from the early, all-too-easy success. His was a face without empathy.

They walked into the *Gazette* to find Lancaster, in his power tie and power suspenders and those wine-colored shoes with the dreaded floppy tassels, dictating his column to a pretty, collegiate-looking thing, who tapped his words into a word processor while he paced about with grandiosity.

"How can I help you gentlemen?" he said with marvelous annoyance, as if they were interrupting a Leonardo at work.

After they stated their business, he dismissed his assistant with more of the same self-importance and offered them seats. "Well, how was I to know?" he said. "You just didn't have the look of federal agents. Not much of a clothing allowance, huh?"

Bunko was already imagining stuffing him into his antique rolltop. It was a beautiful old piece, though, much too good a place for the likes of Lancaster.

"I see you're a connoisseur of fine things, Inspector," Lancaster said, noticing where Bunko's attention was at. "Well, there's quite a wonderful story about that marvelous rolltop. Obviously you know it's a Dellachise, whose value had increased a thousandfold over the years. Magnificent piece, isn't she? Well, here's the great part," he proceeded,

96

eagerly. "The old coot who was here before me, Walter somebody or other, had absolutely no idea of her worth. Do you realize—and you may find this hard to believe, as I did—but old Wally was actually using her as a working desk. Can you believe?"

Now Bunko realized what was bugging him. The rolltop was completely clean, absolutely free of objects. The old beauty was just there for show and tell. He looked around the rest of the office and saw that the walls were plastered with ancient *Gazette* front pages, beautifully lacquered and mounted. It was a nice old smell, of varnish and better days.

"Yes, I bought the paper only last year," Lancaster was saying in his rich, smug voice, a voice that came by way of Exeter and Princeton. "I'd been in commodities—and, well, I don't want to brag, but let's just say that I'd done rather very okay, if you catch my meaning here. I mean, I'd made a ton of money, *as if* there was some god-awful trick to it."

At this point, Lancaster laughed, as if they were all in this together, as if they were following any of it. "So anyway," he said, composing himself. "It was a little dream of mine, you understand. To retreat into the country after I made my fortune. To run a little shop, as it were. Money hardly enters into it. I'm sure it's the same with you boys. Can't be for the money; I'm sure it's a pittance, but then I'd only be guessing."

"After I pay the Chinese girl who does my laundry, it's a moot point," Bunko told him.

"Right, exactly," Lancaster said, not getting it. "You know, this is the life, though. Rugged. Light-years away from Wall Street. You know, I even bought one of those four-wheel-drive range vehicles—"

"Mr. Lancaster, if I may be so bold as to interrupt," Bunko said, anxious to get out of there, "Jack said you might be able to help us. What'd he mean by that?"

"Well, he could have meant many things, but he was probably referring to the articles. Really nothing, actually—"

"What articles?"

"Well, it's a trivial little thing really, but we run a weekly feature highlighting some of the better student athletes in the area. Nothing to write home about, just a few hundred glorified words on the boy or girl who—"

"Yeah, so what?"

"Well, we'd featured two of those boys who'd disappeared. The Jakes's lad and Greg Hohenberger. Greg was a star back on the Ashland High football team. Call themselves the Tigers. But there's no growl to them at all—no one remembers the last time those pussy cats had a winning season—"

"Mr. Lancaster, if we could just get back to the articles—"

"Well, let's see. The other boy was some sort of Little League star. You know, I don't write these things. Marjorie Walpole does about fifteen articles a week for us. We don't even pay her. She's this crazy old octogenarian, and I suppose she thinks of herself as some kind of ace reporter, which is actually kind of frightening. God knows. Anyway, 'Star Athlete of the Month' was one of those things I was going to phase out at some point. I mean, who really wants to read about some pubescent volleyball champ or what have you? It's my thinking that our readers are interested in—"

"Mr. Lancaster, did these pieces appear at around the times of the disappearances?"

"Yes, that is strange, I suppose. It's a weekly feature, and I think, if I'm not mistaken, but don't hold me to it or anything, that each boy was missing within a week or two of the story. Perhaps it's just one of those amazing coincidences we're always reading about. Well, I'm sure it's beyond me. Oh, but there was one other thing. That murdered girl—"

"Gertie Johnson—"

"That's right. We'd featured her at some point, too. But, like, last year, months and months before her murder. Tragic, very tragic."

"She was an athlete?"

"She was a member of the boys' freshmen wrestling team.

Oh, there was a big to-do, you wouldn't believe. First girl and all. But apparently she was quite good. Of course, she was rather large. I suppose we'd refer to her as chunky."

"Jesus Fuckin' Christ," Bunko said, exasperated. "What the hell is going on around this goddamn town? I hope the FBI got all this information. They did find this out, didn't they? Just nod your head like you know something, Lancaster."

"I wouldn't have the foggiest. Never did come in to chat with me and—"

"Lancaster, I'll need copies of those stories. Besides that, I'll need a complete *Gazette* subscription list. Further, for the time being, I'm going to ask you not to run any more of those student profiles."

"I don't suppose there'd be a problem in any of that. Gives me just the excuse I need to get rid of that hokum. In fact, I think I'll tell Miss Walpole that she can't write for us until this darn thing is solved. That's rich, very rich—"

"Lancaster, is there anything else I should know about? Think carefully. Anything unusual at all. Any letters to the editor that stick out particularly? Any strange phone calls?"

"No, nothing like that. But you really should take a look at my editorials, as long as you're here. A whole series devoted to giving old Sheriff Marvis Moron the boot. I don't mean to brag, but they've been quite hard-hitting, very à la Mike Wallace—"

"I'm sure they were terrific, Lancaster. Let me ask you something: Is there any possible way that the sheriff could be involved in any of this?"

"Marvis? God no, he's too stupid to kill anybody. But getting back to my editorials, and I don't want to harp on this, but . . ."

Bunko stopped listening, he'd heard enough. Evan Lancaster was still going off at the mouth, in his dandified suspenders and forty-dollar necktie, the prince of fop, with that marvelous moneyed inflection, a privileged member of the new America. Bunko didn't like the son of a bitch, that was for sure, but it was much more than that. It was the *whole* thing. It was what he represented; it was about what the hell kind of place would even make an Evan Lancaster plausible. It really wasn't about yuppies, that overused word to describe pricks in their Beamers wearing outdoorsy bullshit from L.L. Bean, or even really about the money fever. All he knew was that his America was changing, none for the better, and that dinosaurs like himself were becoming less and less welcome everywhere you went. He wasn't really sure how to put it together, how to *formulate* it, but Evan-Fucking-Lancaster—Mr. Amero-Trash—figured into it somehow. It was getting harder to be a slob, to eat a T-bone smothered in onions. Not another word about cholesterol levels and oat bran, please. And damn if it wasn't getting harder to have a little drink somewhere, to find a spot of quietude, a dim place where you could light up a smoke and watch the time pass in the reflection of the bottles. He wasn't *exactly* sure how it all fit in, all these different things. But you weren't ever going to find Bunko chowing down on brown rice and working out in some goddamn health club and then scooting off in some German sedan to some transparent skyscraper to do hostile takeovers or leveraged buyouts or whatever the hell these creeps were doing these days. Hell, he just wanted to go to Pimlico with his pals, to lay a few place bets, drink a couple of bottom-shelf whiskeys, forget all about it.

He stared at the bastard, sure that Evan Lancaster was part of a great and all-encompassing conspiracy, one that was making life more miserable every day.

Day Two was rapidly going the way of toilet water. They kept making mistakes. Mistake Number One had been going over to the sheriff's house. But Bunko had started thinking, and the more he thought about it, the more he became convinced that nobody could be as stupid as Marvis Smitty. He remembered what it said in that book about serial killers, about them sometimes using badges and guns and posing as cops, and then he decided that a real cop was probably going it one better.

Eamon tried to talk him out of it. But when Bunk got a mind to do something, there wasn't much anybody could do. So they knocked on the door, and he asked Mrs. Smitty if she wouldn't mind showing them the basement. She was a burned-out housewife with a couple of cats at her feet and the soaps blaring in the background. She was in this crummy housecoat and she wasn't wearing any makeup, and it was fairly obvious she'd been drinking. But it was her hair that grabbed Eamon's attention, really greasy and unkempt, sticking up in places, like she didn't care about nothing in this life. She didn't even bother to ask what it was all about until they were already on the stairs. Bunko tossed her one of his ever-ready lies. Gas company, he said. Here to check your radon level. She just shrugged. And the basement turned out to be just another oak-paneled rec room with a Ping-Pong table and some card chairs.

Mostly it had been a long, unfruitful day, the kind where you drive around a lot and look out the windows and wonder about unrelated things. It'd been inordinately sunny and much warmer than the day before. The roads were sloppy, oozing with mud and slush, but the snowy landscape dazzled with brightness, reflecting back the sun like it was sprinkled with diamonds. They'd gone up to Fish Kill, a small, nothing hamlet, thirty minutes from Ashland, looking to speak with the Hohenbergers, but had learned from a neighbor that they'd left town only hours earlier, ostensibly to go on vacation. Theirs was just a plain square redbrick house on a wide tract of cleared land. In the back of the house there was a small mesh-wire pen crammed with Siberian huskies. The neighbor, a talkative sort, explained that Mr. Hohenberger was a disabled vet and that he raised them to augment his monthly disability check. The black and white dogs with their bandit masks jumped up and down and whimpered like crazy. They were dirty and scrawny, and Eamon noticed that the feeders were mostly empty. It was as if Hohenberger had suddenly stopped taking care of them. He knew huskies couldn't bark, but just the same, their high-pitched whining sounded like a cry for help, more than anything.

They'd gone back to the Choo-Choo for lunch, another mistake, opting for the meatloaf special, a rank, odious decision that they were still burping over. Afterward Eamon called the local humane society to let them know about the dogs.

There were more calls to make. Bunko checked in with Anal, who chewed them out for sharing information with Montrez. News certainly traveled fast. Then Bunk called Mister Tony to let him know about the *Gazette* connection. Montrez in turn let him know that the town would be crawling with agents tomorrow. As a sign of good faith, he also ran down some of the Bureau's own findings, none of which seemed particularly telling or particularly helpful. Bunko had the distinct feeling that Mister Tony was holding on to a card or two.

Now that it was almost nightfall, the sun just a dying ember, they had one last stop to make. They tried phoning the Lauterbergs—not wanting to duplicate their earlier wasted effort—but it just rang and rang. Rosie's Range wasn't far, six or seven miles to the north, worth a shot, at the very least. They rode along in tired silence. Montrez had told them very little, actually. Beck Lauterberg was fourteen and, according to teachers and everyone else who knew him, slightly disturbed. A juvenile delinquent who'd already had a few scrapes with the law. Nothing too major, though. He threw a rock through a butcher shop window for no real reason, because he felt like it, and he stole a couple of tires another time. The last anyone saw of him, he was out in the high school parking lot, kicking a can. Montrez's men had interviewed practically everybody who'd seen him that day and come up with nothing they could term unusual. The problem, of course, in this case and the other two, was that too much time had passed, making it that much more difficult to catch a lead. If things were done right, investigators hit the turf running within twenty-four hours. There was no telling what vital clues were simply blown away, a note, a telling cigarette butt, whatever, lost to the wind; and it was a lot easier to remember a strange car in the lot the very next day than it was half a year later.

There was moonshine in the night, and the snow appeared blue and luminous. Rosie's Range turned out to be just a ramshackle grouping of convenience stores. There was an Exxon and a 7-Eleven and a post office the size of a mailbox. That was all she wrote. The Lauterbergs were a few blocks away on State Street, a quiet, maple-lined stretch of nineteenth-century homes, each proud house slightly different from the others, but all of them three stories tall with magnificent gable roofs. The Lauterbergs were the last house down, right there behind a yellow DEAD END sign, the ugliest one on the block.

The house was peeling badly; it was hard to tell which was the last paint job, the way it was flaking gray and blue in some places and pink in others, and the front was a veritable junkyard, with rusted cars scattered about like so much scrap metal. There was an ancient Volkswagen Beetle, missing its hood, that was used as some kind of planter. A van, painted like some kind of psychedelic rainbow, was smashed up pretty good, with a shattered windshield and a body that reminded Eamon of an accordian. There were several others up on blocks, in varying states of decay, a Ford Pinto and an early Honda Civic, staring back as if they were haunted or something.

There were even some old rotting jack-o'-lanterns on the crumbling porch, most likely left over from Halloween. They rapped on the door a few times and then shuffled about, waiting. There didn't seem to be any lights on in the house. The front windows were dark, hung with old, moth-eaten lace curtains.

They were about to give up when the door opened a fraction and a woman said, "Yeah, what is it?" The voice was anything but friendly.

"Federal agents, Mrs. Lauterberg. We were hoping to have a word with you."

The door opened wider, revealing a pregnant woman in a long knit dress with strings of beads and crystals around her neck. Her black hair went almost to her waist, and she was barefoot. Her face was sallow and unwholesome, but she couldn't have been more than thirty, almost too young to be Beck Lauterberg's mother.

"Got nothing to say to you," she said, through the tattered

screen door. "I'm in the process of becoming a Buddhist," she dropped out of the blue.

"Why is that, Mrs. Lauterberg?" Bunko continued, unfazed.

"Because it is the way of things. If you asked Beck, I'm sure he'd tell you the same. It's not surprising, all things considered."

"Have you seen Beck?"

"No, Beck is dead. It is only to say that Beck was always getting into trouble and that his karma was poisoned. His natural karmic color was a beautiful aquamarine, but at the end it was streaked with brown. It's not like he deserved it—but you could have predicted it. Let's just say that."

Her voice was almost otherworldly, like she wasn't there, and her eyes were blank and undiscerning, even though she looked right at them.

"Mrs. Lauterberg, maybe we could come in and chat some more?"

"No, I know that wouldn't work out. You're not with my kind of people. Your auras are all wrong. I bet you haven't been to Katmandu. Have you now?"

"No, ma'am. Is your husband by chance home? Perhaps he'd be willing to talk to—"

"He ain't here," she said, shortly.

"Will he be back soon?"

"He ain't here, just like I told you. We'll have to be ending this conversation now—"

"Mom, what's going on?" It was a boy, right about Beck's age, in back of her, in the hallway. Their antennae instantly went up.

"Who is that, Mrs. Lauterberg?"

"He's not for you. I don't want you spoiling him. We just got his color back. Agent Mathews spoiled his color."

Bunko was losing his patience with the loon. "Hey, kid," he called. "Come here."

The boy approached the door, warily. He had spiky blond hair and was draped in a too big Alf for President T-shirt. His face was unnaturally pale, almost as white as the moon.

"You Beck Lauterberg?" Bunko said.

"He was my brother," the boy said, deadish-like. "We were twins. I'm the one who's Figg."

"Identical twins?" Eamon said, suddenly.

"Yeah."

"What do you mean *was* your brother?" Bunko said.

"I know. Don't you think I know?" the boy said, looking down at his laceless sneakers. "I felt it. Beck got hurt bad. Real bad. Somebody done tore him apart."

"See what you're doing?" his mother said. "You're ruining his color. I'm sorry, but you'll have to leave now."

"Just a few more questions, Mrs. Lauterberg."

She didn't bother to reply. Just backed away from the door with the boy. Then shut it, as if they weren't even there. They stood in the moonlight, on the broken-down porch, in the warped silence, slow to move.

Eamon lifted the fresh Rolling Rock to his lips and took a healthy swig. It was number eight—eight exactly, not thereabouts. He kept track with a primitive but nonetheless accurate system that depended on the removal of the labeling. They were carefully peeled off and then placed in a sad, dilapidated pile alongside the shot glass. He had yet to devise an arithmetic to account for the Jack Daniels. Every now and then, out of boredom and neglect, he'd pick one up and hold it to the feeble light, twisting it, trying to squeeze sense out of its incidental characteristics, pressing his eyes to the small print, putting to memory the Extra Pale's start-up year, 1939, taking note that it was "Brewed from Mountain Springs," but just as soon forgetting it, finally losing interest altogether in his diversionary tactics.

Bunko had turned in early, but he'd been restless with the spirit and taken to the road. The Caddy was beautiful to drive and so he drove without a destination, into a starry night, availing himself of the road. He had little idea what he was doing or where he was going, but he put his trust into the road. And the road took him there.

The beauty just about overwhelmed him. There was

something about driving late at night with the radio on, cruising through a sleeping land, on your own, everything so dreamlike. He lit up a cigarette with the glowing lighter.

Mossy's Tavern was there, just as he knew it would be somehow. It was just a warm winking off the road, not near much, as far as he could tell. He pulled in, not even thinking about it.

The rest came naturally.

The bartender seemed to know him. He was a tough-looking dude with a ponytail, but he said real friendly-like, "Glad to see you. What'll you be having tonight?"

It wasn't his plan to get shitfaced, but it happened, happened just like everything else, with a bad ease. Now he was in that weird, inarticulate place, all slow and murky, submerged inside of himself. It was hard to get out when you were in the deep place. It was hard to talk, and if you somehow managed to start with the words, they rolled out all loosey-goosey, all wrong.

He watched them play pool in the middle of the sawdust. They were bikers, and he couldn't tell them apart. His eyes were on the girl anyway. She was playing with the cue chalk, blowing on it. She blew blue dust on the backs of their leather jackets, then laughed hysterically.

He drank back some more Rolling Rock. It had no taste anymore and he drank it like it was water, because he was thirsty.

Eamon Wearie was too far gone to notice the other woman, the one at the end of the bar. Her name was Dorie and she definitely noticed him. Dorie came there all the time. Her old man, Coot, drove the big rigs for a living and was gone up to two weeks at a time. Coot beat her up often enough, fact of life, when he was messed up on the uppers and the Wild Turkey. When she'd been sixteen, Coot rode up to her mom's trailer on his Harley. It was hard to believe that she thought the creep was once gorgeous; a lot could happen in two years.

Eamon didn't know how it happened exactly. Suddenly some girl was asking him for a ride home. They were talking, or maybe, come to think of it, she was talking. But

106

stuff was going on in his head just the same. She told him her name, but now it was just blackness. And he could've sworn that she said something about being married—but he must've heard her wrong or something.

He didn't know where they were. She was just a changing face in the moonlight, in a rented car. They were in the crushed red interior and she was on top of him, warm and gooey. He realized he would never be able to remember her, whoever she was, tomorrow or any other day, because he couldn't even remember her right now. She was hair and breasts and the warm goo. She was nobody.

It happened and it all had to happen and it was still happening. He was somehow up over himself, looking down, somehow seeing it, somehow. She moved on him faster, side to side. He couldn't feel anything at all, but she moaned the thing about getting closer and closer. Then he realized she'd come and felt her body relax on him.

10

It is the way that we remember things that makes me believe, James, that there is great poetry in human beings. I do not believe for a single ordinary minute that real life can ever match the heavenly way we remember it. Our gilt-edged memories happen in beautiful, languorous slow-mo takes, as we isolate the good things, those things that we choose to remember. I think that is the way of most memory: we make it up as we go along and we have the final cut, the final say, changing what we don't like, lifting our roles to more glorious stature. Thank God, we have some place, albeit a small place, inside of ourselves, where we are free of the obvious strictures.

As always, James, I get carried away, hoping that my words have import, but you know me, you always knew me, you see through my misguided efforts to make that deeper statement. I was going to say, James, before I realized what an ass I was making of myself, that there is another kind of memory, one far more unsettling, the kind we have no control over, like an—if you'll allow me this—antediluvian shuttering, charging through our bloodstream like so much memory heroin, toppling us.

I was thinking about us again, James. Or, it just surged through me. I cried awhile, for everything that is lost. I went to the bleachers, to the top row, all splinters and October memories. You can hear the shouts and cries of Games Past up there, you can, it fills the ghostly air, the cheerleaders, the smell of franks, the muddied players. You kissed me up there once, in our big bulky sweaters, on another cool day, a day thick with the burning leaves. You kissed my eyes, as tenderly as God—no one had ever done that before. But that's not what triggered my jag. That's one of the good memories.

Behind the bleachers, the white birch are spotted black, skeletal in the mist. I'm writing to you on one of my long yellow legal pads, the kind I always have with me. As if someday I will suddenly ignite, rip into that novel that you say is in me. Now and always it is for my jottings, for the ever-small reflections of myself. I know you still carry your sketchbook around. Your sketches are so complete, so unalterable, they just come out of your head full-bodied and magical. You do not need to practice. In you it has already been realized. Aren't you smart.

It was that time in New York. At that hotel that we couldn't afford. We were counting our dollars; we had just enough.

We had such high hopes.

You came so close.

Really close, darling.

There was nothing to say to you, nothing that you might listen to. Your work, all those years, your great work, set up in one of the very few galleries that counts. I'm sorry to dredge it up, I'm sorry. It is what you said anyway. You said that when you were young you always thought that everything would work out. Everything. You were going to paint and live and be famous for all of it, for the living and the painting. You had no doubts and you strove in the one direction, but that day in the gallery you confessed to me something. I don't know if you remember. You just said that as you had gotten older that you understood it might not happen. That was the strange thing, you said, to wake up one terrible day and know in your heart that it might all come to naught. That might not've seemed like a big revelation to most people, you told me, but for you, for you who never looked back and only wanted the one thing, it was like staring down into the abyss.

We stood glumly by. They walked in, they looked, they made faces. You never got to feel the feeling. No red dots, no sales, all over.

I remember you wouldn't let me touch you in bed that night. You couldn't utter a word.

Months went by. You refused to get up. You stopped shaving. You ate out of cans. I didn't know if you'd recover.

When you did start to paint again, after all of it, all the crap, you were different, you were better, baby. When I walked into the barn to find you there, I held back tears. That's when I loved you for sure. I know most people wouldn't understand. But I knew what you'd given to it. I knew that you'd spent your whole life in pursuit of the one thing, given it everything you had. That made you better than a lot of people. In my book it did.

That is what I was thinking about up on the bleachers. Seeing you there. Seeing you smile again. Holding a brush, like it was Excalibur. God, I'm not sure why it tears me up so much. Who knows why our lives turn out the way they do; you deserved better, all the way around.

Ever your friend, Netti

He read her letter while soaking in the tub. He couldn't really explain it, but he heard her voice inside his head, and it was a voice that touched something in him. It was fiercely intelligent, it was fraught with compassion. He could see her sitting up in the bleachers, bundled up from the chilled, smoky air. She was a beautiful, untouchable vision. Why hadn't he had a woman like that in his life?

Eamon thought again of the girl from last night. His girls

110

were nameless, wordless things that fucked him in the backseat of a car. He was just as bad. He hurt. The booze had made his body sick and he felt weak and feverish. He wondered when he would learn.

It was late afternoon and the day had passed him by, like a long shadow falling over him. Bunko had gone out on his own to see if he couldn't talk to that sheriff. Bunko also wanted to check out Dip's, the one really hard-core newsstand in the area. Maybe the owner knew something. Maybe one customer stood out.

The Driftwood depressed him. The carpeting was seaweed green, and the walls were supposed to be ocean blue. It was a little after four o'clock, according to the thing that looked like a ship's wheel. Over the dresser there was an oil painting of a schooner going down in stormy seas. Men in yellow slickers were being swept off the watery deck to certain death.

He flicked on the color television, a bolted-in RCA. Oprah had on women who couldn't get dates because they were too attractive. Yeah, right, he thought. Geraldo's panel of guests appeared in shadow, and their voices had been electronically altered. He didn't even want to know. HBO had a Stallone movie. He was shooting at a car. With a flamethrower. He began zapping through the channels.

When he heard the knock at the door, he assumed it was Bunko and yelled back that it wasn't locked.

A man stepped in. He was six foot something, in a dark three-piece suit with a starchy white shirt and black tie. His face didn't have a whisker, and his short hair, parted neatly to one side, was combed wet. If such a thing was possible, he looked like 1960, the year. And Eamon immediately pegged him for one of Montrez's men.

"Special Agent Mathews," he said. "I was instructed to deliver these to you. This is what we have from our end." He was holding a load of files. "You Ryan or Wearie?"

Eamon felt at a distinct disadvantage. He was sitting up in bed in a pair of old jeans and undershirt, an unshaved television junkie. "Lieutenant Wearie. My partner's out interviewing."

"Perhaps that's better. Gives us a chance to talk," he said, still standing in the open doorway. "My commander has good things to say about you."

"I have good things to say about him," Eamon said a bit skeptically.

"He was one of your instructors at Q, wasn't he," he said, like it wasn't a question. "You've done good work here. My men missed a few things. We're a little upset. You picked up the pieces. To tell you the truth, we were surprised." His tone was measured, sure. "It's time you left, though. I'm sure you understand that."

He waited, even though Eamon said nothing. "This is just way out of your jurisdiction," Mathews said.

"I know," Eamon said, slightly defeated.

"Yeah, well, my commander says you're a good man. There are some other things. Your supervisor, Marcus Brown, is causing us trouble. He's been calling members of the media with the story. So far we've been able to deflect him."

"Well, he's a stupid asshole," Eamon said, a bit more harshly than he intended.

"Well, that's our general perception of him," Mathews said with a straight face. "I can tell you I wouldn't want to work for the prick."

"Can I ask if there've been any new leads?"

"Just what you boys have uncovered. My men are right now going through the *Gazette* files. We're making lists of names. Kids who've appeared in the paper over the last year. I don't know if you know this, but even Beck Lauterberg's name made it to print. He wasn't profiled or anything, but he made the police blotter column once or twice. And of course, we're doing crossovers. Checking if any name comes up in connection with one or more of the missing boys or the dead girl."

"You think anything will come of it?"

"I don't know, Wearie. I've worked on these types of cases before. And anything could be up. It could all be coincidence. It could all just to be to throw us for a loop. You never know what the deciding factor is going to be when you're dealing with a psychopath. Usually they just get careless. Just get tired of it themselves. Like a Bundy or something. I worked on a case for three years down in Waco and we had twenty-two filing cabinets full of clues and possibilities, and the killer just hangs himself. Doesn't show up for work and they find him swinging in his house with a shitload of evidence. And you know what's so funny about that?

"What's funny is the guy wasn't even a suspect. His name never came up in those twenty-two filing cabinets. I'll tell you something, Wearie. Be thankful you're going back home. This thing could drag on for . . . hell, God only knows. My advice to you is to just get on with your life. Do yourself a favor. Make believe you never heard of something called the Executioner. Tell yourself you've never even been to a town called Ashland. Tell yourself that."

Then he paused to take in Eamon's room at the Driftwood. "And really," he said, grinning, "how hard could it be to forget a place like this?"

11

Sometimes you just need a friend in this world. They don't have to do anything very special. Sometimes all they have to do is listen for a little while. Not much more than that.

It's late afternoon, golden late afternoon. The sun should be beautiful, the way it streams through the living room, all that flecked perfect light, but it leaves me empty, like it was raining in my heart. I know, I know, James. I tend to overdo it. But that telephone just sits there, a big clunky thing, as I try to think of someone to call. I have that little book in front of me, filled with all the names I've accumulated in this lifetime. They don't really add up to that much, if you think about a person's whole life. And when I go down the possibilities I can only think of the reasons why I shouldn't. I have nothing urgent to say to anyone. I have no parties to invite them to, no news to tell. I just hunger for a friendly voice. I think it is the hardest thing in the world to find a true friend. I should just be grateful for the light, for the warm light. Or I won't even have that.

I wouldn't dare bother you at this time of day, James.

I know it's when you take your walk up Byer's path, to that muddy pond you like so much, Monty leading the way, his funny red tail going a mile a minute.

I'll just help myself to more wine. Yeah, that's what I do best these days. It feels warm though and in the warmth I find the tiniest bit of salvation. Just the tiniest worst little bit. You should see me. I drink my wine and I just want to think of old times. It helps get me there.

Once when we were a lot younger, when we were at college, can you remember back that far, and we were home for the holidays, how nice the lights looked on Main Street, my mom was alive back then, and we were walking hand in hand in the Christmas snow and you tried to kiss me and I wouldn't let you because . . . I don't know why. Because I was playing hard to get. Because I was going out with another boy. Because it was back then. I always remember that night for some reason. I always remember your face, that hurt little boy look, even though you were trying to come off as a sophisticated college man. You were in a green turtleneck and your new hound's tooth Harris tweed and you had cut yourself rather badly shaving and you had put on way too much smelly cologne. And you were really quite handsome. Really. I don't remember for the life of me what I was wearing, but I have a feeling you could probably tell me. It is the best, truly the best, to know someone that long, to go back that far. I'd sure hate like hell to start all over with someone new. But you know that, you must know that.

Ever your friend, Netti

Eamon looked up to find the Command Post as quiet and gloomy as a morgue. A federal judge had been killed in D.C. by a letter bomb earlier in the day, and Anal had assigned most of the other agents to the case. Not much was known yet, but Judge Bertrand Boysee had recently handed down a particularly stiff sentence to a member of the Medellin drug cartel. Eamon and Bunko badly wanted to join in the hunt, but Anal insisted on keeping them on the Executioner, even though they were increasingly relegated to mop-up duty. The Bureau was getting first crack at everything.

Anal had locked himself in his office, in a state of panic over the letter bomb, while Bunko and that crazy Lipsick sorted through the Executioner mess. The Bureau's paper trail, thousands of unorganized single-spaced pages, documented an astounding story of miscommunication and misadventure. One fuck-up after another. As Bunko had said, "You ever hear of the Chisholm Trail? Well, what we got here is the famous Fuck-up Trail."

It had been news to learn that Sheriff Smitty had sought outside help with the disappearances almost from the very beginning. After the second boy, Greg Hohenberger, had turned up missing, just a few weeks after the Jakes kid, he was quick to go to the Williamsport police for assistance. It seems Smitty wasn't such a pea-brain that he couldn't see a connection between two missing teenage boys in a county not known for so much as a missing cow. Williamsport sent up one of their own detectives, Roy Esposito, and his report, included in the Bureau files, shows that he snooped around for two weeks before deciding that the boys were not runaways and that the cases bore too many similarities for them not to be related. Noting the absence of ransom demands, he supposed the kidnappings to be either sex-related acts or revenge-motivated. Esposito further decided that he himself was not up to the task and promptly contacted the FBI. And this was where it got complicated.

Esposito called in a Harrisburg field agent by the name of Bernard Tupper. Tupper was a notorious fuck-up with a drinking problem who'd already been transferred five times; it was the general hope of the placement committee that he might just disappear in the woodwork of Harrisburg's one-man bureau. It seems that Tupper was overwhelmed by the magnitude of events, and instead of following procedure and requesting higher-ups in Philadelphia's main office for additional man power, the five-time loser became a six-time loser. Instead of keeping it within the Bureau, Tupper went outside to the Philadelphia Police Department's Task Force on Sexual Exploitation of Children. They promptly, even though it was clearly out of jurisdiction, sent in Detective Donnie Howser and another detective, William Boot, from the Thirty-seventh Precinct's homicide division. It did not get any better.

The boys' families and friends were put through exhaustive interviews, but finally, without any new leads, the detectives were recalled back to Philly. It was at this juncture, most certainly, that Tupper should have—and perhaps he would have—contacted his superiors at the Bureau to ascertain a logical next step. Except for one small thing. Tupper suffered a massive coronary occlusion at the wheel of his car. With Tupper dead, a management decision was made in Washington to close the FBI's Harrisburg outpost altogether. Agents were called in to gather up Tupper's files. The steel gray filing cabinets, which contained somewhere in the neighborhood of fifty thousand folders, dating back to the Truman administration, including all pertinent materials relating to the mess in Ashland, were shipped whole to the FBI's 309-Auxiliary Classification warehouses just outside of Tallahassee. Which was where they remained until one of Montrez's thinkers put two and two together, which happened little over a week ago.

It was all there in numbing black and white. Since they'd returned from Ashland, Eamon had spent most of his time on the Fuck-Up Trail, but he was worn-out by repetition and official dreariness. The police and FBI reports, in carbon triplicate, with their misspellings and unusual verb conjugations, were full of superfluous physical description and trite, misguided attempts at psychoanalysis:

"The subject, a white female, of average height and build, or within those established parameters, appeared to this official observer depressed and anxiety-ridden. It is possible that the loss of a loved one, particularly a son, plays no small part in generating this outward appearance . . ."

Besides being remarkably free of noteworthy detail, the reports had so far established no new leads. Not a one. It was slow death to skim through the transcripts, interviews that were utterly mind-boggling in their worthlessness.

Eamon picked up one on his desk and shook his head in wonder.

Interview: 223
Subject: Gil Doogmeir, school chum of Beck Lauterberg
Conducted by: Agent Silver
Date: 4/5/90 (2 P.M.; between classes)

Agent: So tell me Gil, what do you know?

Gil: What are you talking about?

Agent: We're talking about Beck, son. Beck Lauterberg. I think you've heard of him.

Gil: Yeah. So. (a potential attitude problem here)

Agent: Gil, did you see Beck the day he disappeared?

Gil: I might have. I'm, like, you know, in his classes, you know.

Agent: I don't know anything. You tell me.

Gil: Beck was cool, man. What do you think, man.

Agent: We're not interested in what I think, son. What do you think?

Gil: Like I said, he was cool. Beck was cool. What else do you want?

Agent: I want to know if you know anything.

Gil: You're a waste, man. I'm trying to tell you I really didn't talk to him that day. Talk to his brother man, that wimp. (subject continues to be uncooperative)

Agent: Did Beck talk about going anywhere? Did he seem to have plans?

Gil: We all got plans, man. Like what do you mean, man?

Agent: Son, I don't have time for this.

Gil: Hey, this wasn't my idea, man. I got things to do, you know. I'm only doin' this 'cause Beck was in good standing. He was cool, like I keep trying to tell you.

Agent: Let's start at the beginning . . .

Gil: Oh (expletive) . . .

Agent: Why don't we can that crap right now, son . . .

Eamon found himself examining Lipsick. Lipsick was such a horrid sight under the crackling fluorescent tubing, pasty-faced with that ridiculous Beatle cut, every gray strand of hair that much more pronounced, his pink eyes lost in a sea of white. There was a story. There was always a story. For Lipsick, it had been the old coming home early from work one day to find his beloved in a merry configuration with the cable television installer. Eamon watched as Lipsick tapped telephone numbers into the IBM terminal. They'd requisitioned Ma Bell's records, going back a year, of the families of the missing boys and dead girl. With any luck they might match a number or two. Looking for crossovers, as Agent Mathews called it. Anyway, Lipsick seemed content with this small job, secretarial work really, as if concentrating on minutiae was his ticket out of there, out of that scary head of his, even if it was just for a short while.

Maybe it was watching Lipsick. Maybe it was just something that had been on his mind long enough. He wasn't sure what he was going to do with it. Maybe he'd just hang up; maybe he'd tell Richard Lonetree something of the truth. It wasn't anything thought out. He punched up Lonetree's number on the touch phone and waited in the dead zone of telecommunications, that wilderness of white noise, as if you could hear your call blipping off satellites, traveling the wires.

I'm sorry. But the number—five-five-five-seven-two-three-three—you have called has been disconnected. At this time no further information is available. Again, that number—five-five-five . . .

In a way, he wasn't surprised by the recording. It had already occurred to him that Lonetree might've moved or cut off his affair with Netti, or both. It made sense. Otherwise why didn't Netti address her letters? Or maybe he was married or something like that.

Undeterred, Eamon entered Richard Lonetree's name and last known address—49 Reedy Hollow Rd., Sandstone, PA—into his own terminal, into the Super Removal Book, a computerized listing of some ninety million Americans and their last known addresses. All post offices keep their own removal books, which tend to look like ordinary phone books, detailing the comings and goings of their tiny provinces and towns, but very few people were aware of the existence of the Super Removal. Eamon knew it was not something the Service wanted to spread around. That's all they needed, to be besieged by the general public and private detectives and whatnot, all clamoring about the Freedom of Information Act; why, they'd wind up spending all of their time tracking down nuisance requests.

He wondered, as it flickered for a long moment, whether he needed the ZIP. Then, bit by bit, the screen began filling up with Richard Lonetree.

Lonetree, L. Richard	SS: 063-20-4486
Single Filing Status	Birth: 01/11/53
****DISCONTINUED	As of: 04/01/89
DD7692333060	
Sept. 1973–June 1976	Harvard Center
	Box 7878
	Cambridge, MA 02138
Nov. 1977–Dec. 1979	American Express
	Main Office
	Cognetti, 23840
	Florence, Italy
Mar. 1980–Mar. 1983	51 Spring St. (apt. 2A)
	New York, NY 10012
July 1983–Aug. 1985	PO Box 477
	Forked River, PA 16933
Nov. 1985–****DD	49 Reedy Hollow Rd.
	Sandstone, PA 16901

So that's what happened. Richard Lonetree had died a year ago. Actually, it explained everything in a way. But it was strange to see a man's whole life—all that we do and touch and say—reduced to a few ionized blips. He had seemed so alive in Netti's letters, as if she never let herself believe for a moment that he wasn't up the road a ways, still doing his painting. He guessed she must have loved him awfully hard, so hard that she just couldn't let go. That said something about Richard Lonetree, all right. And it certainly said something about Netti. Eamon had trouble imagining any woman feeling that way about him.

The screen continued to hold him, and it seemed an easy enough code to crack. From the post office boxes, the wanderings and stop-offs, a clear picture of Richard L. Lonetree emerged. Eamon saw the young Harvard undergraduate, in his new tweed coat and khakis, out of the boondocks of northern Pennsylvania, slightly outclassed. The city of Florence appeared, the one really bold move. Probably some kind of grant or scholarship. It was easy to imagine him lingering in the museums and cafés, sketching, always sketching. It was not so difficult to take it a little further, to imagine lovely signorinas, perhaps even one that stood out, a great love. Why not? Then Eamon saw him touching down in New York, getting the little walk-up in Soho, painting, painting. But was he making inroads? Was his career going anyplace special, or was he waiting on tables or something? There was only so much you could weed out of a mere street address. For some reason, it made Eamon sad to think of him returning to his birthplace, to his hometown, after all those years away. There was just something defeated about it, the end of something, that's all.

Eamon had a lot of questions, but the one thing that he was sure of was that Richard Lonetree died too young. If he had lasted out another week, he would have reached his thirty-seventh birthday. This set him wondering about what got him. Was it some kind of disease? Or was he in a car accident or something? And then he was struck by the fact that that would make Netti about thirty-seven, too. For some reason, he was glad that she wasn't so old. Just a few years older than himself. He wondered what she looked like. He'd wondered that before, but now he had something to go on.

Eamon Wearie wasn't through, not by a long shot. He loved being in the throes of an honest-to-God mystery, unraveling it. The next thing he did was call the *Gazette* offices in Ashland. Evan Lancaster wasn't in, but he spoke to his young assistant. After identifying himself, Eamon asked if she could dig up Richard Lonetree's obituary and send it over.

"Does this have anything to do with those boys?" she asked.

"Yes," he lied. "I'll need assurances of confidentiality, though."

"Yeah, sure," she said. "But do you have like some idea of when this Mr. Lonetree died?"

"Yes, I have it right here," he said, enjoying the chase. "It was April first of last year."

"April Fool's Day. Wow, what a weird day to bite it," she said.

That was strange, he had to admit. Maybe the whole thing was an elaborate hoax, the letters, everything. No, what was he thinking? That would be too incredible. Eamon had gotten so caught up in his little game of mystery that he hadn't even noticed Bunko. Bunko had been eyeing him the last couple of minutes with something quite like scorn.

"Hey, sport," Bunko called over. "That little call to the *Gazette* wouldn't have anything to do with a bunch of dumb fucking love letters, would it? Christ, Wearie. If you spent half the time you spent on those fucking letters looking for the Executioner, you'd have this thing solved, buddy boy. Believe it."

12

.. . . and I can think of nothing better in this world than watching the Hens play a twi-night doubleheader in July. Make it late July, James. It's one of those steamy days and as you look around little Rooster Field, all those men in their white short sleeves, dripping perspiration at the armpits, passing beers and franks down the rows, shouting out to the Hens to look alive, look alive!, c'mon, c'mon, you Muddies! Then Bucky Hatchet steps up and taps his bat down on the plate once or twice and you can hear the crowd noise change, the isolated shouts disappear and something like quiet comes over them, oh it is the beauty of hope. It is like something out of The Natural, the way Bucky looks out to that little chain-link fence, the way the outfielders step back, respecting that power, his stance. Everyone, not just Bucky boy, is thinking long ball. Oh nothing else will do. There is a great wide swath of pink in the muted sky, so perfect that you try not to dwell on it. The pitcher takes his sign. It is all hazy and slow until that moment of release, when the ball shoots in like a bullet, high and tight, and Bucky swings, just getting a piece of it, fouling it off into the *crowd. The sense of release is palpable. Then it begins all over again. The pitcher stares down for his sign . . . and, James, you know, it really doesn't matter if Bucky strikes out, no, it doesn't. Because he's given us our little moment, filled us with the sense of the possible. But Sweet Jesus I sure like it when he gets into one and nails it into the stratosphere.*

They'd started off, as tradition warranted, at the Charles Village Pub, drinking beers and downing kamikazes. Then, appropriately wasted, they'd made their way up to the stadium, staggering through the old neighborhoods, past the nice old houses, the old folks waving from their front porches, past the kids hawking fresh roasted peanuts and Oriole caps, just part of a great old Baltimore scene.

It had been cold and blustery up in the third tier, third-base side, section H, of Memorial Stadium. Most of the fans were in their winter parkas, a bright, floodlit scene of oranges and pinks and greens, even though it was the middle of April. The Birds had lost in a one-run game, the kind of game the cold weather often produces, but he'd had a great time anyway, sitting between Bunko and Gena, passing a bottle of Jack back and forth.

He liked Gena, and he was sorry that they'd broken up before. It was nice to have someone to do things with, real nice; but sometimes it all felt a little claustrophobic, the way she held his arm and nuzzled her head on his shoulder. And he found himself, sorry to say, looking at the other women in the stands, so many beautiful, interesting creatures in the world. Eamon often wondered if all men felt the same way, and if they did, what a great lie it was.

Bunko had sat there, yelling out his obscenities, oblivious to everything around him. Gena, like a lot of people really, couldn't understand his friendship with Bunko. She knew he worked with him and all—but, like, why did they have to hang out together? She just saw this big, massive guy in this really tacky checked sport coat. She couldn't get past the meaty face and that messed-up bulb of a nose to see what lay behind, his good humor, his love for life, all that heart, all that heart. But Eamon understood. Because sometimes, not often, he felt, well, embarrassed of his friend, too. It was a damning, shaming thing to have friends, to have a family, to even have a lover.

After the game, they'd stopped in at the Marlin. There was a new one behind the bar, pulling the Oxford and Guiness. She was a small, curvy blonde, wearing something that looked like a negligee. It had been hard not to stare. The music on the juke was good, a lot of Stones, Talking Heads, and he'd had a lot to drink, and anyway, he found himself in the warm, smoky light, staring dumb-assed. This had not made Gena very happy. Gena was not one to hide her feelings, and so she basically knocked her stool down and stormed out. "If you want your girlfriend back, I'd make a run for it," the curvy blonde said.

They'd wound up back at Eamon's. It wasn't very romantic. He was putting in a Tom Petty CD when Gena just started taking off her clothes. She had made her decision. They fucked each other in the darkness, to the sound of the Heartbreakers. The only light was from the Hitachi, a soft, luminous glow on the shelf.

Nothing ever felt worse. They'd broke up a month ago, and now they were going to have to do it all over again. He was on top of her, but he didn't look down, as if her face held some kind of unbearable truth. He listened for her sound in the darkness, with a heavy heart.

Afterward she cried. Her face was wet and she lit a cigarette and talked to him while looking up at the ceiling. "Life hasn't been easy for me," she said. "My dad was an alchie and he left us, you know. Eight kids, that's a lot of brothers and sisters. I got out of there. Wasn't easy. Waiting tables. Least it isn't Paducah, Kentucky. Least it isn't that."

A long minute passed, where he thought of unrelated things. She lay on top of the sheets naked, and he found himself examining her patch of pubic hair. He thought about one of the better plays in the ball game. Ripkin reached into the hole and threw as he went down. Her pubic hair was mossy brown. He didn't feel much. It was all kind of bland—and he knew he was distancing himself, that he had to.

"I thought you'd be more decent," she said. "We had something going there for a while. You led me on, Eamon. You made me believe that there'd be something else. I know you're not going to talk about it, because that's not the way you are. You'll be nice and then you won't call, and that way it'll be like I never existed. Isn't that right, Eamon?"

What was there to say? You had to admire her clarity.

"I just think you're scared," she said. "Or it might even be worse than that. You just don't feel anything, do you? You're like one of those psycho-killers. Have you ever made love to anyone, Eamon? Or is it all fuck fuck fuck? I think it's the latter, that's what I think."

She got up and started collecting her things. She wasn't the best-looking woman he'd ever seen, but he liked her, whatever the hell she thought. Sometimes nice people couldn't make it happen in that way, that's all.

"I'll be going now," she said. "And, Eamon. I don't want you calling me up in a lonely moment or anything. And, Eamon. I hope you get the help you need, you fucking bastard."

He heard her charge down the stairs and out the door. He wasn't the only one to hear Gena Davio leave, though.

Daniel P. Pinkus was in his own bedroom, finishing up with the time-consuming, even exhausting, nightly arrangements. Of course, he had to say his prayers to all the dead people who were watching him, which was at least a twenty-minute litany. It had to be done the same exact way every night. If he made a mistake, put one person's name before another's, he would have to begin at the beginning and do it all over. It was a maddening exercise, but he had to do it. He had no choice.

Then his shoes and clothes had to be arranged in a particular order. He always set his shoes down next to the bed so that the right one projected out slightly farther than the left. And then he had to make sure that all the coins on his bureau were showing heads. And then he prayed again to God. Because you could never pray enough. He prayed for nothing terrible to happen. Just nothing terrible, please God, he went. He never prayed for happiness or prosperity or the lottery or whatever it was most people wanted. He knew better than that.

Then he got into bed, making sure that his right foot was the last one to touch the floor. To Daniel P. Pinkus's credit, he knew that it was all crazy as hell. But even knowing this did not help him. He had seen a Phil Donahue show only last week where they'd examined his problem. It seemed he wasn't the only one. They called it OCB, which stood for Obsessive Compulsive Behavior. And so now before he went to bed, he said OCB to himself twenty-two times in a row. He was not sure why he did this. But he knew that it was necessary.

The very last thing he did before turning out the lights was read one of her letters. It was his newest nightly ritual.

When Eamon wasn't home, which was most of the time, Daniel P. Pinkus would go into his bedroom and rummage where he didn't belong. That's how he'd come across Netti's letters. He had no idea what it was all about, what her connection to Eamon was or anything, but Pinkus had found them somehow soothing. And soothing was something in short supply in his life. The letters calmed him, and now he had to read one every night before turning in. He was already worried about what he'd do when they finally ran out. After all, there were just so many letters.

13

"I'm having trouble sleeping at night," he said seriously.

They were in the left lane of I-95, going about seventy-five miles per, which was slightly slow for Bunko, just outside of Wilmington. The traffic was especially light at eleven in the morning, just the diesels and other movements of commerce.

"Well," Eamon said, "I'll tell you what you do. You give up the booze and the late hours and the bimbos and the sloppy work habits and your penchant for the track—and then you see what happens."

"Oh, easy for you to say. But that's all I have."

"Have you tried warm milk, Bunk? Works for Trish's cats."

"Yeah, you're a riot, Wearie. I wonder why all those babes keep walkin' out on you."

"Ouch."

"Ah, I should talk." Bunko said with less gristle in his voice. "I ain't exactly Mr. Right. Even got dumped by Mrs. Taglianno. The woman with green hair."

"Wanted a commitment or something?"

"She wanted the or something. Wanted me to take her

dancing. I don't dance. I don't even like watching people dance. It makes me feel self-conscious."

"*Self-conscious*, Bunk? I didn't even think that word was in your vocab, buddy. That's like right up there with *self-awareness*. Next you'll be telling me you like got *feelings* and that we'll have to like *explore* them together."

"You got the fuckin' sensitivity of a crustacean, Wearie."

"That's funny. That's exactly what my last girlfriend told me."

It was warm and sunny, and the highway stretched out before them like fool's gold, sparkling with so many false prospects.

"No, Eamon. I tell you I can't sleep." Bunko sounded serious again. "That sweetheart in the hood. Fuck him, brother. You know what I think? I think he's killing himself. Over and over. That's what I think."

"What are you talking about?"

"Brother, I dreamed it. It's him. You know. The pictures. Everything. He keeps committing suicide. 'Cause he fuckin' hates himself. At least he's got that fuckin' part right. See? The pictures. All the kids have blond hair. Right? Am I right? That's him. He's got blond hair. I'll bet you. No question. And the objects in the pictures—the glove, the record album, the bra—represent moments in the turd's life. I'm telling you. He's killing himself. It came to me during another restless night."

Eamon thought about that. There was something to it. Before, he'd thought it probably had something to do with an ex-lover or somebody who'd meant something to the Executioner. But Bunko's theory had that weird ring. The ring of the true.

"But why's he cutting his dick off?" Eamon asked.

"Hates himself. Or no. Something else. I don't know. Maybe the turd's impotent. No, no. How about he's already been castrated? Check that out. Oughta interview all the castrated folks in Bear County. Find our man, or whatever the hell he is."

"You're forgetting about that fucking picture. Know he's got a dick."

"Not much of a dinkus, if you ask me."

I-95's four lanes split up. I-295, the Jersey Turnpike, took you right to Route 40, and this in turn brought you to the promised land. Atlantic City. This did not escape Bunko's notice, as he stayed left, onto the Pennsylvania Turnpike, in the direction of Philadelphia.

"Jesus, we haven't hit AC in a few weeks," Bunko said. "What do you say we hit Trumptown coming back? What's the harm, tell me that?"

Eamon wasn't sure. "I don't know, Bunk. We got a lot to do today, man."

"I'll tell you what," Bunko said brightly, already consumed with the idea. "We'll just split up our appointments. I'll talk to that private dick. I mean, that's my expertise, right? And you do Famous Buddy or whatever the fuck his name his. I mean, kooks, weirdos, total frauds—that's pretty much your territory, isn't it?"

"Know me like a book, pard. Count me in."

"Speaking of books, what do you think of the Bureau's finding on the turd's bedside reading matter? You know, the ones they identified on the nightside stand, in that *Boy Love* photo."

Eamon hadn't given it much thought. The Babar the elephant book was a little odd. It didn't seem to fit in. The other three were classics. *Of Mice and Men. The Sun Also Rises.* And then there was *The Catcher in the Rye,* a favorite of his and the only one he'd read of the bunch. It wasn't that he hadn't read Steinbeck and Hemingway, just not those two novels. Anyway, Elmore Leonard was more his style.

"I'll tell you what I think," Bunko said, back on the case. "I still think the turd is a teacher. I don't know. I keep coming back to that."

"I don't know, Bunk. What about the elephant book? That's for like little kids. Like, how does it fit in with the others?"

"Beats me, buddy. Beats me. But, you know, there's another thing that bothers me. The handwriting. You saw the sample. Those fuckin' Have A Nice Day dots over the *i.* Doesn't that just kill you? What the fuck is that about? But wait. Here's my point. The handwriting is all fucked up and everything, but in its own way, it's got like a kind of discipline. Yeah. It's like a teacher's. It's full of fuckin' loops and everything, but there's a severity about it that I can't explain."

Bunko had been excited. The words had come out in great big gulps, and color had charged into his face. He didn't know what was with himself lately. This wasn't like him at all. He took a deep breath and exhaled it. He looked out at the road, as if suddenly reminded that he was doing the driving.

"Maybe he's just trying to throw us off," Bunko said, a little dejected-sounding now. "Sometimes I get the feeling the turd is toying with us. That he's tossing lots of junk our way, like almost too many clues. But like with nothing really there. You know. Like the thing with the *Gazette*. See, I think that's a smoke screen. Cat and mouse. Just adding to his titilation. I don't know. Who fuckin' knows?"

"Yeah, I got that feeling when I was talkin' to that Agent Mathews," Eamon said. He was more pensive, looking straight ahead, at the developing congestion. They were just outside Philly.

"Mathews told me anything goes," Eamon began again. "It's been on my mind, too. There's all sorts of little things that have been bugging me. Dumb things. Like the identical twin stuff. It's probably nothing, right? But it stays with me. Beck Lauterberg has a twin brother, and then that Jake kid has twin sisters. Probably just the dumbest coincidences. But you can never be sure. And then why does he suddenly take out the girl?—I mean, if he did it and all."

"Yeah, yeah, I know," Bunko said, disgusted with the whole business. "Too many fucking odds and ends. Even those pictures in that porno magazine were overkill. Maybe he's tired, real tired of it all. He's probably been killing and dismembering these kids for years. The sickness runs through this turd like a bad fever."

The traffic had crawled to a stop. Three lanes were being asked to empty into one. This, evidently, presented quite a challenge for some motorists. Windows were rolled down.

There were exchanges of opinion. Some punctuated their remarks by leaning into their horns. Humanity came to a virtual standstill.

"We've got to get back to what we know," Bunko said, trying to keep cool, to hold down the old blood pressure. "What we do best. Christ, I mean we're just a couple of postal inspectors. So what do we know? We know that the turd used three-cent stamps. It goes back to that mother thing again. Either he's real old himself—which he didn't look to be in that nice picture of his dungeon—or he's living with a mother or grandmother or something like that. Or maybe he's a fuckin' stamp collector. And then we got an interesting handwriting sample. That's what we got. But what do we do with all of it?"

"I don't know. Maybe we check teachers out. The books on his nightstand. Maybe they're from a certain course. You know. Maybe that's what we do. We start looking for a big blond teacher who lives with his mom. Or maybe even his fucking old man. What do we know? We start with something like that. Then we check out local stamp collectors. You might be on to something there. And that's what we do."

"Now you're talkin'," Bunko said. "We go with what we know. It's like with that federal judge that just got blown up. Santos was telling me about it. They came up with a bunch of little shit that's starting to add up. Bomb was wrapped in this meat-packing paper. Judge had been getting threatening letters for weeks. Letters were full of biblical references. Looks like it has nothing to do with that drug cartel. Seems this judge came down with a ruling on the side of the Darwinists a few months back. Pissed off a lot of religio-fanatics. So my point is, they got a postmark. Chicago. So maybe they go looking for a butcher in the Windy City. Big town, yeah. Common profession, yeah. But at least it's something. You got to start with something, don't you?"

Up ahead they could see the blinking arrows and orange cones. A road crew sat around eating bologna sandwiches. Many of the motorists paused as they went by, to offer their opinions as good hardworking taxpayers. A few of the yellow hard hats welcomed the chance to speak their mind. There was some good, spirited debate.

Bunko watched the hyperventilation with some amusement. There was an all-American family in a sleek van right in front of them. Dad shouted out his discerning thoughts to the construction workers while Mom and the three kids flipped them the bird.

"You know, I've been thinking lately," he said. "It's those long, sleepless nights. That's what's doin' it. And yeah, I think about that sick turd, all right. But it's more than that. 'Cause I'm also thinking about the people. About all the people out there. I used to think I was a good judge of character. But you know, lately, I'm not so sure anymore. I think that it all happens inside with people. It's all in there, where you can't see. Forget about all the surfaces they show. Don't mean shit. Can never look into their souls. That's the bitch."

Eamon had never been to Philadelphia before. He was surprised right off by its size. Baltimore was so different, such a slow and lazy town really. He'd forgotten what it was like to be in a real city. Philly had that New York feeling, those same hurried, self-centered movements. He watched as determined businesswomen in Dior suits and Reebok sneakers stepped by as if they were entered in a walkathon, leaving behind only a tantalizing whiff of their perfume. Well-dressed young men, gripping their lovely calfskin briefcases, preoccupied with stock indexes and the prime rate, shoved on by with malice in their eyes.

He felt almost invisible, overcome by the sights and sounds. Green and white cabs barreled through midtown, braking and squawking. Hot dog vendors called out. They lined up at the newsstand for papers and Lotto. The homeless badgered and cajoled, striking bargains wherever they could, a nickel, a dime, being better than nothing. Even though Philadelphia was noisier and bigger than Baltimore, Eamon thought they smelled the same. Black clouds of bus exhaust and last night's urine. Fast food and manhole steam. And city sidewalks were always slimy, blotched with pink gum, slippery with spilt vanilla shakes and old vomit.

Bunko had dropped him off on Market Street, right out in front of the R. H. Lamb Building, a miragelike skyscraper, its silver facade of sheet glass blurring and burning in the noontime sun. Secretaries and mail-room guys sat around a fountain unwrapping tuna sandwiches and laughing among themselves, their words drowning in the spray. He walked past the ugly Caldor, a horribly twisted piece of corrugated steel, its red paint showing signs of rust, through the revolving door, into the quintessential modern lobby, potted plants and a huge, dominating piece of abstract expessionism, over to the elevator bank, where an open car awaited him.

She stepped in behind him. She was quite striking, in the empty, overly coiffed way of a television anchorwoman, which he supposed her to be. Her overt perfume, like raspberry-flavored sex, filled the car. Her face was a perfect oval, her eyes Windex blue, her nose a surgical wonder, and her lemon-colored hair was stacked with verve. He noticed her gold hoop earrings and the pearls that hung from her sublime neck. In a way—and he somehow hated to admit this—she was splendorous. In her presence, he became acutely aware of his own sartorial shortcomings. Even though he was wearing a blue blazer, his best jacket, over a pair of new chinos, his tie was hopelessly out-of-date, and his penny loafers were trade-in material. He spotted her gold Rolex, catching what little light there was, and for some reason it left him vaguely ashamed of his own wristwatch, that black plastic thing he'd had forever.

The elevator doors opened and he stepped out. He glanced back at her fleetingly, in the momentary void. Her eyes were locked on her ruby shoes, evidently this was appropriate elevator etiquette. He had entered into another lobby, spacious and bright, filled with plant life and modern art. Two hefty security guards immediately focused on him. They stood in front of one of the yellow and blue paintings, two fatties with mustaches, regarding Eamon suspiciously.

They looked funny, like a couple of Duane Hansons, just as waxy and perverse.

The main desk was staffed by two beautiful, absolutely superficial-looking creatures, each in her own way as incandescent as the woman in the elevator. The phone lines buzzed repeatedly, but they remained unfazed, picking up with the standard "WKRX, please hold, sir." Their voices were unreal-sounding, like electronic recordings. He waited at the desk for some sort of recognition.

"All messenger deliveries are made on the thirty-first floor," one of them finally said disdainfully.

She didn't bother to apologize. Just told him to take a seat while she called to verify. Two other men were already waiting on the white leather couch. It was all very California, the two Eames chairs, just as white, just as immaculate, the potted palms, the clear slab of table. He plopped down in one of the chairs. It wasn't long before he grew tired of waiting, unconsciously he tapped his feet, swiveled nervously. His eyes flitted about, taking it all in in bits and pieces. He noticed the other gentlemen, how finely put together they were, their expensive accoutrements, the alligator briefcases, those slimmest of wristwatches, the neckties in the latest Italian splashes, their snazzy silk socks and power-shined shoes. They were framed by a large painting of a red circle and yellow triangle in a blue and white field. It made him think of that modern art elective he'd taken at Stony Brook how many years before. He'd only taken it to meet this one girl; always a girl . . .

"Lieutenant, Barry will see you now. You'll have ten minutes. That's all. He's booked up two years in advance. We're making an exception for you. Make the most of your moment. This way."

She was another perfectly turned out specimen, full-chested with a stack of auburn hair, a panty line to die for. He followed her through a narrow corridor, past fifty or more glass offices, each one fronted by another Amazonian secretary.

Famous Barry's office contained two fold-up chairs. That was the extent of the furniture. The walls were covered with a dizzying array of crucifixes. The bloody, emaciated Christs were nailed into wooden and metal crosses of every size. The expressions ran the gambit, from the silent scream to the beatific to a sort of ghoulish nothingness. It gave Eamon the creeps.

Famous Barry, a small, slight, baby-faced, wholly forgettable man, sat in one of the chairs with his eyes closed. He was dressed like a reject from the disco seventies, in an open velour shirt, exposing the requisite gold chains, bright blue designer jeans with fancy pocket-stitching, and a pair of laughable white patent leather shoes. His hairline was badly receding, and the effect, if not entirely pathetic, was one of great vulnerability.

"Barry," she announced to him, "you have a visitor."

He was startled awake. "Uh, what, oh. I'm sorry. Yeah. You're that lieutenant fellow. Right. Were you waiting long? Oh man. Just place your butt right here." He patted the remaining fold-up, which was directly beside him.

"You look pretty tired," Eamon said, taking the seat. Bunko had always taught him to go with the small talk first. You tended to learn more that way, rather than from straight Q & A.

"Well, yeah, it's funny, but it's the only time I can get away from them."

His accent was thick, uneducated-sounding, like a Philly version of that much-denigrated New York borough. "Get away from who?"

"All the dead," Barry said. "You know, it's kind of a bitch, but I'm like the only medium for these poor bastards. And they got their own agenda, you know. And they got messages they want to pass on and all sorts of shit like that. Thank God they can't, like, uh, you know, enter into my sleep. That would definitely be like cutting over the line, man."

"Well," Eamon said, "first of all I wanted to thank you for seeing me on such short notice—"

"Hey, when I heard you were with the Service, you know. Then it was like hey bring the man in. Because, you know, like, I used to be a letter carrier back when, you know. Before this like happened."

"What do you mean *happened?*"

"Oh man, you don't know the story. Don't you watch the show? Doesn't matter. You know, like, I had a bad car accident. I died on the table. Dead for five minutes. You know, had the whole after-life experience, the warm light, the old relatives and friends greeting you, the whole feeling of love deal. You ever see that movie *Resurrection?* Sam what's-his-name, you know, Jessica Lange's hubby, and that chick, who I can't think of her name right now. Anyway, saw that movie and almost flipped out. Just like what I went through. Caught the whole thing good. Hollywood, huh. So anyway, like I was sayin', I died and had the whole big after-life trip. But here's the screwy thing: It like never went away for me. You know, the warm, fuzzy light and all the spirits. Always there, man. In fact, they started to collect the minute you walked in. There's an old guy in a blue uniform wants to talk to you. Barrel-chested. Good shape. Cirrhosis of the liver. Got a funny Irish name. Like Shea-something."

"Seamus? Seamus?" Eamon's heartbeat increased. There was something about all of this. Famous Barry just didn't seem like some big con artist or sharpie; he seemed way too unaffected, much too real.

"I don't know, man. You got to take hold of my hands. That's how I work, man. C'mon, what are you waiting for?"

He felt funny sitting there, holding Barry's hands. But then he felt the heat. Honest to goodness heat.

"Yeah, that's much better, man. Make out the voices clearer now. Yeah, Seamus, that's him. Your grandfather, right. Father's side. Yeah, right. Okay. Now, he's your guardian angel. Okay, now that we got that straight. Yeah, he was in the marines or something. Some kind of officer. Yeah, okay. He wants you to know things. He doesn't want you making same mistakes he did. He says you drink too much. He loves you, but he's worried. Thinks you're kind of like undirected. Letting everything happen to you. You got to take control of things, man. He says the thing with your

137

wife, I don't know what it is, but he says it was for the best; yeah, that's what he says. He says hang in there. He wants to make you an offering. It's something like one of those old-time watches, with the gold chain. Yeah, he wants you to have it. Do you, uh, like, have like any questions for Seamus?"

It was strange, the tears were streaming down his face. He could feel his heart, the crazy way it was beating. His grandfather, whom he had always loved so much. His grandfather who'd come over from the Old Country as a boy, who wound up fighting in Iwo Jima. A marine captain, no less. Came home to find work as a conductor on the Long Island Railroad. That gold pocket watch, which was his most cherished possession.

"Is he," Eamon choked and sniffled, "is he in heaven? Is there such a thing?"

"Oh yeah. Most definitely. Made the Big H. Looks like he had to wait it out for a few years in P Country, but heck, that's the way it is for most of 'em. Oh, he says, let's see, he wants you to know that, uh, Billy and Maureen and, uh, let's see, Maggie, yeah, Maggie, they all, like, want to say hello—"

"Uncle Billy and Aunt Maureen . . ." Eamon's voice trailed off.

"Listen, he has to go now. He says hang tough. Always be proud of your name and what you come from. He'll try to watch over you. He'll do his best, is what he says. Oh. One other thing. He says something about the transmission on your car. I don't know. Have it checked out. And another thing, he says forgive your pa. Says that's the lesson of life, all in the forgiving. He wants you to think about that. And now he's gotta go, but he wants you to help the kids."

"The kids?" Suddenly he was reminded of what he was doing there in the first place.

"Yeah. I forgot to tell you. They've been collecting since you got here. There's about ten or more of them. They have things to tell us, but it's hard to hear. They're kind of unformed, if you know what I'm saying. And they're all kind

138

of talking at once. It's hard to catch. I remember one of 'em, he's visited me before. His mom was here. Chris, right? Yeah, he's too excited. I can't understand him. This is hard—"

"Can they give me a name, anything?" Eamon said, trying to make the most of it.

"I don't know. I'm like getting something here. *H*, that's the first letter. I got an *H*, I got I think an *O*, and then I got an *R*, something like that. I think that's the first name. Now they're like arguing among themselves. They're not really sure. Like, some of them know the lady—"

"Lady?"

"No, no. It's a man. I'm sorry. I'm getting too many thoughts. Their mothers, everything enters into this. Let's see, it's a guy, yeah. He's—"

"Is he a teacher?"

"Yeah, that's it. They're all nodding their heads up and down. I think that's who he is. He's some kind of teacher. Yeah, and he's big and ugly, kind of fat, I think. You know, there's so many different stories here, though. Real confused, man. One big kid, name of Mike something, Mike Winkle, yeah. And another one. They know each other. Sam, yeah, uh, Sam Fair—Sam Farrety. Okay. They were kind of like buddies. Oh, no. Not that. Oh, shit. They're starting to do that screaming stuff. Oh, it's very intense, man. I can't listen to it. Think we'd better let go here . . ."

They released hands. Eamon's brow was dripping. He'd just gone through something, and now he was more than a little disoriented. The little guy in the disco retreads was saying good-bye. "You oughta check out my television show, man." The lady with the panty line was ushering him out. "It changes people," she said, leading him to the elevator. "But don't worry," she added, "all things fade with time."

Outside, it was still very sunny. He bought a hot dog at one of the umbrella carts, more a reflex action than out of any hunger. He looked at his watch. Bunko wasn't due to pick him up for another hour. He went over to the fountain and took a seat. Now he noticed the glint of the pennies, thousands of pennies, on the tiled bottom, so many gleaming little wishes, all of them paid for in full. He thought about that for a moment, about how gullible everyone was, the way everyone was always wishing for things to come true, wishing wishing wishing, how so many beautiful wishes could wind up just coins in a fountain.

Then he wondered if he'd been had.

He took out his little spiral notebook and started writing it down from memory. He wasn't willing to dissect the experience yet, and so his pen ran across the pages, not missing a beat. He wrote it all down, everything that he could remember. Damn, he should have brought a tape recorder.

Bunko was concerned. Here they were, at the Trop, playing blackjack, up a couple of hundred apiece, having these sex kittens in lingerie bring them free drinks all night long—and the guy was Mr. Doom and Gloom. Who could figure Eamon Wearie? He fucking couldn't, that was for damn sure.

Christ, he was having an absolutely marvelous time. The cards were coming out faces, no hard decisions to make, and he was happily toasted on Sambuca-laced coffees. Jesus, what wasn't to like? He was just where he wanted to be, at the blue felt table, with a bunch of shoddy characters like himself. Everyone was smoking and drinking a ton. Just great. Nobody asking him to put his cigarette out. Nobody cutting him off at the bar. And Christ, he was already in love with the dealer. Miranda was nearing the dark side of forty, and she'd done everything in her power to stop the clock. Why, she was a work of fucking art. Her chest was a silicone dream. Her hair was frosted and teased to hell. The blue eyes were those newfangled contacts. Then there was the matter of the world's worst nose job. Oh, it was a beauty, chiseled all to hell. And, the pièce de résistance, for him at least, those exquisite, and most fake, dimples. Christ, he liked that in a woman, or anybody for that matter. Trying to better yourself. Rise above your circumstances.

Miranda was his kind of gal, full of spunk and inner grit. She rooted for the players and wished them luck, but she did it with a wink, because she knew the hard truth of the tables and of life, which was that everyone was a loser, or soon would be. The best you could do, the best you could hope for, was to buy in, get a little action for your money.

The way things were going, Bunko would've loved to stay the night in AC—who knows, maybe even make a little play for Miranda—but Eamon was being a real party pooper, totally unlike him, asking every three minutes when they were going to hit the parkway.

"Listen, ace," Bunko said, at the end of the shoe. "Why don't we go and cash in. Then we hit the Castle on the way out for a quick round. All right? Whatayasay?"

They went up to the cashier's window, never a line there, and Eamon watched as an expressionless young woman counted out $480 in twenties, his denomination of choice. "Have a nice day," she said like death.

He should've been happy, the easy victory, the money, but he was supremely troubled. Walking through the casino, to the escalators, through all that mirrored light and bordello color, amidst all that coin-jangling noise, the ringing slots and communal blood lust of the dice tables, he felt adrift, out of sorts, as if he were having some kind of out-of-body experience. Red cards were sprayed out in slow motion. Roulette wheels spun and spun, never stopping. Grizzled old men and fat circus women shrieked out their magic numbers, like in some Fellini film. Mind-boggling cocktail waitresses, pouring out of their leotards, outrageous flashings of breast and thigh and ass, wandered about with their drink trays, enticements of the devil.

He couldn't say if it was all related to Famous Barry and the events of the afternoon, but he wondered if God would judge him harshly. It had occurred to him, in revelatory enough fashion, that if he was to believe what happened, if indeed his dead grandfather had spoken to him through Barry, which—crazy as it sounded—he almost half bought, then he would have to buy the rest of it too. Heaven. Hell.

The Bible. The whole fucking deal. Instead of giving him reason to hope, he found the whole idea scary. Again he saw Barry's office, a solid wall of crucifixes, that silent scream.

They found the beige Aries where they left it, in the parking garage, up in section 5C.

"Jesus, we may actually leave this town with a little money," Bunko said animatedly. "Jesus, they'll put us in that *Guinness Book of Records*. I'm telling you. TV people will want to interview us. Our legend will grow. When word gets out, the casinos will blackball us . . . What the heck?"

The car had turned over fine, but when Bunko tried putting her in reverse, she wouldn't budge. He restarted her, with the same results. Then he got out of the car to take a look.

He got down on his belly. "Jesus fuckin' Christ," he said, dipping a finger into the big, reddish puddle. "So guess what the problem is?" he called up.

"It's the transmission, isn't it?" Eamon said, as if in a trance.

"Yeah, that's right. A seal broke. But hey, how'd you know that?"

142

14

Richard Lonetree, 36, of Sandstone, an acclaimed artist and former college professor, died Friday at his home after a long illness.

Mr. Lonetree, a Harvard graduate, had won many awards and competitions for his paintings. In 1977 he was the recipient of the famed international Morgan Fellowship, and as such, he was given a stipend to study abroad in Italy and France.

He also taught fine art at the prestigious Parsons School of Design for several years. Susan Israel, a vice-president at the New York–based institution, called his demise "a deeply-felt, even tragic loss for everyone involved."

His paintings, which were described as "old-fashioned and bucolic" by his agent and dealer, Simon Warren, had been shown in some of the best galleries in the world. His last show, "The Cows Come Home to Roost," was at the renowned Boone Gallery in New York City.

"Richard was a very, very fine painter," Mr. Warren said by telephone. "But he was not painting au courant, as it were. In some ways he was hopelessly out of fashion, even strange. But God love Richard, he painted from the heart. He was a minor light, in the best sense of the word. And he will be sorely missed."

Mr. Lonetree was a 1973 graduate of Sandstone High School, where he was remembered fondly by teachers and administrators alike. "Rich was a good kid, hardworking, wish we had more like him," his gym teacher, Mr. Sal Burton, recalled.

He is survived only by his mother, Ellie Winters, also of Sandstone. Burial was private.

Eamon asked Bunko to cover for him while he went down into Dead Letters. He wanted to see if any more of Netti's letters had arrived over the last couple of weeks. He had just left the obituary on his desk, which was where Captain Marcus Brown had found it.

"Lieutenant," he said, addressing Bunko. "Do you have any idea how this relates to our case?" He handed Richard Lonetree's obit over to him.

Bunko was caught short this time. "Uh, lemme see," he stumbled. "It must have something to do with it. I just don't know what at this time."

Captain Brown was frowning. "Communication," he said, like it was a biblical word. "That is what we will need more of if we are ever going to solve this. I've put my faith in you men. I hope I won't be disappointed."

Captain Marcus Brown was more than a little concerned. He could ill afford to keep three men on the Executioner, what with a federal judge being blown up and all. Everyone was breathing down his neck—he'd received calls from Senator Hollins and the FBI director's number two man and even the postmaster general himself—but he was still fuming about the way Tony Montrez had disparaged the Service. He had used a tone of voice with him that was totally unacceptable. There was ridicule and condescension

144

in that smug bastard's voice. But he would learn. Learn like so many others.

That's why they could ill afford any lapses in communication now. Bunko and Wearie and Lipsick were going to have to work together like three Siamese twins. Whatever you called that. It didn't matter. What did matter was teamwork. Teamwork was the key. Without it and you were through, disgraced, washed up. This was the lesson of Richard Milhous Nixon. The greatest president in history had to abdicate his throne because of a lack of teamwork. Basically that was the root cause. It was all there, in Dick's memoirs. He'd explained himself well, explained away many, if not all, of the tiny discrepancies that those liberal extremists were always going off at the mouth about. Dick just had no idea what half his staff was up to. Here he was a man of great integrity, and yet he had scoundrels, men of absolutely no honor, working below deck. Well, Marcus Brown could assure you that this was not the type of thing that was going to happen in his administration. Marcus himself was a great student of history. And he knew that one had to memorize history if one was not going to repeat it. Or something to that effect.

It was at this point that Eamon Wearie returned.

He stepped off the freight elevator with three more of Netti's letters, fairly thrilled with the find and already eager to rip into them. His spirits took an immediate plunge when he saw Anal sitting atop his desk with the obituary from the *Gazette*.

"Well, it's about time, Lieutenant Wearie," Anal said. "We'd practically given up hope of ever hearing from you again. Now that we're all here, perhaps I can address the issue of communication . . ."

While Little Pucker and Big Pucker stood behind him, nodding eternal acquiescence, Anal made a stirring little speech about the fall of Nixon and the dangers of miscommunication. Eamon knew old dickhead was going to ask him about Lonetree, and tried to think up something halfway believable.

145

"So, in conclusion, may I just say that President Nixon was duped by those closest to him," Anal said with some gravity. "As a student of history, I firmly believe that there is a lesson to be learned here."

Bunko clapped and whistled. Lipsick had turned his chair around so that his back was to Anal. The Two Puckers, lapdogs *extraordinaire,* were actually shaking his hand. Eamon wondered how he ever came to be in such a world.

"So, uhmm, Lieutenant Wearie," Anal said, clearing his throat. "Why don't we begin with you. Now, I see there is this, uh, ah, obituary on your desk—I only happened on it in passing—and I'm sure it has something to do with our case. Why don't you inform your partners of its significance."

"Well, sir," Eamon began. "We're just covering all the angles. Don't want to miss a beat. And in point of fact, sir, it is my expert opinion, after a thorough investigation, that Richard Lonetree was, in fact, not involved with this particular case. So there really is no need beating a dead horse here, sir."

This seemed to appease Anal for the moment, even if the Two Puckers appeared totally mystified by this explanation. On the other hand, Bunk had on his hoo-boy, what-a-load-of-horseshit face.

"Well, fine work, then," Anal declared. "But as I understand it, you were down in Dead Letters, following up a new lead in the case. Perhaps you could *elucidate* on your work there. I suppose those letters in your hands are of *paramount* importance."

"Well," he said, buying time. "Actually, these letters, uh, have to do with, uhm, another case I'm working on."

"Lieutenant," Anal said with great officiousness. "You are only supposed to be working on the one case. I want this Executioner thing solved. I do not want my men squandering their time elsewhere. Montrez is way ahead of us on this. We must redouble our efforts. Is that understood?"

"Yes, sir," Eamon said, uncomfortable in the shit-eating role.

"Now, what is this other case anyway?"

"Well, it's really quite a long story—"

"It's not that long a story," Arthur Marlens suddenly interrupted, a crafty little smile forming on his narrow, weasel-like face.

Eamon examined him impassively: that sad thatch of gooked-up hair trying to cover an even oilier piece of scalp, as if sideburn-extensions could ever be the answer; runny eyes with all the breadth and vision of dishwater; the Pee-Wee Herman wardrobe, the geeky pocket pens and calculator, the manly bow tie, shoes only a mother could love. He should have seen this coming. They'd been careless around the twerp lately.

"Yes, Art," Anal said, with mounting consternation. "Is there something that I should be made aware of?"

"Well, perhaps it's none of my business," Marlens jumped in, "but it has come to my attention that Lieutenant Wearie has been pursuing a personal matter on company time. Now, I have nothing personal against Lieutenant Wearie per se, but I've never been one to tolerate indolence. I think you know that to be true of me, Marcus. Anyway, to continue, it was not my intention to point fingers, but as you all know, I am a man of duty and principle. Wearie here has been going down into DL territory and, well, taking things that don't belong to him. As I understand it, he has been bringing certain classified materials home with him. And more to the point, he has been spending considerable time and company effort—well, I don't know what he's doing exactly, but it's just not professional, if you ask me."

"Art, I appreciate your candor on this matter," Anal said solemnly. "I think we all do. Now then, Lieutenant Wearie, what do you have to say for yourself?"

"Well, sir, these letters, well, what they are is love letters. Not what I'd call classified information. Anyway, what happened—"

"I don't want to hear any more, Lieutenant. If there is anything I despise, it is slacking. Slackers are not to be tolerated in my company. I want to make that crystal-clear. Now then. You have an excellent record. I certainly take that into consideration here. I just want you to put an end to this nonsense as of this moment. Do I have your attention? Good. Now then, I want a rundown of your activities today. I want to know what you've been doing on the case."

It was all too fucking much. The Wimp Inquisition. "Well, sir, as a matter of fact, I have not been neglecting my duties. Right now I'm working on finding out the whereabouts of Mike Winkle and Sam Farrety. These were the names given to us by the psychic in Philadelphia. I've already contacted the National Center for Missing and—"

"Am I to understand that we are spending valuable time chasing down the *predictions* of some *soothsayer?* Lieutenant, this is the United States Postal Service's most elite corps. We do not use *sorcery* to solve our difficult dilemmas."

"Sir, if you'd just hear me out on this one—"

"Not another word, Lieutenant. You are dismissed for the rest of the day. I want you to cool your heels. Then perhaps you'll show up for work Monday morning clear-eyed and ready for work. That is all, Lieutenant."

The captain knew you had to nip these things in the bud. Otherwise it was like a cancer that could spread with sickening swiftness. Wearie wasn't such a bad lad, but it would do him no harm to pay closer attention to the work at hand. It was probably that damn Bunko's doing anyway. He was just not a team player, never would be. Not that there was any great loss there. Some men, like Bunko, were neither leaders nor followers, only a great disservice to their country.

The captain and his two assistants marched off, a little too triumphantly. "Congratulations, sport," Bunko said, once they were out of earshot. "Pretty nifty job of getting the afternoon off."

Eamon was infuriated, practically incapable of speech. He should've taken their fucking heads off. He went over to the Command Post's window on the world, that long slat of streaky Plexiglas. He could see them, down below, getting off the elevator. He watched as the boys in blue, regular army, who were riding dollies, or else loading conveyor belts, stopped what they were doing, saluting as the three little men passed their way.

He arrived home, shortly after one, which was certainly new for him, with all the intention in the world of kicking back with a few brewskies and the joy of the remote control, to find the front door wide open. He heard sounds coming from the second floor, from his bedroom.

"Daniel? Daniel, is that you?" he shouted up. What the devil was that son of a bitch doing in his room?

No reply. The shuffling stopped. It finally hit him that it might not be Pinkus at all. He went into the front hall closet and pulled out his Don Mattingly–autographed Louisville Slugger.

"All right, who the hell's up there?" he yelled from the bottom of the stairs. He was ready to bolt in an instant if the intruder had a gun or anything.

A frail, rather dignified, elderly gentleman appeared at the top. He was in a camel's hair jacket and tie, holding a fancy attaché case. He did not look like your standard crowbar specialist.

"Yes?" he said, the voice tastefully British. "I say, what are you doing in Mr. Pinkus's house?"

Eamon released his grip on the bat. "Mr. Pinkus's house? You gotta be kidding. I'm Mr. Wearie, and this is Mr. Wearie's fucking house. Pinkus rents a room from me. I'd say you got some explaining to do."

"Well, I say," he said, descending. "Daniel told me distinctly that this was *his* house. Very sorry, old man. I'm Dr. Elliot Feathers. I'm with the T. K. Smather's Institute. I'm sure you've heard of it." He produced a card out of his wallet.

"Yeah, so what?" Eamon said, examining it.

"Well, Daniel has checked in with us. If you haven't noticed, he's a very unwell man. In fact, I'm not so sure how anyone could possibly miss it."

"Yeah, well, he cries a lot at night," Eamon surprised himself by saying.

"With good reason, I'm sure," Dr. Feathers said, all crusty-sounding.

"I still don't get what you're doing here."

"Well, I came to collect a few of Daniel's personal belongings. He'll be with us for some while, I suspect."

"Yeah, well, his bedroom is on the first floor, over there. That was my room you were just in, pal."

"Well, I don't see how that can possibly be," Dr. Feathers said. "I was given very explicit instructions from Daniel himself. And I found just what I was looking for, right where he said."

"What the hell are you talking about?"

"Why, the letters, of course. Daniel wanted his personal correspondence. That's all I've come for. See?"

Eamon had a very weird feeling in his gut, something like premonition mingling with dread, when Dr. Feathers opened his attaché. He didn't even have to look at them to know. Netti's letters had taken on a life all of their own.

15

... *There is a spot up the Peccote River, just before it swirls together with the White, up towards the Timber Hills, that Dad—God bless his eternal soul—used to take me to in the good old days, so we'd get a chance to talk. It was so nice back then, when everyone was still alive. Mom and Dad were great people—and I always wished, James, that you'd gotten to know Dad better. He had great clarity and integrity and his word was gold. But he could be an old pain in the ass too, I know that. It just never sat well with him when I started going out with boys. And you were the main event, darling. Didn't he threaten you with one of his hunting rifles once?— when you brought me home particularly late?—or am I imagining things now? It all swirls together, like where the White meets the Peccote, that water is fierce and can take you under, James.*

Don't tell me you never thought about it, James. Especially when things were bad, when your movements got so restricted. I never cried when I came to see you those days but when I left you, it would take me an hour or two just to pull myself together. Don't you remember? We watched television together—you like the reruns best of all, "The Twilight Zone" and the old "Mary Tyler Moore Show"—and in the jaundiced afternoons we did crosswords and sometimes I read to you from Henry James, because he can seem the most old-fashioned and romantic of the writers I like. It is a strange and overpowering thing to care about another even more than you care for yourself. You, you. You send me, just like Sam Cooke said. I don't think most people ever experience that. And once you have, it is mighty hard to go back to those old empty ways. I think I'm just toying with it but then again I don't know. I'm a precious coward at heart and I think that's the problem; I'd have to find a very painless way to go about it; and I worry that I might botch it, leaving me brain dead and hooked up to some apparatus.

I've decided the best way is up where the Peccote meets the White. It looks too cold but then death looks too cold too. It's better than swallowing gulps of sleeping pills and falling back into the deep one, fading, fading. I'd rather step into the clear cold water, knowing what I'm doing to the bitter end. If you make the decision to die, you have to make it in a way you can live with. That's kind of a joke, James. I guess I never was very funny, nope, guess not. You were the funny one, always were, always made me laugh, made me see things a different way, always gave of yourself. I'll never understand what you were doing with me—what did I ever give you, really?

I could just drive my Elouise off a cliff, that's what I could do. Don't think it's not in me some nights, that feeling, that little dangerous voice whispering in my ear, saying, purring, let go of the wheel, little darling, just let go and I'll take care of the rest. That's all it takes, how little it takes. Then the state troopers are there with their red flares, marking it off, talking it into the radio, all she wrote. God not that way.

You said it might get rough for me. James, you said, Girl, I'll always be there. You said it with courage and conviction, even though you just weighed a few pounds then. You said no matter what, no matter what, there are still things in this world worth admiring, worth appreciating. And you told me to make a list anytime I was feeling blue. James, honey, I've been making a lot of lists lately. But I think I need to remind myself once more.

Things we like:

We like the rivers and we like frying trout over a fire, the way we used to do.

We like harvest moons and we like making love in their big moony glow.

We like riding around at night with nowhere special to go. What we do is we get ice cream, if we can't think of nothing else.

We like babies and animals and decent folk.

We like the smell of pine cones and tobacco and Juicy Fruit chewing gum. Because that was the first time we kissed, when we were just kids in that glade near Shady Hollow.

We like all four seasons, equally.

We like playing poker sometimes in the back room of the Old Whitaker, or just by ourselves, which is more exciting really.

We like baseball of course and we dream of one of our lowly Hens making the Big Leagues sometime soon. That is reason enough worth living right there.

We like working on something. It's better to work on something, if you can find it, because the time passes better.

We like eating steaks and fries at the Starlight. And we like that with cold beer, don't we James.

And James darling, we like holding each other in the darkness.

I won't make a list of what we don't like, but I feel certain that if we did, it would include high-priced lawyers and auto mechanics, bigots, Rolex watches, most kinds of money, peach schnapps, dental bills, floods (careful of the White in late March), and unflappable people.

James, James.

Would you be really mad at me, if I didn't show your courage?

The Peccote looks like it's up to the job, got enough white water and current to take a person under who ain't resisting so much.

See, I just walk in, a step at a time. Usually that water's so cold it numbs you, but I'm already there, number than hell, darling, sweet darling.

I brought beer with me today. I bought a six-pack of that beer you like so much, that Canadian beer. And I did it just the way you like. I stuck the bottles in the water, keeps them nice and icy.

You always loved your beer. After you finish painting, you always need a couple to wash over you, to slow you down, to take the throb out of your brain.

It always made you mad when we ran out of beer or coffee or the milk to go in your coffee. But if you had all three on hand, you were a happy camper. It didn't take much to satisfy you, darling, and that's a remarkable thing in this world.

Me, I like the beer well enough. But it does the job too slow, if you ask me. Much too slow. And you get sleepy besides. I think I'd rather just take a nap right now than make any permanent decisions about my future. Yes, I think that's what'll do for now.

Oh, James, did I tell you enough? Did I make you believe it? Did you know, truly know? I think of you twenty-three hours and forty-nine minutes a day. Where the rest of it goes, I don't know. If I ever slighted you, if I ever made you the least bit sad, forgive me, please forgive me. I just didn't know any better; who knew we had a timetable?

Netti

Eamon Wearie shoved the letter in the inner breast pocket of his forest green corduroy jacket. Then he took another slug from the pint of Yukon Jack. He marveled, from the vantage point of a park bench, at the soft pink gloaming, settling over the Inner Harbor like a summer dream. It was early Friday evening, at the end of a miraculous day, one so warm and hopeful that only a very few were left unaffected. They streamed out of their air-conditioned glass towers, anxious to join the traffic home or their friends in a week-ending toast, spun out of revolving doors, in full office stride. But it didn't take long for them to lose the purpose in their step, to slow down, to pause and wonder. It was such a sweet, fragrant evening, perfumed by cherry blossom and jasmine, rich with possibility and nostalgia, poignant beyond all belief, an ode to lost youth and lost innocence, as if all our pleasant yesterdays wafted in the balminess. The lost brokers and lost lawyers stood on the corners, loosening their ties, rethinking their hurry, staring up into the rosy, forgiving sky. Secretaries whispered and giggled, pointing out the tall accountants of their dreams. Beautiful, aggressive businesswomen, shimmering in their Armani silk and linen blazers, looking so self-possessed in their lizard-skin shoes and Gucci scarves, let their executive guard down for a moment. There was girlish blushing and furtive glances and stolen kisses. They were boys and girls in the soft gloaming, remembering.

Newly established couples strolled past Eamon, casting disapproving looks in his direction. He hadn't even bothered to brown-bag the Jack. Others peddled little bicycle boats out into the harbor, on the rippleless, velvety water. Across the murkiness, the giant DOMINO sugar sign glowed red. Even when he lost sight of the boats, he could hear the muted laughter, could imagine their ardor.

The Inner Harbor mall was ablaze with light and activity, as the restaurants and bars spilled over with people, winking with the neonic urgency of Friday night. Behind him, the city seemed ghostly, all lit up and transparent, an after-hours skyline. You could see janitors mopping up, and the terminally employed in the upper squares of many of the newer high-rises. But it was the Legg Mason building, a strange, phosphorescent green palace, that claimed his attention. It wasn't so much all that new green glass, an emerald Oz, but the small, forgettable fact that he'd gone out with Belinda Miles for a couple of weeks about eight or so months ago.

Belinda was like a lot of girls he'd been with. She was somewhere in her twenties, and she was pretty and dressed real nice. She'd been to one of those colleges no one had ever heard of, and she'd found a clerical job in Legg Mason's finance department first time out. She didn't make great money or anything, but she never let on to her struggle. She bought the nice clothes on the plastic and she bought the little sensible Honda on time and she shared a bright, airy apartment in Bolton Hill with another girl, who was just like herself. Belinda's parents lived in nearby Towson, and she went there every Sunday for dinner. It was a nice little compact life without a whiff of soul to it.

And Eamon remembered that Belinda had offered up her body to him on the third date, like it had all been worked out in advance, as if she'd read about some ironclad sex timetable in the pages of *Cosmo*. There was an old, yellowing poster of Newman and Redford, from *Butch Cassidy and the Sundance Kid*, up over the shiny brass bed, which was a birthday present from her parents. And there were big, goofy stuffed animals in every corner of the room. They were in the strange place, somewhere between childhood and adulthood, somewhere in time. She undressed with little modesty and told him that she was on the pill and not to worry. She took off everything but the gold crucifix around her neck.

There were tears in Eamon Wearie's eyes as he finished the last of the Jack. He wiped them away and decided to get something to eat. He went into the mall, up a crowded escalator. There were a bunch of fast-food counters on the second floor. He got a big cup of greasy fries and an extra-large draft beer. He wandered about like a zombie, bumping into people, not caring.

Once outside again, he took his beer and went over to the elaborate fountains. The whole thing was as big as an Olympic-sized swimming pool and as shallow as a bathtub. The water flowed through all sorts of complicated channels and locks, gurgling up in unexpected places. It was all lighted, and people had taken off their shoes and sneakers and rolled up their pants and waded out. Some of the shirtless men drank cans of Bud, and there was one drunk teenager cavorting in her underwear.

He thought about girls. He thought about all the girls he'd ever had. He couldn't remember them all. There was Debbie D'Angelo, who was the first. She was baby-sitting at the Calamaries', and he came over and they watched television, and one thing led to another. Debbie wasn't a virgin and she didn't much care. There was that cheerleader from another high school. They were in his dad's Chevy, parked in the driveway. Great flashes of lightning filled an atomic blue sky, as if God were somehow watching. His idea of a date used to be driving around in his car with a girl and a six-pack. Then there was Jenny. There was always Jenny. Jenny and he never did it. She broke his heart and all that. There were others. Other living room sofas and backseat romances. Then it was off to college, and he met Nicole and they lived together in his dorm room for a couple of semesters. She was a great person and they'd had their moments, and now he couldn't even fathom what did them in. Hell, they were young, and that's the way it is when you're young. There were all those spring breaks down in Lauderdale. He got a nasty case of the crabs that one time. He vaguely recalled rolling on the beach with this coed from Saint John's, and a cop waking them up with a flashlight. Too many times like that, in the bad hours before sunrise.

It left him cold, the emptiness stretching out into more emptiness. He heard Gena again telling him that he had no feelings, that he was some kind of psycho-killer. He shook his head vigorously, although Gena was nowhere near.

Two punky-looking girls were checking him out. They were sitting alongside him, totally bored with the fountain scene. They were from Salina, Kansas, which was already seeming like a very long time ago. Right now they were hungry and in need of a place to crash. They were looking for something to eat or a pack of cigarettes or maybe even a little change. Eamon didn't even notice them. He didn't see anything but the burning, haunting past; he danced with someone called Roxy in the dark club-land of his mind.

"So you got a light?" one of them said.

He looked up and saw a butch babe in a motorcycle jacket that was covered with buttons. Greenpeace. Billy Idol Rides On. Dying Is One Good Option. You're a Toxic Dump Site. FOREVER RAD. She was in metal-toed boots and spiked wristbands, and her haircut must have come from Razors R Us. Strangely enough, she wasn't that bad-looking, if you didn't mind it served up that way. Her leatherette friend, on the other hand, was an audacious beauty. The raven hair was streaked with silver glitter, and her flaming red mini-skirt didn't hurt matters.

He patted his pockets for matches. "Sorry, ladies, you're out of luck."

The butch one took out a book of her own. "So what's your name?" she said, blowing smoke.

"I don't got one tonight," he said.

"I'm Paula and this is my best friend, Wiley. Don't hurt her. I don't like it when guys hurt Wiley."

"I'm not going to hurt her. How can I hurt her if I don't even know you?" He was messy-eyed and indignant.

"I don't know," Paula said. "But if you ask me, guys don't even need a reason." She had taken her makeup brush and slashed two thick marks under each eye, like Indian war paint. They both couldn't have been more than seventeen.

"Let's just brush by the shit," the long-legged Wiley said with some attitude. "We could use something to eat. You want to feed us?"

"Yeah, let's all go have a candlelight supper," he said with a laugh.

"You feed us, maybe we'll do something for you," Wiley added, seriously.

"No shit," Paula said.

"Not interested," he said.

He didn't know how he got talked into it really. But he took them over to one of the outdoor cafés, jutting out from the mall, that looked out over the wharf and harbor. They sat under a Cinzano umbrella wolfing down roast beef clubs.

He got a pitcher of beer for himself. The *Trump Princess,* the billionaire's yacht, as big as an ocean liner, complete with helicopter landing pads and a hundred lifeboats, was docked in front of them, blocking the view. Tourists crowded around with cameras and dopey awed expressions.

"Too bad about him and Ivana," Paula remarked, her mouth full of sandwich.

"Yeah, absolutely heartbreaking," he said. "How will the man ever cope?"

"Ain't no rich men in Salina," the red mini said, her eyes as big as saucers. "I'd fuck ol' Donnie boy, if I thought it would get me anywhere."

"That's what I like about you two gals. Your unwillingness to sell yourself short. What's your story? What are you doing so far from home with no money or anything?"

"We're on our way to New York to meet Lou Reed. We're gonna take a walk on the wild side," Paula said, wiping her mouth. They'd cleaned their plates of everything, the chips, the pickle, the garnish.

"We grew up listening to his records. They still hold up, you know," the red mini offered, her eyes filled with ocean liner. "Yeah, we would have got there sooner. But we got sidetracked. We had this ride, but he turned out to be a real creep. Like, he started masturbating in the car when he was driving and all sorts of shit, and we just told him to let us out, you know. This happened a couple of weeks ago, and then we started hanging with the Murdered Seals, this totally retrograde band. Anyway, they dumped us here in the middle of the night, which really sucks, if you want to know the truth."

There was plenty of Midwest twang to their voices, which was kind of funny considering they didn't look like the Bobsey Twins. "What about your folks? Don't they give a shit? I mean, you girls don't look that old to me."

"Fuck them, that's what they get," Paula said, suddenly agitated. "Wiley's father was—"

"Stepfather," she corrected.

"Yeah, well, what's the difference? The thing is, he was going into her bedroom at night and doing it to her. You know, what was we going to do and all? I mean, Wiley's mother was spooked and couldn't find it in her to do nothing. So I'm her best friend. And I knew I had to be strong."

"Yeah, the sicko used to wait until Mom dozed off, and then I could hear him coming up the stairs for me. I couldn't sleep no more and I'd just lie there in my canopy bed—which was something that my real daddy had built when I was just a little girl and all—and I'd be lying there thinking about all the ways I'd like to cut his dick off. Scissors always seemed like the best idea, if you really want to know."

Eamon was quiet. It was a bad night and it was an ugly little story. It made him think of the Executioner. The whole idea of castration; it gave him a sick little feeling in his stomach, just thinking about it. It struck him then that the Executioner should have been a woman. It would have made more sense, that's all. Only a woman would want to do something like that to a man, he thought.

He looked out at the *Trump Princess*, lit up like a Christmas tree, all of her windows glowing with warm yellow light. He imagined tuxedoed men, and women in long, satiny gowns, dancing to an orchestra, in a sea of champagne bubbles. Some people lived real good, that was for sure.

Down on the wharf a fire-eater had gathered in a small crowd. A child, possibly his daughter, walked around with a hat, collecting coins. She suddenly seemed to Eamon like some character out of Dickens, a wretched little thing who lived by her wits, though he had no idea if this was true or not. And then this young black man, in gym shorts and expensive new sneakers, wandered into the café, going from table to table, aggressively panhandling. "Yo, now you had a nice meal. What 'bout my kids, man?" A waiter came out and told him to get lost. "Yeah, I'll be back. Count on it, motherfucker."

It was such an obvious contrast, rich and poor, the hungry and the gluttonous, that he didn't bother to linger on it. He just smiled at the two girls, not with lechery or anything, but with that weird feeling of being in the world at the same time, knowing all the wrong turns everything could take. They weren't such bad people, they'd had some bad things happen to them. He'd give them twenty bucks or whatever else he had on him. He wished he could do more. He was worried about them. They were tough and streetwise, but there was a lot of hardened scum out there, and sooner or later they'd meet up with it. Girls from Salina, Kansas, didn't stand a fighting chance.

There were so many lights out tonight, a dizzying variety of lights, that golden yacht, glowing like Fort Knox, the kinetic light from the restaurants and bars, all wink and blink, the ghostly hue of the city skyline, a specter hanging over everyone's pleasure. The myriad colors played on the velvety water, like a rainbow in a wondrous oil slick, all of it beautiful and beautifully obscene. It was a giant carnival of light and color, and all it needed was a Ferris wheel to complete the picture.

16

James, I'm going to have to take a leave of absence. There is no other way. They are so young and they are so lucky to have all of their good years ahead of them. I see them by their lockers, gossiping. I see them in the hallways, sometimes snatching a kiss just before the bell. Their faces are fresh and bright and untainted. They are so lucky. They do not yet know about mortality and the very finiteness of living. How I envy them. How I wish I could turn the clock back. I know there are people who will proudly and pompously admit to having no regrets, but my heart aches with a hundred thousand regrets—and if I could go back and change things, I most certainly would. I would change everything, dear sweet James.

You may not understand. You were never one to churn over the dead and gone past. What's done is done, you used to say. But to be young again, to be back in your arms, in your father's pickup, in the moonlight on a cool autumn night, the radio on, in your arms, in your arms, I would sell my eternal soul. And it would be a bargain at that.

He didn't wake until late in the day. By that time the girls were long gone. Before leaving, Paula and Wiley had taken the liberty of emptying his cupboards of all the canned goods, which really didn't bother him so much. They'd be slurping Campbell's Alphabet Soup all the way to Lou Reed's apartment. What did bother him was that they also filled their humongous green duffel with his last two six-packs of Old Boh. Now, that was just short of unforgivable. Perhaps he should have been grateful that they left the TV and VCR alone.

There was a half-filled pot simmering on the Mr. Coffee, and the sink was full of breakfast dishes. You didn't have to be a detective to see that they'd helped themselves to bacon and eggs and the last of the English muffins. He got himself a mug of the java and added a healthy dose of milk. He was suffering the effects of either a world-class hangover or a brain aneurysm. These things were hard to tell.

It was like picking through the shards of an accident, the way it came back to him. Last night's music still thumped in his head, especially that overplayed song by the Fine Young Cannibals. He felt the coarse stubble on his face, like it was braille, like it might offer up some clue. They dragged him off to some pitch-black club, some Dante's Inferno, and the three of them danced to the ravings of some deranged band in the flames. He didn't remember how they got back to his place. He knew they'd done some drinking. There were glasses and an empty bottle of tequila in the living room. Somewhere in the middle of it he went up to his room, alone. Later, the lights were snapped on and there was Wiley in her panties at the foot of the bed, laughing. She was demented. She said, *Don't you want to fuck me? Don't you want to fuck me? Everyone else does.*

He didn't do anything. Not because he was some kind of saint. It wasn't like that. She was some sad, fucked-up kid, and that was all there was to it. Someone else would fuck her. Someone else would do that sometime soon. You could count on it.

Now he knew what was troubling him. Besides the

hangover. Besides all the rest of it. It was the damn milk carton. On the back there was one of those poorly reproduced pictures of a missing kid, with his height and weight and where he was last seen. This boy was five six, 134 pounds, and last seen in the vicinity of Ashland, Pennsylvania. His name was Chris Jake.

It was just one more something. He wasn't quite prepared for any of it. Lately everything seemed a little beyond his grasp, and he had the feeling, not a good feeling at all, that he was being hurled forward by too many odd occurrences and unseen forces. And if he wasn't careful, if he wasn't very careful, he'd soon be hurtling into darkness.

He needed a drink. Fuck the coffee. He set about the task of making a pitcher of Bloody Mary. He collected the Worcestershire and the Tabasco and the vodka before he realized the girls had absconded with the V-8 juice. He had to settle for Finlandia on ice with a lemon rind.

Although Eamon Wearie didn't know it yet, the missing V-8 juice was the least of his worries. He would be more upset to discover his wallet gone. Paula and Wiley had filched it when he passed out the first time. Nor would he be pleased to learn that Gena Davio had stopped over that morning. She had been concerned about him lately, and when he didn't show up at the Marlin for his Friday darts, something he never missed, her concern had turned to genuine worry. Also, she had been feeling rather guilty about some of the things she'd called him last time out. After all, Eamon Wearie was *hardly* a psycho-killer. What Gena hadn't anticipated was two seventeen-year-old girls, naked as the day they were born, frying up eggs in his kitchen. At first she thought she had the wrong house. When she asked what was going on, Paula explained that they'd been sent over by the escort service, that in fact Mr. Wearie was one of their better customers, which left Gena dazed and speechless.

So as Eamon settled into his La-Z-Boy recliner and flicked the big thirty-six-inch Zenith to life, he was just hoping to ride out the rest of the day. Fortunately, judging by the dwindling light slanting through the bamboo blinds, there wasn't much of it to go. He sat there in his underwear with a double vodka watching men in lemon LaCoste shirts and madras trousers stroll leisurely up a heavenly blue fairway. He didn't play golf himself, but he liked watching it. He liked the far-off, sun-splashed courses with the famous relaxed names like Pebble Beach and Dorral and Augusta. He liked the godly, unreal quiet, the way the announcers did the play-by-play like nervous librarians. He watched Curtis Strange concentrate on a ten-foot putt, in a perfect circle of green, a putt worth a hundred thousand dollars if done right. Nice, Curtis, nice.

He worked his way through four more of the vodkas, going from the PGA tour to bowling to stock car racing. Whatever required the least amount of thought-exertion. If he could only hold out until the Oriole game, he'd be home free. He was doing his best to ignore Trish's cats, Pacino and Brando, who sat quietly, patiently, at his feet. He kept forgetting to feed them; Pinkus always took care of that. "All right, all right, in a minute," he said, aloud. "I'm getting to it. I'm just a little slow today. What, you never had a day like that?" He'd feed them at the next commercial break, unless, of course, Paula and Wiley ran off with the cat food too. It was just that he was very tired right now, very tired.

Drinking through a hangover wasn't an easy business. Sitting there, nodding off, he realized how little time he spent in his own house. Half of the things were Pinkus's anyway. The bookshelves were lined with his psychotherapy bullshit, Jung and Freud and R. D. Lang, from when he was a graduate student at Chapel Hill. Poor bastard. Eamon should've talked to him a little bit more, given him the time of day at least. His eyes went to the huge oil Pinkus had put up shortly after arriving, displayed prominently over the downstairs fireplace. Pinkus had crucified one of Wall Street's young turks, nailing the phony, power-tie-knotted, suspender-stretching would-be Gordon Gekko to a glittering, bejeweled cross. The joke was, the poor crazy bastard had talent. That was a helluva lot more than most people had. At least Pinkus tried. Tried to do things. What had

Eamon ever done? His only contribution was a framed photograph of a Ferrari Testerosa, bought in the famed K Mart gallery.

The cats were becoming impatient, making demands. "In a minute, for Christ's sakes. I'm getting to it." His eyes were heavy-lidded, and they flickered precariously. He barely noticed the blinking answering machine, just within his periphery. Probably Bunko. Probably pissed about missing darts. Just before falling asleep, he drifted to Trish's Chinese rug, lingered on its ancient and most elaborate weave. If you examined it closely, in small sections, you could begin to decipher the beautiful stitching, make out the many different flowers and birds that were lodged in her corners, begin to understand the gardens of thought that went into it. But if you just looked at it whole, without really thinking about it, you'd think it was just this nice paisley rug. In seeing the big picture, you'd be missing out on all the little pictures in between.

When he came to, to the bleeping ring of the portable phone, he was amazingly disoriented. His dream was already on the outer edges of consciousness, receding away from him. It had been bad, whatever it was, as if someone had been reaching into his sleep, trying to pull him down. But now it was lost to him, which was probably just as well. He picked up the still-ringing phone.

"Yeah?" he said uncertainly. It was really late; the digital on the shelf flashed 2:12.

"Eamon, man! Is that you, bro? How's it hanging?"

Brian. His brother. "Brian?"

"Man, you oughta be down here, bro. It's the life, man. I'm telling you. You can only dream how good it is, man. Man, how long has it been, huh? Been a while, bro. I missed you guys up there at Christmas, man. Just as well. Christ. You know how the old man gets. Always on my case, man. So anyway, what's happening? What's going on?"

Brian was high as a kite. You could tell. He got excited and talked too fast and didn't listen. "Everything's okay, Brian. I've been doing some—"

"Excellent, man. Just excellent. Man, you should check out my new digs, man. Got me a swimming pool and cabana and this like gold Jacuzzi. The ocean's like right down the fuckin' street. Paradise, I'm telling you. You gotta come down. Man, we gotta hang together. You know what I'm saying? You're my brother, man. Get your ass in gear and fly down, man. C'mon down tonight. Just say the word, bro."

"That's sounds nice, but—"

"Believe it, bro. Believe it. Hey, I want you to say hello to a new friend of mine. Say hello to Rhonda, buddy. Man, you gotta see this babe. I'm telling you. She's done some modeling, man. Wait. Let me put her on. She wants to say hello."

"That's all right—"

"Hi, are you Brian's brother? He's like told me so much about you. I'm Rhonda."

Her voice was Barbie-doll-dumb. He didn't know what to say to her. "Hi, Rhonda. Have you known Brian long?"

"Like not exactly. We met last night. But I feel like I've known him a lot longer. Like, don't you know how that is?"

"Sure, I—"

"Wasn't she something, bro? Like I said, c'mon down, man. I'll fix you up with one of them. They're all over the place, on the beach, everywhere. Hey, man. It's been excellent talking to you, man. You take care of yourself, bro. And, like, if you need anything, you know, like cash, or like anything, you call me, man. Right? Okay? All right. Okay, my best, man."

He held the phone, dumbly. The television was still on, spilling its eerie blue light, making the living room radioactive. The astronauts were planting the American flag on the moon. Some kind of look back. Then those pictures of the National Guard firing on Kent State.

Brian's voice had come from so far away, so damn far away. He was wasted somewhere in the south of Florida. He was just another fucking dealer, blowing it all.

In the inky blue darkness, Eamon began to cry. Sometimes he forgot he even had a family.

17

It was an awful big letdown.

He had gotten his hopes up much too high. It had all seemed so perfect. All right, too perfect. He should've listened to Bunko. Bunko knew enough about disappointment not to get excited about anything.

But everything fit. In one beautiful perfect morning it all seemed to come together. That Harold Kingsley wasn't the Executioner—well, that in itself was extraordinary. Harold Kingsley, standing six feet three inches tall, was a blond, blue-eyed, left-handed English teacher who'd taught in Philadelphia ten years ago. To top it off, he lived with his invalid mother, a septuagenarian whom nobody had seen in years, and collected model trains. Furthermore, two of the missing boys, Chris Jake and Beck Lauterberg, not to mention the dead girl, Gertie Johnson, had passed through Kingsley's junior high school English class.

That Harold Kingsley wasn't the Executioner—well, it just seemed grossly unfair. It had been such a nice piece of detective work that had led them to him in the first place. The first break, extraordinary in itself, came from the National Center for Missing and Exploited Children. Amazingly enough, at least to everyone else, they were able to trace those two names that that psychic had supplied. Famous Barry had been absolutely right about Mike Winkle and Sam Farrety. They *were* best friends who'd disappeared ten years ago, right off a Philadelphia street, on their way to school. Several eyewitnesses saw the boys get into a gray Dodge van, the last that was ever seen of them. Apparently they were not coerced or forced, leading investigators to believe that the boys knew their abductor. In fact, in the intervening years, the case had become kind of a cause célèbre, having been rehashed in the papers and by several national television shows. All of which made Bunko plenty suspicious. If this case was so well known and all, why wouldn't Famous Buddy, or whatever his name was, have heard of it too? Eamon didn't know the answer to that one, but he had little doubt that Famous Barry was on the up and up. After all, what did he have to gain out of all of this?

Eamon called Montrez and relayed the story, and was surprised to find a willing listener. It turned out that Montrez had crossed paths with psychics plenty of times in the past, mostly with dubious success. However, in one particularly astonishing instance, a Madam Zola was able to pinpoint the location of a mass grave in the Winnake Forest; a serial killer had buried ten prostitutes in the middle of a ten-thousand-acre wildlife preserve, but she was able to lead agents to the exact site in little over an hour. So although Montrez did not place a great deal of faith in their chances, he was not above taking the unorthodox approach. His men, in short order, found out that there were only three teachers in Bear County's two school districts to have taught in Philadelphia at the time of Farrety and Winkle's abduction. Two of them were women. The other was Harold Kingsley. Eamon was particularly interested in the first three letters of his name. Not only did Famous Barry say that the Executioner was a teacher, he practically spelled out his name. He said something about an *H* and an *O* and an *R*. Harold was close enough, that was for damn sure.

And the fact that he was blond and left-handed just about clinched it. The FBI's National Center for the Analysis of Violent Crime had concluded with little reasonable doubt that the man who killed Gertie Johnson was also responsible for the disappearances—and, indeed, likely murders—of the three boys. And the man who killed Gertie Johnson was left-handed and blond-haired. That was conclusive. The Bureau had Gertie's body exhumed and brought in their own people to perform the autopsy. Old Doc Viola, at Ashland's Lady of Mercy, had not been up to the task first time around; he'd even managed to misplace the semen sample taken from the body. The Bureau's boys, though, were able to establish that Gertie had been strangled by a left-hander, a big, strong left-hander, a man capable of breaking Gertie's neck like it was some kind of twig. They were also fortunate enough to recover hair samples, and DNA testing established that they were dealing with a fifty-year-old white male with blond hair. When they were done with their thorough postmortem, they even knew his brand of shampoo and conditioner.

They also knew his blood type, AB. Unfortunately, that certainly seemed to prove that Harold Kingsley hadn't killed Gertie Johnson. And his fingerprints, on file with the selective service, did not match any lifted from *Boy Love* photographs. Agents also interviewed him, finding Kingsley to be genial and cooperative. He was only too happy to supply a handwriting sample; only too happy to allow investigators into his home; only too happy to introduce his mother, a kindly, wheelchair-bound woman suffering from multiple sclerosis. Harold Kingsley was just not the Executioner, which was just too bad.

Eamon Wearie knew it wouldn't be too much longer before they were pulled from the case. Anal would give them another week or two at the most. No matter, Montrez's men would continue with their extensive interviews, combing the county, block by block, bloodhounds in relentless pursuit. Something would probably just turn up, something so small, so utterly dismissive, some tiny, unmistakable clue. A footprint, a tire track, a credit card receipt. Or else somebody—a next-door neighbor, the meter reader, a newspaper delivery boy—would step forward with what seemed a most negligible and unnoteworthy sighting. Maybe they'd recall a strange vehicle parked in a key place. Or it might be they'd report an unusual sound or smell coming from somewhere. Whatever, whatever it was, it wouldn't leap off the page. He knew that. But you could count on something happening. Something logical, that had been there all along.

He must have been out of his mind to think that a man who claims to talk to dead people could give him the Executioner on a silver platter.

Captain Marcus Brown, seated at his executive desk, in what he liked to call the Oval Office, even if it was a dingy little rectangle of a room, had just gotten off the phone with Francis Cummings, the postmaster general's right-hand man. Francis made it quite clear, even if his threats were spectacularly veiled, that if dramatic progress was not made on Judge Bertrand Boysee's murder, it was entirely likely that Marcus would be passed over for promotion.

The very notion that he might have to spend his remaining years at Depot 349 had thrust his brain into overdrive. The first thing he was going to do was assign every available man to that damn letter bomb thing. He knew Red Team was apt to give him trouble, so his mind was busy formulating just the right approach. Bunko and Wearie had spent so much time on that Executioner nonsense that he very well expected them to be their usual unreasonable, stubborn, boorish selves. Why had he ever listened to them in the first place? Why, he had known from the very start what a wild-goose chase it was. After all, this whole thing started snowballing over some ridiculous photograph. Who knew if it was real? Who knew if it wasn't some silly hoax rigged up by that Ivy League showboat? He wouldn't put it past Montrez, that arrogant bastard.

He only knew that everyone would have been a whole lot better off if they'd only listened to him from the very first. It was a good thing, he knew, that he'd been blessed with the powers of motivation. He was a *motivator* of men. Oh, the men didn't often like him—but surely, rightly, without question, they respected him. And now it would take those skills, refined over a lifetime of public service, to bring out the best in his troops. In some ways—and in no way was he bragging—he was a little bit like the Great Communicator. Now, Ronald Reagan knew how to give a speech, that mellifluous voice, that deft way of turning a phrase. Maybe he wasn't as crafty, as wily, as Richard Milhous Nixon, the greatest president the twentieth century has ever known. But Ron had had his moments. Who could ever forget tagging the Soviets as the Evil Empire, which they most certainly were. Gorbachev-schmorbachev.

Then it came to him. A workable approach. He remembered then how Dick had handled that Vietnam thing, a war passed on to him by that Harvard smoothie, JFK. Just thinking of that drunken, womanizing, silver-spoon-fed hairdo sent his blood pressure soaring. Why, his philandering, bootlegging father used all his tainted money to buy every election that Johnny boy ever won. Why, everyone knew that. Oh, don't even get him started. To even think of that television debate, with Johnny surfer boy and his Hawaiian tan, talking such gibberish with that fake British accent. And there's Dick, the grand statesman, full of good common sense, trying to reason with all those swooning, Kennedy-lusting pom-pom girls . . .

He had to calm down. It did no good to be reminded of old, festering injustices. Imagine how Dick himself must have felt. And yet Dick had lasted, had triumphed in his own way. Because he'd outlived the bastards, which was vindication enough. Today Richard Milhous Nixon remained an inspiring, beloved figure. A man for all seasons.

What he would tell Red Team is what Dick told America about Vietnam. Peace with Honor. That was the ticket. Oh sure, it would have to be reworked a little, but it had a certain ring to it. They would not be simply abandoning the Executioner nonsense, they would be withdrawing from it with honor. Something like that, yes. Withdrawal with Honor. God, that was good. He was a *motivator* of men, there was no denying it.

* * *

DEAD LETTERS

At lunch, Eamon Wearie ripped open Netti's latest letter. It was dated not two weeks ago. He noticed two things right away, before reading one word. It was the shortest of the bunch, just a paragraph long, and her exceptional handwriting seemed somehow diminished. That had been the case, too, with the earliest letters; the stroke had been lighter, and at times her sentences appeared to trail off. Later, after discovering the truth, he'd chalked it up to grief. But Richard Lonetree had been dead over a year now.

Most cruel mornings I can't decide if it's worth getting up for. Hemingway did it with a shotgun, pulling the trigger with his toe or something, I believe. I don't suppose my funeral will be any great shakes, which makes me sad for some odd reason. I mean, if you're dead, you're dead, what's the difference? But I'm afraid it will be a pitiful little send-off, some teachers, some students, your mom and Paul. It will no doubt rain, shortening the whole dreary affair. They will scurry away, headlights in the gloom. For the longest time I believed you would just walk through the door and save me, as if none of it had ever happened. But you haven't done that, James. Why don't you send me some kind of sign? That way I'll know for sure.

Ever your friend, Netti

Eamon didn't have much to work with. He knew, from the obituary, that Richard Lonetree's mother was named Ellie Winters. Unfortunately, her telephone had been disconnected. There was a good chance that she'd moved on after his death, simply to make a clean break of things. But when he sought out her current address in the computer, in the Super Removal, she was listed at 49 Reedy Hollow Road in Sandstone, the same as her son's.

It was time to think smart. What did he have? He had the name of a dead man's mother, that's all he had. Well, that wasn't quite true. He had Netti's first name. Or some shortened form of it. Or perhaps it was even a nickname. He knew that she was a teacher somewhere in Bear County; most likely in Sandstone, where the letters had been mailed from. What was he going to do—start calling all the schools asking for someone named Netti? Yeah, right. He needed Bunko's help. This was the kind of thing he was good at. Finding people.

Bunko, for his part, munched potato chips out of one of those snack-sized bags with mounting disgust. He saw what Wearie was up to and didn't approve at all. In fact, he was sick to death of those stupid love letters and the trouble they'd brought. Wearie had already been put on notice; to top it off, he missed their Friday darts. As far as Bunko was concerned, it was all related. But it wasn't just those stupid fucking letters. That fucking Executioner entered into it, too. He'd had enough, for Christ's sake; he was ready to cry uncle. Let Mister Tony and his boys take care of things from their end. For crying out loud, they were the fucking FBI, weren't they? He just wanted to get back to what he knew, back to the business of being a federal postal inspector. Christ, a week ago they had a letter bomb bury some judge. Put him on that, for Christ's sake. Where he could be of some real use. And all that kiddie porn wasn't going to go away by itself. Let him get back to business. Let him close down scumbags like Rube Fuchs in Ocean City. Fuckin' A Right.

This, then, was his mood when Eamon passed over Netti's letter.

"For the love of Christ, don't tell me you believe this shit. It's like I keep telling you, she's some little old lady in some psycho ward somewhere. The reason they locked her up in the first place was she was boring everyone shitless."

"Not this time, Bunk. Netti's the real thing. That's a goddamn suicide note. Now, I need your help in figuring out how to—"

"Christ, Wearie, get with the program. People who write suicide notes and go around talking about it all the time never pull the trigger. It's a little fucking game, buddy boy. That lady ain't going to do nothing to herself. It's all a joke."

"Thanks for your expert opinion, Dr. Bunko. Now, if I was going to try to find her anyway—"

"Forget it, pal. I ain't helping you with this bullshit. And hell, let me just add, since we're on your favorite bullshit subject and all, that if there was one iota of truth to it, she'd be dead by now anyway."

"Fuck you."

"Fuck you back."

"My, aren't we a couple of grown-ups."

Bunko picked this moment to start singing the theme from a popular television show. Strangely enough, his singing was melodic and on-key, which gave "Suicide Is Painless" a certain poignant quality.

That was how Captain Marcus Brown found them when he emerged from the Oval Office, with Arthur Lyon and Arthur Marlens following close behind.

"Attention Red Team," he announced in true Elmer Fudd style, across the empty rows of steel gray desks. "I want to make it crystal-clear before I begin that my decision, which is final and irrevocable, has nothing to do with your performance on the case. Men, let me just say that your work is not at issue here. At this time we will be withdrawing our efforts from the Executioner, not with any bitterness or apologies, but with the full knowledge that it is the right decision at the right time. We're withdrawing with honor, as it were. Our credibility intact, our pride restored."

"God bless America," Bunko muttered.

"What's that, Lieutenant Ryan? Do you have something you'd like to share with the rest of us?" The captain, his arms folded, one foot tapping, was prepared for the worse.

"Not at all," Bunko said. In point of fact, he was delighted.

Eamon spoke up: "Sir, maybe we could just have another week to—"

"My decision is final, Lieutenant Wearie. As of right this minute, you and Ryan will be shifting your attention to the Judge Boysee matter."

"Sir, you already have too many men on that—"

"Lieutenant Wearie, I've had just about all I can take from you lately. You are in no position to tell me how to do my job. Last week you were formally reprimanded after it was called to my attention by Art here that you'd been involved in questionable job-related activities—"

At the drop of his name, Marlens nodded with the sanctimonious conviction of the lifetime whistle blower.

"—and just a couple of days ago, you reported your inspector's shield missing. In the twenty-two years that I have been commander-in-chief here at Depot 349, I cannot recall that ever happening before."

"Jesus, I had my wallet stolen—"

"I am in no mood for a discussion about your personal life, Lieutenant. You have your marching orders. Now, march."

"Fuck you," he said under his breath, without thinking.

"What was that, Lieutenant? I demand you apologize, right this instant. I will not tolerate insubordination. I'm waiting."

Eamon Wearie reached his breaking point. His head burned and he visualized untold destruction. His rampage began with the hurling of a VTD and ended with a kind of kinetic power, à la Stephen King's *Carrie,* in which he proceeded to splatter the captain across the universe like some Jackson Pollock painting.

"I'm waiting, Lieutenant."

"You're a little bastard, you know that?" he said tightly, on the very edge. "Nobody likes you. Hell, nobody even respects you. You're just a little cocksucker."

"I will . . . I will not tolerate this. I demand . . . I demand . . . that you take it back," the captain stammered, visibly shaken.

"You know what the men call you?" Eamon continued. "Do you? You know what their nickname is for their beloved captain? Captain Anal Retentive. But hell, they say it with the utmost respect for your asshole, sir."

Bunko sat there, not believing his ears. The kid had lost his fucking mind. Little Pucker and Big Pucker, pale and stricken, looked like candidates for intensive care, coronary unit. And Anal kind of looked like that Captain Queeg at the end of *The Caine Mutiny,* the way he was trembling and snorting. Bunko actually felt sorry for the dumb shit, the way his whole fragile world had come crashing down about him.

"You are . . . you are . . . sus . . . suspended indefinitely, Lieutenant," he stammered out. "Indefinitely. Do I make myself crystal-clear? I do not want to see your face when I return. Is that clear?"

"Yes, your analness."

After they'd retreated, like three scurrying little mice, Bunko started in. "Nice work, sport. Way to go. That Dale Carnegie training really paid off."

"Yeah, thanks for all your support," Eamon returned, sourly. "Right there when I needed you, partner."

"Pal, you were way out of line. If I was you, I'd go cool my heels somewhere. And then when it all started making sense again, I'd go in and try to apologize to your commander-in-chief. Wouldn't hurt to bring some flowers or chocolates. I hear the captain likes his bonbons."

"Yeah, you're a million laughs, Bunk. Why don't you go fuck yourself."

"Making friends wherever you go, Wearie. What's your secret?"

He didn't bother with the earplugs. The roar of the huge old sorting machines in Docket C 14, *chunk-chunk-chunk-chunk*ing away, was no match for the grinding, gnashing sounds of his own brain. He drove the scooter recklessly down the narrow aisles, toppling cartons here and there. Every so often he'd see one of the big gray rats, the size of possums, scampering away.

At another point he saw Friedberg's dogs ferociously attacking a package on one of the conveyor belts. He slowed down. At first he assumed it was a drug find, but on closer inspection he saw that the black Labs were chewing and tearing their way into a shipment of Hershey's chocolate bars. It was about par for the course.

Out of force of habit. That must have been it. He hadn't

177

taken a ride back in some time. In the old days, when he first arrived at Dead Letters, he used to go there often. It was his escape. He'd even brought in an old, battered armchair; he'd found it out on the sidewalk, an eviction leftover, one of those unfortunate stuffing-oozing things that are the province of poor college students everywhere.

The novels were almost always terrible in the Unpublished Novelists' Hall of Fame. That was practically a given. It was too easy to side with the publishers. The would-be authors usually dispensed with plot and characterization altogether. Most of them didn't even attempt to hide the fact that they were writing about themselves. And that was the beauty of it. These men and women, mad dreamers all of them, wrote for posterity; they wanted to tell their own story, the great and tragic and always strange saga of a life lived. And that was something Eamon could appreciate. He loved the fact that these people weren't satisfied with mere, ordinary anonymity.

It really was the library that time forgot. He waved away at the cobwebs, a gossamer curtain at the doorless entrance. He entered into a dark warehouse of human emotion, where thousands of lost and defeated manuscripts lay dormant, shelf after dusty shelf, rejects on top of rejects, a place of no return. It did no good to imagine all the hard work and mental perspiration that must have gone into each one. Why, even typing that many pages was job enough, if you asked him.

He yanked at the long string, and the lone hundred watt bulb flickered and buzzed ominously before flaring to life. He found the misshapen, ugly-duckling armchair a comforting sight. He wasted no time choosing one of the moldy, forgotten works; in the long run these things made no difference.

He settled back into his chair, already feeling the calming influence of an old, familiar ritual. This one had been sent without return address to the sedate, old house of Charles Scribner's Sons, which refused to open it, let alone even consider it. The crisp, clear postmark showed that it had been mailed out of Caribu, Maine, on July 12, 1972. Almost twenty years had passed, and Eamon wondered if the author was still in there fighting, churning it out and waiting for Godot, or if he or she had had the good sense to just let go.

It was always strange to open one of the Hall's lost manuscripts, as if his touch could bring those long-buried pages back to life, as if he alone could release their words and power. The author's name was Frank T. Izzo, and the name of his book was *The Ghost Detective.* On the title page, Frank had written a personal message, just above his home and work numbers. "I do not as yet have an agent, but I'm quite willing to negotiate," it said.

Eamon began to read:

Detective Jack Johnson had staked the house out for over a week. He drank plenty of piping hot coffee from his new thermos. And he listened to the AM/FM radio a lot. He liked country music, for some unknown reason. The time passed as slow as a night at the opera. Nobody came out or came into the tiny brick house. It had a white picket fence and geraniums in the flower boxes. It was pretty average but nicely maintained. Perhaps the lawn needed to be mowed.

Jack was not a happy man and he often wondered why it was that he was not happy. He looked out his car window—of his sporty 1966 red Ford Mustang convertible that also had whitewalls—to see a beautiful summer day, the birds were chirping and the trees were full of lovely green fruit, dogs and children played. But it left Jack Johnson cold. As cold as Eskimo pie. After all, he had a job to do.

Jack liked his work, even if the hours were not too good. He was always coming home late. He did not have time to smell the roses, or the coffee.

The house, at 13 Cherry Lane, that he was staking out belonged to a recently widowed bombshell with the saucy name of Peg Peterson. She had a chest that could suffocate a normal red-blooded male. And it was rumored that she was easy. Very. Although, Jack, at this point, could not personally verify that.

The problem was that Detective Jack Johnson was dead. This was the thing that Jack didn't know. He was not just tired from not getting enough sleep, which is what he thought at first. No, Jack Johnson was the ghost detective.

18

The last two days had been a blender-blur of sallow faces and leftover tabs and pathological liars. Lipstick-smeared women, twice-divorced and learning to live with herpes, tilted their heads back and shrieked in laughter. Hoary bartenders, who drank more than the customers, spat out hundreds of off-color jokes into their open-ended spittoons. Willy Loman types, dead souls on the Fuller Brush trail, always had time for one more.

Eamon was one of the lost, and last night he danced in tainted strobe with three garrulous secretaries at a downtown hotel. He wound up with one of them at some piano bar—somewhere else, he couldn't remember now to save his life—with a twinkling view of the city. They were the only ones there. The used-up lounge singer crooned "Young at Heart" as he looked into the polluted eyes of a woman he hardly knew.

Struggling to consciousness somewhere around noon, trying to grapple with the sunlight and those skittery, hellish images that are part of all our lost nights, the drink and the mind-numbing conversation still reverberating, he found himself examining his bedroom, half wondering if some strange woman would just appear, sticking her head out of the bathroom or something. Luckily, no such demands were placed on him.

He really wasn't sure what he was doing. He had wanted to get totally fucked up. He had wanted to forget. He had managed to take a pretty decent hack at it. He wondered, in the void that was all his own making, in that hollow place reserved for the morning after, when he was going to call it a day. There was the matter of his job, or former job. He really wasn't ready to deal with it yet. There would be no apologies, that was definite. The rest was speculation. The rest would happen, whether he liked it or not.

But there was something else, too. Something he wasn't quite willing to even admit to himself. It was there, though, this thing, bubbling up, a little too crazy to really even analyze, this thing that was trouble all the way. But all too soon he found himself in the red vinyl world of Bonnie's Bar & Grill, where he was following his tap Buds with sinus-clearing shots of peppermint schnapps, following up where he left off yesterday.

He wandered into the Marlin at the dinner hour. All that drinking had made him hungry for animal fat and fried greasy stuff. He wanted a bacon cheeseburger with onion rings and more beer.

Boxcar greeted him with: "Bunko's been looking for you like crazy. He must have left twenty messages for you to call him when you came in. I think he was like kind of worried about you, if you really want to know the truth."

"Yeah, well, I've been kind of worried about myself, to tell you the truth."

"Well, that's a good thing," Boxcar said, leaving to attend to another customer.

Gena Davio was at her waitressing station, doing her best to remain calm. She'd known she'd see him sooner or later. Still, she wasn't exactly sure what she was going to say; all she knew was that bastard had it coming to him.

"Hi, Gena," he said, glad to see her.

"You are one sick puppy, do you know that?" she said in a rush of anger. "You are one sick, sick, sick bastard. Those girls weren't even legal age, you sicko. And here you're sleeping with me without protection and you're doing this shit. Don't you worry about diseases? 'Cause I swear to Christ if you gave me anything, so help me God I'm going to cut your fucking balls off. Do you read me?"

He never had a chance. Before he could even ask what the hell was going on, Gena Davio took his beer and splashed it in his face. She wanted him to know she wasn't kidding this time.

He went home and took a long, hot shower. Then he packed a bag of clothes. Before he left the house, he put out water and plenty of dry cat food for Pacino and Brando. There was no telling how long he'd be away.

The one thing he hadn't anticipated was the car. Someone had smashed in the passenger-side window—it could've happened anytime during the last week—and removed the stereo system. There was plenty of broken glass on the seat, and the dash looked weird with that hole there. Fuck it. It was the third time it had happened since he'd lived there. He put the Pontiac in reverse and backed out of the garage.

It was a long ride, and it was going to feel even longer without the radio voices to accompany him.

The cold night air rushed in through the empty space, jarring him awake.

19

The white farmhouse was something Norman Rockwell might've painted. It was that sweetly cherished, that purely remembered, that kind of an American memory. It was in the middle of a large, grassy clearing, protected by a split-rail fence and the blue forest beyond that. The sun burned brightly in a sky that was a cobalt wonder, not a wisp of cloud in it. Out front, surrounding the freshly painted lattice porch, the azalea and lilacs were in full purple bloom, attracting honey bees and monarch butterflies galore. As he stood on the stoop, he wondered—not for the first time that day—about his sanity. Eamon rapped the brass knocker again.

Sleep hadn't come easy last night. He'd driven as far as he could before stopping at one of the blinking motels off the roadway, a shabby, nameless experience. The walls were paper-thin, and he was kept awake by the epic thrustings and bloodcurdling cries of a particularly energetic couple. The man liked to talk dirty—favoring everyone with a hellish play-by-play—while the woman moaned that thing about wanting to die. Eamon, for his part, lay with eyes wide open, in the dirty brown darkness, thinking about the many and varied people who make up a world. At daybreak he was off again, in his shattered Pontiac, barreling to an unsettling destination, a place that seemed to belong to·his unconscious as much as anything else.

He went around the house to try the back door. He noticed the freshly turned soil back there, not a big deal, just enough for a good-sized vegetable garden. There was a friendly red barn a short distance away, but from the looks of things, there hadn't been animals or any real farming done in quite some time. A rusting snowplow sat at the top of the drive. He could understand that. The driveway must have gone a mile long, not something you were likely to shovel by hand. He still wasn't even sure if it was the right place. There'd been no number or name on the mailbox at the bottom, and since the houses were so far apart, it was hard to tell.

"Hello? Anyone home?" he called out, to no avail. He started toward the barn, stepping through the tall grass, which was sprinkled with daisies and dandelions, buoyed by all that warm, dappled light.

The barn doors had been left wide open. Again he called out, and again no one appeared. It took a moment to adjust his eyes to the cool, dank darkness. He had been right, after all. Richard Lonetree's studio looked as if it had been left totally undisturbed, as if he'd been there that very morning. In fact, a dog, probably his, an old red settler, was curled up at the base of an easel. He raised a tired eye and seemed to frown at the sight of Eamon, before returning to the comfort of sleep. Lonetree had done his best to make the barn workable. He'd put in a hardwood floor and insulation, and there were two kerosene heaters in a corner. There were also open tubes of paint and coffee cans filled with brushes and rolls of blank canvas. But it was his paintings that drew all your attention. The huge, bright pop art canvases were hung from every available space, and there were many more leaning sideways against the walls. Eamon thought they were incredibly beautiful, even if they were mostly just pictures of cows.

But they were great, wondrous cows. He'd painted them in the greenest, most golden pastures imaginable. The background skies were just as bewildering with their great fits of color. In Richard Lonetree's paintings it was always the magnificence of sunset or sunrise, nothing in between. Eamon had never seen the ordinary look so extraordinary. In fact, he had gotten so caught up in admiration that he failed to notice her. She had grabbed a pitchfork.

"State your business," she said from the big doors, a shadow in the noontime brilliance.

"Ellie Winters?" he said, trying to make her out.

"Who wants to know?"

"I'm a friend of your son's, from college."

He had worked it out in advance. He knew that it was better to lie to people. The truth only scared them.

"Richard's dead," she said, still on edge.

"I know. I came to pay my respects, ma'am."

"What's your name then?"

"Eamon Wearie."

"I don't remember Richard ever mentioning you before."

"It's been a long time, ma'am. Harvard."

"You don't look like no Harvard man I ever met. A little young-looking, too, if you really want to know."

"People tell me that."

"Well then, I guess that's who you are, all right."

"I'm sorry about your loss. I really shouldn't be intruding. He was a wonderful painter."

"Yes, he was," she said, putting down the pitchfork, entering the sublime darkness. "He was a great man, my son."

She was a white-haired lady in farmer overalls. There were muddy patches at the knees.

"I've been working out back in the garden; you'll have to excuse me. I thought I'd heard somebody out there. Quite a pretty day, isn't it? I saw your car. Someone done broke in, I guess."

"Yes, last night."

"Where you coming from?"

"I'm out of Baltimore."

"Oh, that's quite a ways. And you just come up here to pay your respects. Richard's buried at the little Indian cemetery up near Roundoak, which ain't that far from here. His father was a full-blooded Iroquois. But I suppose you knew that. It would be hard to miss and all. How did you hear about my son's passing, if you don't mind my inquisitiveness?"

"In a letter," he answered.

"Yes, that does seem to be the way news is passed. I thought it might be in that *Harvard Alumni Magazine*. They did a very nice feature on Richard. Very nice indeed. Well, you must want something to drink. Where are my manners? Let me go fetch you some lemonade."

He found himself following her back out of the barn. She continued to talk unconcernedly, as if she had known him all her life. "I can't get over this weather. This is truly my time of year. You picked a funny day to arrive, Mr. Wearie. I'll tell you that. This morning Monty was acting mighty peculiar. That's Richard's dog. Well, he hasn't been the same since Richard left us. He just sort of mopes around now. Well, that's not your concern, I suppose. But he was scratching and pawing to be let into Richard's barn all this morning. And Monty, well, he never goes near there since what happened. And anyway, it was awful peculiar. But I opened it up—I keep it locked and all—and I didn't see what the harm was giving the whole place a little taste of the honeysuckle. It can get awfully musty in there, you know. But here you are. And isn't that strange, my oh my. You and Monty and everybody wanting to get into the barn on the same day. You must have been led here. That's what it must be. What do you think, Mr. Wearie?"

She seemed strong and friendly and very much out of her mind. She didn't look him in the face and she didn't wait for the answers to her lopsided questions.

"Yes, it's what Richard's woman friend was always going on about," she said, walking ahead of him. "It's his Iroquois spirit. He probably brought you here for some reason. Oh, it wouldn't surprise me, Mr. Wearie. Some nights I'd just about swear to hearing his footsteps in the house, and sometimes I look out my window and I can tell you that the light's on in the barn, and I know it's my Richard working late again. These things are of the land and they are mighty mysterious, and I do not hesitate to believe that it is all very true. I believe that. I most certainly do. I believe it is all very real and that it is up to us to acknowledge it. What do you think, Mr. Wearie?"

They reached the house, and she had one hand on the screen door when he asked his one and only question. "That woman friend you were just mentioning wouldn't happen to be named Netti?"

"Well, that's interesting you should ask. But that's not Sarah Lumiere's real name. Oh, it's a hoot. The way those two were always making things up. They had their own little language, the two of them. Why, sure. And Richard was James, and they called me Elouise, heaven knows why. Ellie's short for Ellen, for goodness sake. Anyway, let me get you that lemonade and I'll be able to give you the directions to that cemetery, Mr. Wearie."

She disappeared into the shadows. It didn't matter. He had what he came there for. He debated whether or not to stick around for that drink.

He was getting closer. Sarah Lumiere lived at 7 Johnson Street. It had been right there in the telephone directory. For some reason, he kind of wished it hadn't been so easy. Because now that he was closing in on all this strangeness, he was forced to deal with it. What he was doing up in Sandstone in the first place was anyone's guess really. He hadn't felt too good about invading Ellie Winter's privacy, snooping into other people's business, rummaging where he didn't belong. What the hell was he doing? Tell him that. *What the hell was he doing?*

It was like he was dead or something. In his soul. He felt nothing. Not even trepidation. He just drove the fucking car.

He continued to fight the impulse to turn it around and head on home. He had taken things too far, had gone beyond the dull, mindless edges of curiosity, beyond the safe, tucked-in corners of his world, into a darker, more fervent arena. At this point he had no idea what meeting

Netti might accomplish. He was even beyond hoping. Hoping was not something he was very good at anyway. Sarah Lumiere could've been anybody, and he refused to hope for her to be somebody special. He was just following through at this point. He suddenly wondered what he was going to say to her. Hey, loved your letters. And by the way, that committing suicide idea is just the pits. Yeah, right.

He drove through Sandstone itself, a humble little village on the verge of quaint. The ramshakle town had been built alongside the White, and in fact, a huge old wooden wheel, left over from another century, still churned over the water. It was unfortunate, but the perfectly preserved mill gave the town a melancholy, seen-better-days quality. There wasn't much to look at really. There was an all-purpose café, a darkened real estate office, a Union bank, a post office, a tobacco shop with a wooden Indian standing sentry, a produce market with its melons and oranges displayed out front. Except for the two large lumberyards—the H. F. Finkle Company and Ox's—at the end of the sketchy Main Street, nothing seemed to come in twos. Sandstone was one of those touch-and-go, end-of-the-earth places that depended on the eldest son remaining behind to take over the family business, never that far from having the tumbleweeds blow through.

The Mobil map was spread out beside him, covering the shattered fragments of glass. It was strange not having a radio, a sound to drive to. It was like viewing the land without a context, without a real defining mood. In the perplexing quiet he passed a sprawling trailer park and the adjoining Wampum Trading Post, a dreary, almost unimaginable slice of life, all those clotheslines heavy with the morning's wash. At a railroad crossing, he waited as a long freight train took its time.

He was surprised to find that 7 Johnson Street, a mile outside of town, was the address of the Sonesta Garden Apartments. It was a modest three-story brick building that seemed entirely out of place in this part of the country. There were several senior citizens, out on their balconies, in their rockers, taking in the sunshine. A wheelchair-bound woman, parked on the lawn, watched with undue interest as he passed. It looked like some kind of senior citizens' home. Jesus. What had he got himself into? It just didn't fit with what he knew about Netti. She was in her thirties, just like Richard Lonetree. That much was clear. She had to be. He couldn't have confused that. It must have been the wrong address. Her letters were full of rivers and lakes and the great outdoors. Something was very wrong. But there was only one Lumiere listed, and it was a brand-new directory besides. He turned the car back around. He had come too far not to get some answers.

He pulled up and called out to the woman in the wheelchair. "Oh, yes," she said. "Sarah lives here. Lovely lady. Apartment 2 B. That's where you'll find her, young man. Now, she hasn't been here long, that's true. But she's a lovely addition. What did you say your name was? My name is Patricia Dawson. But my friends call me Pat. Now, I was married for quite some time, goodness. My husband and I raised six wonderful children. And it was a good thing. Two of them died very young, much too young. It is the worst thing in the world when the parent buries the child. . . ."

He stood next to Patricia Dawson, listening, paying homage to her age. She looked about ninety—her skin was burnished leather, and her hair had been reduced to a few white wisps—and it didn't seem fair not to listen for a minute or two. After he had nodded for some time, Patricia said. "Well then. You go right up there through the first archway. There's a little courtyard and you follow the stairs up on the right. And, young man—tell her for me that the day is quite lovely and worth a look-see. Will you tell her that?"

Things looked a little run-down, actually. The courtyard was a bunch of loose bricks. A splintery-looking bench had been built around an old elm, the lone remaining tree. He followed the concrete stairs up, with growing anxiety, with the sense that it had all been predestined. It wasn't déjà vu exactly, and it wasn't like he was expecting anything. But it was a bit like watching yourself in somebody else's movie. It was that removed.

The curtains were drawn tight across her bay window. The apartments looked like motel rooms, just as dour, just as anonymous. He rang the bell and waited. Like a damn fucking ghoul or something.

She came to the door in jeans and a plain white T-shirt. Her chestnut hair was set back in a ponytail, and she looked just fine without any makeup. Her face was kind of plain, though, the nose wasn't small enough, and the cheekbones weren't high enough, and her lips, thin and thinly colored, would probably not have inspired the Bard to poetry. But it was her eyes, greener than God, that threw you for loops.

She was pretty. And she was almost beautiful.

"Yes? Can I help you?" she said. He could tell right off that she'd been drinking. It took one to know one.

"Yes, I was hoping you could help me, Netti."

She took a step back. "Who are you?"

"I'm that sign you were looking for," he said, his voice hollow and peculiar-sounding. The words weren't thought out at all; they came from unknown parts.

"What the fuck are you talking about?" she said, looking more agitated than scared.

"James. I'm talking about James."

"So? So what am I supposed to say to that? I don't even know you. And I'm not sure I want to . . ."

She was about to close the door on him. "My name is Eamon Wearie. And I'm a federal inspector with the Postal Service. I've driven a long way."

"It's those letters, isn't it? Am I in some kind of trouble? Is that what this is about?"

"Yeah, I guess that's what this is about. I've read your letters—"

"Are you even allowed to do that? I still don't understand what's going on here. I didn't break any laws. As far as I know, it's not a crime to mail a fucking letter. And anyway, how did you find me?"

"You put Richard Lonetree's name in one of them. I tracked you down from there. I was out to his studio earlier. I met his mother. Take it from there."

"You were what? I don't understand what's going on here

at all. Do you have some kind of identification or something? I mean, I don't know you from a hole in the wall."

He fished out his new wallet and flipped her his new badge.

"This is all so weird," she said. "This just doesn't make any sense to me."

"I was working on another case in the area. I thought I'd just stop by. I wanted to meet you."

"So? So what?" She was working herself into something. "You don't have any business here. I don't know you. I don't know who you are. What gives you the right to read my mail?"

"An act of Congress," he said, deadpan.

"This is so fucked up. *You just wanted to meet me.* I don't understand. I don't understand any of this—"

"I'm sorry," he said, feeling defeated. "I'm sorry I thought this would turn out differently somehow. I read the letters, you know. I read them. They were good. They were different. They kept coming up. In different ways. I was worried, kind of. Talk of suicide. Things like that. I was in the area."

He'd mumbled the whole thing out. She didn't say anything for a long moment. She seemed to be trying to compose herself. When she suddenly broke down into sobs and clutched him, he just stood there and let her.

He didn't know that she'd been in her tiny cell planning it. Sarah Lumiere was going to have to be good and drunk to go through with it. That's what she kept thinking. She'd put the barrel of the gun into her mouth. She had really done that. Not twenty minutes ago. She was just playing with the idea. She didn't even think it was loaded. She went into the bathroom and stared at her face in the mirror. That's when she put Paul's shiny silver Colt in her mouth. She wanted to look at it, as sick as that was. She'd done the same thing yesterday. And the day before. But then she thought about it, like she always did, and she thought there must have been other ways. Better ways.

She thought she might take what was left of her money and have one last fling. You know. One last holiday. Check into the Plaza in New York or something. Order up champagne. Jump out a window. She'd seen that in a movie. Or maybe she'd go to California. She'd never been there. Rent a bungalow on the beach. Wait for a perfect moonlit night. Take a walk out into the sea. Come to think of it, she'd seen that in a movie, too.

Or maybe she'd take the fucking pills. It was easier that way. She kept coming back to that. They were right there in the medicine cabinet, just in case.

"Do you ever just want to die?" she suddenly spouted.

"No," he answered truthfully.

"I think about it all the time. All the time. It's always there, you know? I can't seem to get away from it."

"I didn't think you'd live in a place like this," he said, hardly listening. "Your letters always describe such nice places. Rivers and fishing and stuff like that."

"I only moved here a little while ago," she said pulling away from the stranger. She wiped her face and blinked her eyes to make them clear. "I lived in a nice house over by O'Darney's Dairy. Oh, what am I thinking? You don't know where that is. Paul's there now. We couldn't make it work."

"Who's Paul?"

"That's my husband. Who'd you think? Oh, it's a long story. And I guess it's not really any of your business."

"Nothing is."

"Yes, that's true. Do you want to come in and have a drink?"

She surprised herself. But it hardly mattered, after all. A few minutes ago she was putting a gun in her mouth. Counting heads at her funeral. What was the worse this guy could do? Let it happen. Let it happen. Whatever the hell it was. Besides, she had never been scared of good-looking young men. He was not bad, she'd give you that.

It was dark and small, and the place was a wreck. Everything was in and out of cartons. There was only the one place to sit, a Salvation Army relic of a couch. Books and records were scattered about the stricken carpeting, a sick stained yellow. He noted the open photo albums—next to the jug of Gallo white—on the makeshift brick-and-plywood coffee table. A black-and-white television with a coat-hanger antenna was on without the sound. The rose-patterned wallpaper was faded and peeling back at the tops. Eamon knew she was in serious trouble, because she didn't even bother to apologize for the state of things.

"You like beer?" she called from the kitchen-alcove. He sat on the unfriendly green couch staring at the curtained-off bay window. He heard the frige open and shut behind him.

"Not too many places to choose from around here," she said, returning with two Molsons. She plopped down beside him. "You want an apartment, you either have to live with Dan Wheely, this lecher up High Point Road, or you come to the Sonesta and hunker down with the geriatric set. You won't find swinging singles' complexes with hot tubs in good old Sandstone."

He swigged back half his beer and waited for the good feeling to come. "Yeah, makes sense," he said, smacking his lips. "It surprises me that you're married and everything. I thought . . . well, you know . . . Like you said, it ain't any of my business."

"We're separated. For a couple of months now. I know. God knows. People carry on in strange ways. Sure, I was married. These things happen. Don't you think? Besides, Paul knew. Which I guess makes it even more perverse somehow. I guess he had his own hopes—of course he did—probably thinking we'd just go back to our old ways after James died. But it just got worse for me somehow. You lose respect for people and it's all over, that's the truth. And the funny damnedest thing is that Paul is a very sweet and gentle soul, and that's what makes it so terrible, of course. I'm ashamed to admit that I hate the fact that he is not some kind of bastard. That would make everything so easy. If he was some kind of fucking bastard . . .."

For some reason it disturbed him, her use of the f-word. He used it all the time himself. It wasn't that. He realized he did have certain expectations. He wanted her to be something that she wasn't. He wanted magic. She kept talking.

"The best way I could describe Paul is to say he's like that

194

short story. Do you read? It's important to read. James Joyce is such an amazing writer. You must have read 'The Dead'—anyway, it is one of the most beautiful stories ever written. That ending. You know. The snow falling on everything, you know. Anyway, that's who Paul is. He's Gabriel. He suffers because he's left out of my deeper feelings. Does that make any sense? I hope it does. So I'm here, you know. That's me. I don't know about you. I don't know why you're here. That doesn't make sense still. Why are you here? And what's your name again? I seemed to have forgotten it already."

"It's Eamon. Eamon Wearie. Not that it matters. I drove most of the night. Did I tell you that? Yeah. It was a long nowhere ride, you know. Your letters. That's what I keep coming back to. I have this boarder—or had one—and you wouldn't believe it. Pinkus is reading them and I didn't know it and he's fucked up anyway, but they were becoming part of things. They just kept coming up. And they were good. Really. They were. In my line of work you see a lot of stupid letters. Most of them are so boring, it kills you. Most people just write a bunch of how-are-you, miss-you-loads, see-you-soon bullshit, full of that kind of crap, all insincere like that. You know. Like nobody cares enough to write anything true or real. Still, I don't know why you sent them, you know. What'd you think would happen?"

"I thought they'd just go out there, into the void. I didn't think anything really. It's funny, I didn't even feel that strange about putting stamps on them and shoving them in the blue box on Main. That didn't strike me as all that peculiar. I sent them off with my telephone and Visa bills. I guess I acted like he just moved away. To tell you the truth, I didn't think about that aspect too much."

"It's all right," he said. "Last week I went and saw a guy who talks to dead people. This psychic guy. And yeah, I was talking to my dead grandfather through him. And I didn't have much trouble believing it. I mean, there's plenty of strange stuff out there if anyone wants to pay attention to it. Got another beer?"

It was strange sitting in her crummy living room on her

crummy couch. Her eyes were great and she had a smart little body, and the thought crossed his mind. But it didn't seem like playing fair somehow. She wasn't in any condition to make those decisions. Not that he was in any great shakes himself. He downed some of the new beer and watched as she went over to the crummy record player, which was on the floor, next to a couple of withering potted plants.

He recognized Sinatra's inimitable voice. "My friends think I'm crazy," she said, rejoining him. "They don't understand my thing for Frank's voice. It's not that I don't like other things. I have a whole stack of old Crosby Stills and Jim Morrison and my-generation things. But there is something strong and reassuring in Frank. He was my father's favorite. Maybe that's what it is."

"It's okay. I have a partner who's a Sinatra nut. When we head down to AC, he's got to have him in the tape deck. One time we even saw him at the old Golden Nugget. He was good, but he looked older and more frail than I thought he would, and so it was weird but I was kind of worried about my friend. I wanted the concert to be good, you know, because like Sinatra is one of his heroes. Wanted him to be able to reach those high notes, you know."

She lit up a cigarette. "I really should quit," she said for the millionth time in her life, thinking it really was a stupid thing to say. What did she care? An hour ago she's got the gun in her mouth.

He asked to bum one, and the two of them sat there, quiet, not too uncomfortable, taken in by the drifting smoke.

"Frank's just one of those things for me," she said after a time. He was singing about Indianapolis in the summertime. "Him and Roy Orbison, and then I like Rickie Lee Jones, and I'm sure there are others, even if I can't really think of them now. You know, and I've been rereading Cheever a lot lately, and that comforts me. His stories strike the deep chords in me. I don't know. What was I talking about?"

"Things you like. I know the feeling. Me, when I'm down the blue river, I put on my Elvis Costello and get me an

Elmore Leonard paperback. Or Ross Thomas, he's good, too. Or Parker. You know. Doesn't matter. It's good just to get out of your own head for a while. You're a teacher, right?"

"I was up until a few months ago. I'm on leave. I don't know what I'll finally decide. I have until the summer. I teach English over at Sandstone Junior High. It's not bad. Although everyone else complains. They sit in the faculty room smoking their Pall Malls and complaining for eternity about how dumb kids are today. But I don't see it quite that way. I'm kind of curious about your job . . ."

He found it easy to talk to her. He told her some about Dead Letters. She was good enough to act intrigued, and he appreciated that. He got to the part about the Executioner and how that tied in with her. She'd read about the missing boys in the local newspaper. But the stories didn't mention anything about any Executioner. He tried not to get into too many details. He could see the whole topic made her squirm a little. So they sat there smoking cigarettes and downing beers, talking about nothing too particular. He brought up baseball, and she rhapsodized about her Muddies and their chances for a class A pennant. He told her he liked the stuff in her letters about that slugger whose name he couldn't think of. Bucky Hatchet, she said, smiling. And they would've gone to a game if those damn boys had been in town. As it was, they were making a swing through the Carolinas. She may have been suicidal, but at least she had the presence of mind to keep track of the schedule. There were other things. Personal things. He told her a little about Trish leaving him. No, she didn't die or anything, and he wouldn't ever make comparisons. Just thought it might make her feel better to know that other people had gone through shit. To illustrate this point, he told her about his suspension. He was lost in the world, too, and he wasn't exactly sure where he would wind up. There were lots of people going through lots of things. They weren't the only ones. He sounded like a jerk. But he couldn't think of how to put it. How to make it right. Don't worry, it's okay, is what he always said. It's what his father always said. The best he could come up with. And it wasn't good enough. No one had to tell him that.

They finished off the last of the beer and moved on to that jug of wine. She matched him drink for drink, and he doubted that any of it was real. When he looked at her, it was not with longing, not really. She was pretty and she had a pretty name, but she was messed up all the same. He'd be going soon. He saw the road in his mind, lit up for night travel. But then she suggested getting some more beer and maybe a pepperoni pizza. What the hell. He could put his life on hold a couple of hours longer. Why not? Nobody was waiting up for him.

She was delighted with what was left of the day. "God, it's so gorgeous," she said ten times or so. She knew the country so well that she hardly minded the road. She talked and lit cigarettes and fiddled with the radio dial, and they scooted up and down the hills as she conducted a little tour. The first thing they'd done, though, was stop at Smitty's, a liquor shack, to pick up a case of beer, and she got herself a couple of quarts of vodka and some more wine. Evidently she was planning on living just a little while longer.

"That's Spruce Road," she said. "You head up that dirt for a mile or so and you come across some of the best trout fishing in the state. It's supposed to be a secret, so don't tell anyone I told you."

She was wearing big round tortoiseshell sunglasses, and they hid her green sparklers, which was a shame. Her Honda was a midget car, and although he wasn't the tallest guy in the world, a shade under six, it made him feel big and clunky, like he was right up on top of her.

"Gone fishing," he said. "That's one of those things for me. Brings it all back. My dad and my brothers and going camping and crap like that. I picture it a lot."

She liked him. He wasn't really her type. He wasn't an intellectual, but there was something frank and open about him. It was an odd thing this stranger coming to her door. She was starting to think that James had something to do with it. That restless Indian spirit. It was as crazy as anything else. Believing was easy, she thought. Believing was the way of the world. It was probably worse not to believe, then all you had was what was out there. You'd be left with nothing, just what you saw. The most peculiar thing about Eamon Wearie the messenger was that he didn't seem to want anything for himself. She kept half expecting that he would make some kind of move on her and reveal himself to be some kind of rapist in waiting. Something. Kept waiting for the sound of shattering glass. Okay, she was attracted to him. But she didn't want anything to happen. She just wanted it to go on, the same way as it was going. It was enough to know there were signs of life in this old girl yet.

She decided to show him the Pit. It wasn't for everyone, but he looked as if he might appreciate it. The road twisted through the hilly, green country, and it was way too easy to miss. There was a little off-ramp that led to a little guardhouse and a chained-up metal fence. VIOLATORS WILL BE PROSECUTED, it said beneath the larger SAND-STONE QUARRY sign. She pulled up right to the fence and got out. There was a chain wrapped around the gate, but it was all show. The locals had hacked her apart years ago, at the same time they'd vandalized the little house, smashing out her windows and scrawling the ugly words. In her prime a thousand men took home their living out of there. Beer bottles and cigarette boxes were littered about. The kids still liked to come up and make out and spook each other or what have you. She removed the heavy linked piece and swung open the gate.

"What's going on?" he said.

"I'm taking you somewhere."

They drove up the old road, the weeds growing through in so many places now, to the top of the hill, the farthest you could go on wheels, where you could take it all in. It was like a tiny city down there.

Those abandoned offices and warehouses and rusting cement mixers. They had sifted and bulldozed down hundreds of feet, had in effect hollowed out Old Henry Mountain, leaving behind only steep red clay walls and the ghost

199

town. And then they'd just left. Didn't even bother to pack up or clean their mess up. It was American as hell. You could see the colored piles, leftover hills of sand and silica and quartz, red and silver-gray and phosphorescent green, ugly and prepossessing at the same time.

They got out. She rummaged in her hatchback-trunk and came out with a pole and a tackle box. He thought she had to be kidding. She told him to carry the beer. He did as he was told.

She led him through a battered section of fence, posted with No Trespassing signs, curled with barbed wire at the top. Then they skidded down a dirt path, grabbing hold of bushes along the way. "This better be good," he said at one point, after sliding on his ass a ways.

It was eerie to walk through the wasteland, in the unnatural quiet, the way the ground was covered with a fine gray powder, dusty and chalky-smelling. He knew it was crazy, but he had the feeling he was being watched. He walked faster. He didn't like all those rusted-out sheds and storage bins. He didn't like the way you were aware of your own footsteps. It was a ghost town, all right, and it wasn't that difficult to bring it back, the rumblings of the long-dead machinery, the yellow hard hats calling out to each other, the tractors, the lunch whistle, the diesels pulling out with their loads. All of it faint and shadowy now. But there, still there nonetheless.

She had been right, after all. It had been worth it. After you went a little farther you saw the shining lake, only a hundred yards from that dead industrial village. In the distance it looked like a giant pool of quicksilver.

"There can't be anything living in there," he said.

"Plenty of rainbow in there. C'mon, I'll show you." She took his hand and led the way.

It was incredible. You could actually see the big fish in places, so still, in groups of three and four, just sitting there. He got excited just seeing the trout. Most of them were spotted, but every once in a while you'd see a gleam, a flash of silver.

"We're probably wasting our time," she said. "Not their time of day. But we can give it a try."

He was still perplexed by this slice of heaven in the middle of such a grim place. The lake must have been about ten or more acres wide. It was absolutely clear, and all you could see were the fish and that fine sandy bottom and some green weeds.

"I don't understand how anything can be living in there," he said again. "There's gotta be too much minerals or chemicals in there. Where'd it come from?"

"The White," she said, busy tying a lure. "It happened one year not so far back. Tributary opened up. Started filling up. It was all the talk around here for a time. People were hoping the Pit would just become one big reservoir. But you know. The sandstone company, they came and they closed it off. But it's still here. Water's even been tested. Just fine. I guess it's kind of a small miracle. Here, try this."

She handed him the lightweight pole with its homemade fly. A piece of glass and aluminum foil with a red feather. It was the oddest bait he'd ever seen.

"I've learned it really doesn't matter what you use as long as its shiny and catches the light," she said, anticipating him. "I used a piece of broken Coke bottle, and that feather was something that came out of my pillow. What you waiting for? Go give it a whip."

He flicked it out sideways the way his dad had taught him, and was pleased by that familiar yawning, winding sound. Casting was half the fun. He couldn't get over the fact that he could see his prey so clearly. He was much more used to deep-sea hunting, never knowing what lurked in those murky depths, such hit and miss. He saw one he liked and he tried to grab its attention. Easy, easy now. Oh baby.

She twisted open one of the Rolling Rocks. The sun was going down. It was a bleeding orange in a pastel sky. "It's good to have a secret place. Someplace to go. The thing is, I have lots of secret places. I'm always hiding from something."

"I envy you," he said, flicking it out there again, toward

his rainbow dream. "Living in the city, you never get away from nothing. It's always staring you in the face. It can get ugly and you can forget about the nice things out there. I feel like a kid right now. I swear to Christ."

"James had lived in New York, and when he came back, he was like that. He would shout and jump and touch the leaves on trees. There was so much joy in him. Crazy, isn't it?"

"What did he die of?"

"It was bad, it was truly terrible," she said, softer, staring out at some memory. "Just when you're flying along, you know. It just shakes your faith. Everything only lasts a second and a half."

"Well, we got a whole hour here."

For some reason, that made her laugh. "Now I know you've been sent here. That's just the kind of thing he would have said. You would have liked him. He wasn't some tortured artist or anything like that. He was my friend more than anything. We made love, but he was my friend. More than anything."

"You're lucky," he said. "At least you've known something deeper. I've wished for a long time, ever since I can remember, for somebody to save me. I've never known that woman yet. And I'm starting to think she isn't out there. But the weird thing is, I've never given up hoping completely. It's always there, somehow. In the way back of my mind, this person, this imaginary woman, shimmering in beauty, if you know what I mean. It's such a jerky, stupid, dumb thing to think. After you've lived a little, you should just see it clearly, plainly. Why, shit, it's as bad as religion. All that waiting, all that deluding. Sometimes we'd just be better off if we let go of the old lies. What do you think, Netti?"

"I think you don't know how to catch fish," she said, laughing. "Here, I want a try."

"Fine with me. I'd rather just drink the beer and watch the sun go down."

The day had turned into something manageable, something bordering on the ordinary. He basked in the normalness of it all. It was downright wonderful to drink a bottle of beer and watch a pretty woman get her feet wet. She had taken off the sneakers and rolled up her pants and waded out into the shining water. She laughed at how cold the water was, and he could see the goose bumps pop up and down her arms. The sun had done her setting, and the dusk was turning out to be deeply blue and deeply satisfying. He couldn't imagine ever wanting to die.

"Hey," she said, "don't drink all the beer. Save some for me."

"Hell, I'd like to. But it's so fucking boring watching you catch nothing that it's the only thing that helps me pass the time."

"Hey, that's not funny," she said, laughing.

"Those are like plastic fish in there, right? I haven't seen one of those trout—if that's what they are—move in the last hour. They're either plastic or visually impaired. Trout from the Helen Keller Oceanic Institute. You tell me if I'm right. Fucking plastic fish. That's what I think. This is like some elaborate hoax. The whole town rigged it up for dumbshit visitors like myself. It's to promote tourism. I can just hear the mayor say, 'Yeah, we got plenty of damn fish up in these parts. Coming out of our assholes. Why, just look at the damn quarry.' Hell, you probably don't even have a mayor. You probably elect a game warden around here."

"Hey, we got a mayor," she said, all touchy-sounding. "A matter of fact, Bob Cutley is a fellow teacher of mine."

"I wouldn't go bragging about being a teacher," he shot back. "We've got our suspicians that our friend the Executioner is also a teacher. At least me and that guy who talks to dead people tend to think so."

"Oh, that's good enough for me," she said, laughing again. "As long as it's coming from such a reliable authority."

"Actually, I got a question," he said, suddenly thinking of something.

"Shoot."

"Well, it's funny. But maybe you could help me here. Since you're an English teacher and everything. There were these books. Maybe it doesn't mean anything. But what the hell. Maybe you'll see something that I don't. Okay. Now, let me get this right. Okay, there was *The Sun Also Rises* and *Of Mice and Men*. And let me think. And *The Catcher in the Rye*. And then there was this kids' book thrown in the mix. You know, Babar that elephant who drives a car and everything. Now, do these books have something fairly obvious in common? Is there some course even where they'd all be taught together?"

"No, I don't think so. I mean, those books are all important, of course. And each one of them is assigned. Just at different grade levels. In fact, I teach *Mice* in my seventh grade English. And we do the Hemingway in my eighth grade honors. You know, you'd have to almost be a substitute teacher to do all of them. God, *The Sun Also Rises* is such a great book. Don't you think? I always loved Brett. She's someone I could never imagine being. But I love her hard impetuousness."

"Me, I'm a big fan of the *Catcher.*" He didn't bother telling her he'd never read *The Sun Also Rises.*

"Oh, I liked it when I was young, I suppose. But you know, what did it in for me was every time they'd find one of those mass murderer types, you'd find out it's his favorite book. You know, the thing with Hinckley and the guy that shot John Lennon. What's his name?"

"Mark David Chapman," he said, glumly. "Yeah, that's true. That hurt it for me too. All those psycho jobs identifying with Holden. Fucking sensitive psycho jobs, huh?"

"I could never understand Salinger in the first place," she said. "I mean, the whole Zen Buddhism thing and locking himself up in some kind of concrete igloo. I mean, turning your back on Hollywood and all the fun of being a celebrity. Because writing is the hard part, the boring part. You sit there and you develop back problems. That's being a genius. Me, I like the idea of going to parties and having people fawning over you and telling you all sorts of lies. I guess I have a lot to learn. But I know that if I wrote a novel, I'd do it just to be rich and famous."

"Me too," he said, staring off.

"Hey, you," she said kind of rambunctiously, coming out of the water. She fell beside him on the fine red sand, and one of those sweet diabolical looks passed between them. Her eyes were wet and shining and reflecting. He saw his face in there. It didn't take much to start to kiss. Boy, that was nice, kissing someone you liked. It was all kind of harmless, perhaps even meaningless. He liked her and she liked him and they rolled in the sand.

It might not have been *From Here to Eternity,* but it was something, all right.

20

I suppose it's a matter of faith. But it is my feeling that you have to believe that it will all turn out okay in the end. We are just human beings after all. I hope you will call me, not just if you need to, but to say hello if you feel like it. Or whatever. I've never been very good at these things. My words always strike me as clumsy. I wish I could put it better. But I just know in my heart that everything will be all right. Not just with you but with me too. That is my misplaced faith.

He didn't know how to sign it. With Love seemed too suggestive, too strange. Very Truly Yours or Sincerely obviously didn't cut it. He finally decided on Take Care of Yourself, and after slashing his signature, he remembered to add his number and address.

It was raining like crazy outside. Shit. He'd forgotten all about that hole in the car. It was coming down something terrible. He heard it last night drumming against the windowpane, while lying on the couch. It was a scary, lonely sound, and he'd felt far away from home. He debated going back in to look for some wax paper and tape. But he didn't want to wake her, have one of those awkward morning talks.

The Pontiac was a mess, all that water on the one side, and when he started driving, it sprayed in like he was out at sea or something. And it didn't help to feel so hung over. He needed a big breakfast and he needed a couple of aspirin and he probably needed a good shrink. Work this out. His life was all over the place. He tried to remember a time when things were workable. He found himself going back, way back. Things hadn't been good in a long time. He realized he was probably an alcoholic. He didn't like that word, and a little voice in his head kept saying, No you're not, no you're not. But he probably was, nonetheless. He drank every day, and he didn't think he had it in him to give it up. It was the one thing he looked forward to.

His dad would come home at nights totally toasted. Sometimes they would watch from the windows as he vomited in the driveway. Finally their mom would come and shoo them away. They would laugh and think it was funny. He could always tell with his dad. His face got colorful and he seemed to have extra life in him, the way he would talk and laugh, so animatedly. He took it hard and straight, bourbon, just like his brothers—and their wives, forever in the kitchen making dinner, accepted it, one way or the other. They smoke and drank and lived hard. And now they were dying hard. Uncle Fitz had lasted only a few months with the lung cancer; and Uncle Paddy was having serious problems with his kidneys, and it looked as if they were going to have to hook him up on that dialysis machine. The last time he saw Paddy, one of the most robust men he'd ever known, he'd lost a lot of weight and he looked gray and funereal, as if all his reason for living had been flushed away.

The little voice told him he was exaggerating. It told him he didn't really drink the hard stuff. He just had a little beer now and then. Okay, every day. So what? it said. What was the harm in that? He was a man, after all. Eamon remembered his mom taking him aside after she'd had a particularly nasty argument with his dad. Don't you ever start drinking, she told the little boy hiding in the closet. I won't, Mom, he promised with tears in his little eyes, never ever. What a laugh.

He wondered, however fleetingly, about how you checked yourself in to one of those Betty Ford centers the celebs were always gushing about on Carson. Boy, he hated the reformed. They were like fucking missionaries. They could never be satisfied with just cleaning themselves up; no, you had to listen to their tired shit about how great they feel ever since they picked themselves out of the gutter and so on. Fuck them.

It was the rain and the gloom and that damn hole in his car. He had to get home. He had to get back to work, hear Bunko's reassuring thunder, make a living, have a place to go, even if it was the fucking Depot.

He stopped just outside of Ashland at the Choo-Choo Diner. He was so soggy and wet that his shoes squished and squeaked walking across the tiled floor to the counter. He ordered eggs and Canadian bacon and extra hash browns from a haggard redhead who never once looked up from her pad. There were no other women in the diner, only hefty woolen shirts, men of bulk and appetite.

He hadn't noticed the one stiff, starchy-shirted, Windsor-knotted fellow in the place. "Well, look what the cat dragged in," the man said. When Eamon looked up, he was surprised to see Agent Mathews.

"It's a long story," Eamon said.

"I'll bet," the G-man said with an easy smile. "Mind if I join you?"

"You'll have to wait your turn. A whole line of people clamoring for my company."

"I'll bet," he went again. Then he let the easy smile disappear and aimed straightaway. "I wasn't told anything about Postal being back in the region. What gives?"

"I'm up here on a personal matter. Has to do with a certain woman. So don't worry. We're not here to steal your big case, big guy."

"Oh, a woman, I see." Mathews's eyes seemed to cloud over, as if he'd already lost interest. "Can't live with them, can't—"

"Yeah, I know that one. Save it."

Eamon wasn't sure he liked him. He was a pro, no doubt

about it. But there was something else, something distant and judgmental. He was perfectly turned out, all six foot whatever of him, not a wrinkle, not a lint hair on his serge blue suit. The black lace-ups were probably buffed this morning, the Gary Cooper face was stinging of after-shave, the short, straight hair was parted like the fucking Red Sea. The guy was living proof of J. Edgar Hoover's successful gene-splitting experiments. To top it off, he was eating a bran muffin. Jesus Fuckin' Christ, as Bunko would've surely said.

"Got caught in the rain, I see," he pointed out.

Eamon was aware of the growing puddle under his stool. It didn't take much to remember the first time he'd met Agent Mathews. The Driftwood Motel. He was hung over. He was always hung over. In a dirty undershirt zapping television channels. Now this. At another disadvantage.

"Yeah, I love to walk in the spring rain. It makes me feel so alive," Eamon said with some glumness.

"Women will do that. I was married twice. I try to stay clear now. I spend my time going after psychopaths. It's easier."

"I was married once," Eamon said, staring into his coffee. "It wasn't worth the price of admission."

"Tell me about it."

Eamon decided Mathews wasn't so bad. At least he wasn't some fucking android. "So what's new with our friend the Executioner?"

"Nothing worth talking about, frankly. We've set up shop in town. Why don't you come over and take a gander? I'll show you how we're proceeding. You take a few days off? Is that it?"

"I've been suspended, if you can believe," he said, embarrassed about it.

"That a fact. You must have done something truly damning, Lieutenant Wearie."

"I dared to voice an opinion to my commander-in-chief."

Agent Mathews chuckled at that. "Yes, Marcus is possessed of one of the smallest minds it has been my privilege to encounter in twenty-five years of law enforcement. And that includes Ashland's very own Sheriff Smitty. What are your immediate plans?"

"I don't know really. Go home. Feed the cats. Important stuff."

"Sounds taxing. Have you ever considered coming over to the Bureau? I could use another man up here. These things can be arranged."

Eamon Wearie was liking Agent Mathews better by the minute.

Like it or not, he found himself with time to kill. Mathews had said to stop by their makeshift headquarters at noon, errands to run and all that. The rain was just an ugly little drizzle now, all in all an unfriendly gray morning. The only thing you could say for it was that it wasn't cold. It just wasn't anything. He'd parked the battered Pontiac on Ashland's near-empty Main Street, that wide avenue with the glint of yesterday's trolley tracks, and he just stared out through the teardrops making their way down the windshield.

He was sad for all the old familiar reasons. He didn't even have a radio to play the memory-inducing songs, that music which triggered the sorry chain reaction, lighting up odd moments of your life, all haphazard, all because it made you think of where you were, who you were with, when you first heard it. So you'd be sitting there, right, listening to God knows what, maybe Neil Young singing "Cowgirls in the Sand," and you'd start to think about feeling up Sue Moody in your dad's car. Just that luminous dial and the scratchy music and all those flickering, tugging memories. He didn't even have a fucking radio. You had to admit that was pretty low.

He lit up a cigarette and seemed about to cry. But it didn't come. The Wearies weren't made like that; they just got all hollow-feeling and bitter-empty inside, like there wasn't anything left. When would he ever learn anyway? Nobody was ever going to come and save him. He was going to have to do that all by himself. That is, if he even cared to be saved anymore. All he knew was that no one out there was going to make it their business to put Eamon Wearie's screwed-up life back on track. Which was probably just as well. He wouldn't know what to do with a woman like that anyway.

Suddenly he felt bad for Netti. She didn't have anybody to care about in this world either. She was nice, real nice. Smart as hell. And pretty. You bet. Lots of things. Best of all, she had a drinking problem too. Could never have too many drinking buddies in this lifetime.

He lit another cigarette and got out of the car, in the gray wet, no umbrella or anything, and started walking. He walked down to the park, a damp zombie, rehashing the whole bizarre adventure. Some sicko killing young boys. He puts a bad picture in the mail. That's how it got started, all right. No one had to tell him. The funny part is, he winds up in northern nowhere Pennsylvania not because of any Executioner business, but because he's got a hungry, hurting heart. Terrific. Sort of came up here for love. Or at least the possibility of it. Something like that.

Was there any such thing as love?

He wasn't sure anymore. You loved people, absolutely. Family, friends. You were grateful to be alive and grateful to go on living. At least he was. But he was talking about the love in storybooks, the love that went off like bright fireworks in the movies, that kind of love. Oh, there were always moments, no matter how short-lived. You became infatuated all the time. Someone was beautiful, and she just seemed to appear when you'd least expect it. But in the end it was always like some kind of drug that wore off much too quickly. He thought of Netti again, thought of her devotion to Richard Lonetree, and it helped in some small way. Sure there was love like that, how could there not be? Keep on believing.

When he got to the deserted park, he made his way to the bandstand, planting himself on one of the rotting, splintery steps. He tried to imagine a warm summer evening, a real dusky purple number, Old Glory waving in the foreground. He could practically see the high school band, with their tubas and French horns, playing for an audience of folding chairs, their cigarette tips glowing in the new darkness.

There must have been nights like that. It wasn't hard to picture the Executioner after that, among the good townspeople, a heavy, brooding presence. Suddenly Eamon was reminded of all the shit again. It didn't really go away, but at times he would relax and experience a kind of forgetting, as if Ashland were just another town and he were just another stranger passing through.

But he had the distinct sensation he was supposed to be here, a feeling that couldn't be shaken or really explained. It frustrated him, this uselessness, as if he personally had let those poor boys and their families down. He'd been over everything a thousand times in his mind, at least that many, sifting through all the little oddities and incongruities, as if the answer was to be found in the infinitesimal, in the tiniest clue. He was not one to seek out the big picture, in his work or in anything else, always feeling slightly outclassed, as if he could only take on so much. Just that there was no way to make sense of this world, the way it spilled over in every conceivable direction, a crazy, messed-up spilling of lives and living, so much of it beyond comprehension really, so much of it falling just short of meaning. When he'd get to thinking about all the different people out there, of the millions upon millions, numbers that defied imagination, all of them reaching out for their own peculiar brass rings, marching to their own deranged drummers, so much madness in that music, he'd feel so damn small and inconsequential, almost as if he didn't matter at all. It truly frightened him, this aspect of life. Maybe he'd be on the Beltway, in that unending stream of red taillight, or maybe he'd be in the middle of doing The Wave at Memorial Stadium. Whatever, it would just hit him, just like that, this overwhelming sense that he was just a speck, no more, invisible to most everyone. At these times of personal eclipse he would fill with terrible regret. Living was also about death and what you would leave behind, if you were lucky enough to leave so much as a trace. Among all those others, lost in traffic and the cries of the ballpark, Eamon would find himself wanting, just wanting to believe in God, in something, just something that might elevate that crazy mass of life to a higher purpose.

It was hard enough to give reality to just the ordinary parts of a day, from waking up to talking on the phone to watching foreign corners of the globe materialize on the ol' TV, to make it real. Then you throw in something like the Executioner business. How did God enter into that? That wasn't fair, he knew that wasn't fair. But Jesus, sweet Jesus, how did things ever get that out of whack? There was no understanding this sort of thing. There just wasn't. It was like what Netti had said in one of her letters. She said something about God not being inside of everyone, that you could see that, see people with no God in them. He wished he could remember her exact words, do them justice. He thought about it some more and he decided, not with any great conceit or anything, that he carried God with him. He certainly meant no one any harm, always tried to think the best of people. Sometimes he was too simple, not deep enough; shit, he knew that. But he wasn't a bad person. No, he always did the best he could and always regretted it when he fell a little short. He'd sure been lucky in life. God, he knew that, how could he not? He had great loving parents and a bunch of good brothers to grow up with and play games with, and they all lived pretty normally. That was a lot. He hoped someday, not too far off, that he'd get a chance to start over and have kids with someone new and that he'd return the favor, do what was done for him. It seemed only right, somehow.

He looked out at the muddy expanse before him, at the lake-sized puddles and general gloom, wishing it were a day for Frisbees and tawny girls in shorts, wishing for salvation. But all he saw was the diminishing rain and the uncomfortable sight of his own failure. At that moment he found himself missing Bunko. He'd never let something like a little rain dampen his spirits. The man knew not to dwell on the lost times, on those things unchangeable. That crummy old world just seemed to come right off him, like he was water-repellent or something. Why, if something was bothering him, getting him down, he'd just go to Pimlico and make one of his legendary, totally deranged bets. Put it all on a 300–1 shot and settle back with a double whiskey on the rocks, pal. Make it all go away. Damn straight. The man sure as hell didn't go blubbering on about what might've been, bore you shitless with the forgettable details. He knew enough to let go when the letting go was called for. Knew enough to live in the moment because sometimes the moment was all you had. Eamon wished he could have been a little bit more like him. Might've been easier that way.

He checked his watch, blinking the time like it was of some urgent concern; had to laugh at that. All he had was time. There was time to do everything now, all those things he'd been putting off, fishing trips and painting the house and reading all the classics he'd never gotten around to. Yeah, now he could go to fucking Club Med or something. Read *The Canterbury Tales* on the pink sand. Yeah, right. He had plenty of time, just not enough money probably. Yeah, it was a great time to be out of work. The papers were talking about a deepening recession, and he'd just lost his one rent-paying tenant to some psycho ward. Great. He was on a roll. Right off a fucking cliff.

With some effort he got up and started off again in the diminishing rain. He wondered if Mathews was serious about giving him a job. *Yeah, well, like, I'd have to think it over. Of course, as you can probably imagine, I've got me a whole bunch of other promising opportunities.* Yeah, right. Snap that sucker up in a lightning moment. Man, you had to have a way to make a living, have a place to go. The guys he knew out of work, shit, he didn't even want to think about it. He walked up Main, past the empty parking spaces and boarded-up storefronts, all that decay and loss. Ashland was just another ghostly town, lonely and desolate and godforsaken, past the point of no return. You could feel sorry for a town, you really could, like it was some out-of-luck person or something. The only light seemed to come from Buzz's Tap Room, neon winking in the darkened window, pale and somber. Put his face to the sooty glass and squeezed a peek. Okay, he was thinking about it. But what he saw quickly changed his mind. A blue-haired lady sat at one end of the vinyl bar, in front of an old, forgotten Christmas tree, a brittle little white thing with a hanging bulb or two. A tired barkeep used a rag on a mug. End of the earth, he thought. Last stop on life's long train ride. Take care, pardners. Ain't ready for that just yet.

You couldn't even go to a movie on a rainy day in Ashland. Imagine a town like that. The old theater, a beautiful, frightful Art Deco palace from the thirties— etched right there in the concrete, Our Playhouse, a Place For Laughter and Tears, All Are Welcome, 1935—seemed doubly mournful in the misty, sickly light. One of the glass display cases had been smashed in, while the other still had Luke Skywalker battling Darth Vader with a glowing angel of a sword. You could look in through the smudged doors, the wax fading in places, make out the ticket booth, the barren candy counter, the chewed-up maroon carpeting, all of it haunted now in the worst way, conjuring up days of magic and plenty, the piercing cries of children at a Saturday matinee.

It was a town without children. You didn't see them anywhere. He knew it was a school day, but it was more than that. There weren't any video arcades or pizza parlors to hang out in, no places for good times, not even a bowling alley as far as he could tell, as if no one cared enough. It would've been a bitch to grow up in a town like this. Eamon decided he probably would've wound up smoking a lot of dope in his room, gotten high listening to Springsteen or something else lonely-sounding.

Was the Executioner born here? Or was it, he wondered, more like bad places drew bad people? Whatever, Ashland was the right cave for the monster. It was hard to believe that the son of a bitch walked among them, went about his business like everybody else. He watched a big, slovenly fellow get out of a Ford pickup and hurry into the First National, her Greek pillars oppressive in the gray. For all he knew, that was their man. How could you tell? *How could you?* It was unbelievably strange that somebody could do so many normal, everyday kinds of things, their banking, the

215

grocery shopping, even mailing a letter, but then go home to mutilate kids in their basement. But people, he realized, even good, sane people, could do plenty, without even blinking, that went against their conscience and their God. In fact, if you really thought about it, most of us were full of contradictions, full of dirty little secrets, following certain rules at certain times, separating and differentiating the many parts of our lives, some more unsavory than others.

If only he could get this guy, stop him.

He started going over it again. What did he have to lose? His job? He'd already lost that. So what did they know? They knew nothing and everything. They had pictures, a postmark, a handwriting sample. They even had his finger-prints. Jesus, maybe it was about time they just went house to house with that. What the hell were they waiting for? Sooner or later he'd get hungry again and he'd be back out there, on the prowl, in a killing way. Or worse. He would just move. Go to a new place and start all over again.

It was there somewhere. Something they overlooked. It was probably obvious, too stupid to believe. And in a way, that would make the most sense. Because this guy was not a career criminal, he was some psychopath sociopath nut job. Why the hell wouldn't he make a mistake? Tell him that. He kept coming back to the original picture, to that little chamber of horrors. There was a beer can. So what? The guy drank Old Mallory. Not enough there. There was that elaborate model train set. But the Bureau had already canvassed every hobby shop in the area, looking for just anything really, customers that stood out, anything the least bit unusual. They even went so far as to check out Bear County subscribers to *Model Train Magazine,* doing every-thing in their power to narrow the scope, to find that one name which might crop up a second time. They'd done the same with the porno magazines too, finding to their chagrin that most of the subscribers were old hermits and widowers. Montrez and his men had gone the extra mile on every single element in that photograph. They'd gone to drug-stores and supermarkets interviewing clerks, searching for a man who bought yellow hair dye in bulk. It seemed as if they'd done everything in their power, just about.

Go over it again. Resist the feeling that it was pointless. Put your heart into it.

Bunko would've told him to stick with what they knew. Go with their own expertise. Those envelopes. The postmarks. Those three- and four-cent stamps. Thirty-year-old stamps. What the hell was that about? Was it about anything? The Bureau had interviewed stamp collectors in the area, gone to some trouble there. But they hadn't found anyone interested in those particular ones, commemorative stamps that didn't seem worth the trouble, worth only a few pennies more than when they were first issued. Stamps that, in 1957 and 1960, had been printed in the tens of millions, nothing rare about that. Think. Push. Go over it again.

Just then he thought of something stupid.

Too stupid.

He started to laugh to himself: It was just too idiotic.

What the hell. The post office was just across the street. There was no harm in asking.

He walked into a time warp. The framed portraits that dominated the snug office were of Benjamin Bailar and Gerald Ford, several postmaster generals and presidents ago. Anal probably would've approved. Other than that, it wasn't much, some letter boxes, an American flag, a small counter run by an old clerk with serious muttonchops.

"Can I help you?" he said genially enough.

Eamon approached. "I've got kind of an odd request, I'm afraid."

"All the better. Not much doing today anyhows."

Eamon pulled out his badge. He wasn't keen on pulling rank, but he thought it might help to jog the guy's memory.

"Oh my. One of the Pony Express boys. Oh my. I've read about you fellas. Mighty glamorous work. Sure, sure. I know all about it. You fellas are kind of like the James Bonds of the Service. Sure, sure. You got guns and everything. Good for you."

Eamon was embarrassed. It wasn't quite like that. But

there was a world of difference between the federal inspectors and the work Muttonchops did. But in some odd way, Muttonchops and Eamon shared a kind of bond. Maybe it was all those years surrounded by mail, hip-deep in the letters and their sealed secrets, privileged holders of the people's trust.

"Well," Eamon said, "I don't know about James Bond or anything. I mean, shit, we're not exactly secret agents, if you know what I mean. And what I've got to ask you is bound to seem a little weird, not the kind of thing Mr. Bond would likely be interested in."

"Go ahead, shoot," Muttonchops said, happy to be included.

"Well, what I want to ask you has to do with some old stamps. A couple in particular. And I want to find out if anyone you know has inquired about them or whatnot . . ."

Eamon knew it was practically ridiculous. Most people weren't going to go to the local post office in search of their collectible stamps. *Yeah, let's see, I want a roll of twenty-five-centers. And while you're at it, why don't you get me a Franklin from 1887.* Yeah, right. But he didn't have anything else. Who knew? Maybe this was the Executioner's bonehead play.

"Here's the thing," Eamon continued. "I was wondering if anyone had expressed an interest in, let's see, this three-cent stamp from 1957 that has this—"

"Sure, sure, that one about the teachers of America or some such thing. Oh, I told Purvis that we didn't carry stamps from no 1957. Wouldn't hear of it. Went on and on. Real oddball, that one. Finally directed Purvis to use the Scott catalogs, to order them in the mail."

Eamon was practically stunned. "What's Purvis's last name?" he managed to ask.

"Oh, no, that is the last name. Just can't think of the other part at the moment. Kind of odd-sounding, just like Purvis. Never liked that one to begin with. Screwball type, you know. Can't think of it, darnedest thing."

"Okay, that's all right. Do you know anything else, like what kind of work Purvis does?"

"Teacher, of course. But not just a regular one. Some kind of substitute teacher. Darnedest thing. Having a person like that around kids. Purvis just ain't right, if you ask me."

In that instant Netti's throwaway line came back to him. About the books, on the nightstand next to the bed. *You'd have to almost be a substitute teacher to do all of them.* Jesus Christ. He had to get to Montrez.

Their operations center was in one of the boarded-up storefronts on Main, right next to what had once been Woolworth's. They had done some job of transforming the old dress shop. New industrial carpeting had been slapped down, and they'd put in enough fancy computer hardware to give Houston Control a run for its money. It was a picture of activity: phones continually bleeping; a dozen display terminals lit up for business; men and women, dressed with the same starchy, well-groomed care of Mathews, moving around the room with the same supremely confident manner. There was a map on one wall that looked more like a light show, flickering with red dots.

"Called a pattern map, latest new toy," Mathews told him, noticing where his attention was lodged. "The computer puts in possibilities, and we use it in an educated attempt to gauge our man's next move."

"I see," Eamon said, even though he didn't really see at all. He was impatient as hell. "Listen, I really got to talk to you."

"C'mon, let me introduce you around first. Over here is Hal Linse, our main strategist. Hal, Lieutenant Wearie, Postal. I think you're aware of his work. I'm hoping he might join up. Why don't you tell him what we're up to."

"Yes, of course," the blond Aryan said perfunctorily, extending his hand. Eamon thought of that second banana on "Man From U.N.C.L.E.," the one with the funny-sounding name. He hadn't seen that show in years. "Kept us in the ball game, Lieutenant. I thought we almost hit a home run with that Harold Kingsley business. As strange as it seemed. With the involvement of parapsychology. Because Kingsley certainly fit the bill. Even collected model trains."

219

"I know, I know," Eamon said. "Listen, there's someth—"

Before he could finish, Linse said: "Yes, we're certainly convinced it's someone connected with the schools. In one capacity or another. For all we know, it could be a bus driver. Or someone who works in the administrative offices. Certainly we keep coming back to that Royal 500 typewriter."

"Listen," Eamon said, anxious to get a word in. "Something just came up. I have no idea if it's a false alarm or anything. Old-timer who handles the counter at the post office just gave me a piece of information that seems a little unbelievable. Seems there was this guy Purvis who was asking about buying three-cent stamps not too long ago. Get this, this Purvis fellow is interested in that one about honoring the teachers, that one from 1957. And wait. Here's the kicker: Purvis is some kind of substitute teacher. He's a fucking teacher. Hey, why are you looking at me so funny?"

It was Linse. He just stood there, his eyes momentarily vacant.

"What is it, Hal?" Mathews said. "You've got me worried. You look like you've just seen the devil or something."

"Purvis. That name." He was coming to, adjusting to this new information. "Came up just yesterday. For the second time. That ditzy girl at the *Gazette* remembered some unusual calls. Seems this Purvis teacher volunteered candidates for that student athlete of the month column."

"Well, that doesn't strike me as particularly unusual, Hal," Mathews said.

"Thing is, I got the feeling that Purvis was very forceful and adamant on the phone. Perhaps even a little demented."

"Jesus," Eamon exclaimed. "This is almost too much, too good to be true. Just sounds like this Purvis fellow is our man."

"There's one problem, though," Linse said, still looking a little vacant. "This Purvis isn't a man. She's a she. But there's something else, something more. She was on that short list. You know, the three teachers who taught in Philly at the time of the abductions. The boys. Farrety and Winkle."

Eamon asked, "What's her first name?" He said it in such a way that it came out sounding like a demand.

"Horatia. Horatia Purvis," the strategist replied.

The rain had stopped, but the sky was dark and billowy. There weren't any children out on the playground, just empty jungle gyms and seesaws and swings, all looking somewhat desolate under black skies. School buses had already positioned themselves in the circular drive out front of the Birch Avenue Elementary School. It was a long, rectangular, one-story structure, red brick and windows, nothing special. Mathews pulled the company Lincoln in the empty space reserved for the principal.

They hadn't said much coming over. Actually, there wasn't much to say. There was no sense getting worked up yet. After all, they had an ugly little picture of the Executioner naked—so they knew the guy owned a penis. But maybe someone else was involved. Eamon had to credit Mathews: He was smart enough, or curious enough, not to discount anything.

Horatia Purvis was substituting for Stella Brinkman, who'd broken both legs in a skiing accident. Her third grade class was in room 18. They had a few minutes to kill before school let out. It was odd being there. Everything was so small. It brought back old memories from long silent corners of Eamon's mind. He noticed all the bright lunch boxes under the coat racks in the hall and remembered that he'd begged his mom for a Green Hornet box just like the other guys'. Dumphey Rickles, a spitball enthusiast and ardent collector of Matchbox cars, was his best friend. Dumphey had gone on to own a chain of successful tanning salons across Long Island. A putz, just the same.

They passed the gym and heard the screams and shouts. They looked in—the doors all had window-heads—and saw that game with the red rubber balls. Dodge ball, that was it. The boys and girls were doing their best to assassinate each other.

221

Mathews shook his head and let out one of his friendly chuckles. "I forgot about all that pent-up energy. Takes you back, doesn't it? Always loved gym and recess and cookies. The rest of it always made me want to pee in my pants," the federal tough guy concluded.

"I know what you mean." And he did. Eamon hated going to school. He would bury his head under the covers and oversleep and pretend to be sick, just do anything not to go. But in a way it was worse if you showed up late. Then you had to walk into that room with everyone staring, or worse, laughing like fucking banshees as the teacher examined your note.

They walked down that silent hallway of the mind, Eamon remembering Mrs. Polesky, the battle-ax of battle-axes. He dreaded being called upon—and you could be sure old Polesky knew this. He'd sweat and he would look up at that clock whose hands moved so interminably and he would pray not to hear his name. She always got him. Then that slow walk up to the blackboard, as bad as facing any firing squad.

They looked into classrooms, seeing the serious, pouty-eyed expressions. Little girls still had pigtails, and little boys still didn't know the correct answer. The tiny desks still had slats for your pencils, and they still opened up so that you could put your books and other junk in them. At one point, Eamon caught the old note-passing ritual in progress, the teacher's back to the whole thing. Some things never changed, and it pleased him somehow.

The halls were plastered with all sorts of crayon drawings. The same ones from when he was a boy. Big, bright yellow suns and green green trees with little red apples on them. The kids still drew their moms and dads in stick figure, and the boys especially liked to make fighter planes with bullets shooting out of them. They passed a hall monitor, a freckled fellow with a silver badge, and he gave them a little salute.

They were still a couple of minutes early. They stood there, outside the room, fidgeting, glancing down at their watches, trying to make small talk.

"So anyway, what's our man look like?" Mathews joked.

Eamon went to the door, and what he saw stopped him cold. Forgetting for the moment that Horatia Purvis was a huge, dumpy-looking woman with a mop of yellow hair—which in itself was hard enough to forget—what seized his attention was the blackboard. They were doing arithmetic. But it wasn't the simple addition and subtraction that held his attention. It was Horatia Purvis's name. She'd written it in the top left-hand corner of the board, under the letters of the alphabet, that sequential series of green cue cards.

It was the way she dotted her *i*'s. With that fucking Have a Nice Day happy face.

His heart began to race like crazy.

21

The yellow tractor sat in the yard, useless. It was too delicate a job for that, unearthing bodies. He watched from behind the white picket fence—yes, if it wasn't a white picket number—and police barricades. It was a nice little house, white shingles with baby blue shutters, three stories high with a mansard roof, nowhere hinting at the darkness. She was an avid horticulturist besides, planting begonias and yellow roses everywhere the eye could see. Of course, they had to dig most of them up.

It was strange to think that at the same time they were also excavating around her old house in Philadelphia. They'd already found ten bodies there, including the mother's. Add to that the five so far in Ashland and you had one sick little story they'd be telling for some time. You could count on it. There'd be movies and books and all sorts of stuff, anything to cash in, and it might not ever go away. It was weird to think that his name would forever be linked with that of Horatia Purvis, the Executioner. He had always dreamed of a kind of immortality, doing that something which would be remembered. For a bad moment he wondered if Purvis had also had dreams like that.

The reporters and the photographers and the TV crews

were camped outside with their scopes and scanners, whirring and flashing. It was funny, you got used to it after a short while, like it was no big deal. It seemed like you could get used to anything really. He even recognized a famous anchorman from one of the networks wandering about, a little lost-looking really. Neighbors collected and pointed, the expressions on their faces not so much of shock or surprise but of tasty speculation and interest. They stood chatting and gossiping across the street, in the terrible sunshine, as if none of it was very real on this buttercup of a day.

And Eamon had to agree with them. There was nothing very real about any of it. Not that he didn't believe the story of Horatia Purvis. Though he had to admit he wasn't very grounded on the subject of hermaphrodites. People with two sets of sex organs was not the usual conversational fare at the Wearie dinner table. It had been all but impossible to tell from that picture that the hooded Executioner owned a pair of sagging breasts and a vagina the size of a buttonhole.

Sick and sordid were the words he kept hearing the TV people use. He guessed they were as good as any others. There weren't any words to convey the horror, nothing so short and sweet, that might make it all go bye-bye. There was no way to look into the minds of the Purvises of the world, sick, swirling places where rhyme and reason slipped under like so much waterlogged debris. Who'd want to look in there anyway?

Words were something in short supply today. Eamon had never been interviewed before and was having trouble coming up with good, new things to say. That woman reporter from the big Philadelphia paper was only too happy to help him out, supplying the sharp, newspaper-sounding blurbs. He nodded his head a lot and Gail would say that's good, just what I need. She was thinking about writing a book about the case. Wanted to get together to discuss sewing up the rights to his story. Told him she'd already been on the phone with her agent. He nodded some more. Gail was quite attractive, and it didn't seem like the worst thing in the world to get together for dinner and taping sessions. We'll cut you in, she kept saying. Whatever, he said. Whatever.

Of course, Gail wasn't the only one interested in his story. Ted Koppel was going to interview him later on for his show "Nightline." And he was already fielding requests from that "Current Affair" program and lots of local news shows across the country. On-the-scene producers kept telling him about their satellite hookups and the miracle of instavision. Some of them were even willing to pay for his Warholian fifteen minutes. He didn't know about that, or any of the rest of it for that matter. He sure as hell didn't want to be just another viper, another moron going off at the mouth because the meter was running.

Mostly he was just worried because he didn't have a suit to wear for the Koppel thing. He'd have to make time to break away, go to some store. Hell, his mom and dad would be watching. Wanted to come across right. He was already busy putting to memory certain choice phrases. Didn't want to sound like a complete imbecile.

One other thing bothering him: What if they figured out what an accident it all was? He'd come up there looking for Netti, for God knows what reason, and wound up—by some dumb stroke of luck—solving this whole sick business. Try explaining that. *Yeah, I was fucked up, you know. Got in my car—yeah, the busted-up Pontiac over there. Drove to see this chick. No, didn't know her exactly. We're pen pals. That's it. Well, you know, she was suicidal and I was pretty down and so what the hell. That's your story, Ted. Nothing to it.*

Not on your life. He'd try and keep it to what they knew. They'd managed to put a lot of it together already. Like they had a pretty good idea that Horatia had spent the first thirteen years of her life as a boy named Howie. Then you threw into the mix some nut of a mother who was too ashamed to bring Howie to a doctor at the first sign of his budding breasts. Something like that. Freak of nature. So good old Mom just changed his name. Changed his sex. Put him in a dress and said he was a she. Something like that.

And so they lived with that dirty secret for a while. Nice. A real family affair.

He'd have to work on it. Iron the kinks out. All he knew was that he didn't want to take too much credit, go that whole hero route. He'd been lucky from the start, gotten more breaks than anyone really deserved. Don't think he didn't know that. Here he was thinking of the first real break in the case, checking out that nauseating little magazine, *Boy Love*. Just went from weird to weirder. Christ, the whole damn thing was mondo bizarro. Forget about Horatia Purvis. What about everybody else? They'd encountered plenty of strangeness along the way. It came to him in like some kind of fast-forward montage. Thinking of that degenerate Rube Fuchs in his Sistine Chapel office. Those decimated families. Barb Jake acting like some kind of Stepford wife. Seeing the pale, haunted face of Figg Lauterberg, Beck's twin, in that moonlight, all that blue snow. Suddenly, for no clear reason, he remembered those girls from Kansas. Paula and Wiley. He didn't know why, what they had to do with anything. On their way to Lou Reed's apartment, for Christ's sake. Just kids, never had a chance. He said a little prayer for them. God look after you, he said into the void. Richard Lonetree's paintings swirled into view. That musty old barn. His red setter stirring at the foot of the easel. But it was those big, bright pop art canvases that grabbed you. Pictures of cows—cows. There were decent people out there, no doubt about it. And Richard Lonetree must have been one of them judging by the way Netti loved him. Kind, sweet Netti, such a lost and gentle soul. To think of someone like that wanting to kill herself. What a waste, what a terrible waste that would be. He determined, then and there, to call her as soon as he got back home. Invite her to Charm City for a weekend. Show her around, take her to dinner, treat her special. Try to tell her that she mattered to this world. And, he had to admit, he could've used a friend like her, someone nice and smart to talk to, who might listen to him from time to time. That's all he asked.

There were other things. Things he'd never really forget.

Famous Barry. Guy who talks to dead people. He'd never get over that. Or maybe he would. Maybe he just wouldn't think about it too much. Seemed like that little fellow in the disco threads got everything right. It got him thinking about his grandfather. If the old man managed to finagle his way into the Big H, well, that was truly a thing of beauty. Somehow it made sense that Seamus Wearie would wind up doing time as his guardian angel. Now, there was a man who could drink with the best of them, who had a big thirst for life, no matter that the taste was often, at best, bittersweet. Shit. Heaven and hell. Maybe he'd have to make some changes in his own life.

That silent tractor just sat there, as if it were there to dig a swimming pool or something. Like what else could it be there for? A special FBI team had been called in to dig up the bodies. That's all they did. That was their specialty. He saw those kids' drawings again. The ones in the Birch Avenue Elementary School, lining the hallways. Those green green trees with all those little red apples. It lasted only a moment.

He had some choices to make, he knew that. Tony Montrez had called with an offer just that morning. It was perfect, kind of thing he always wanted. A call-your-own-shots kind of deal. He tried to picture himself in the J.C. Penny suit and the dark glasses, not to mention the three-dollar haircut, all standard issue. Somehow it didn't quite take hold. Maybe he'd been at Dead Letters too long, lost a certain edge. These things were, of course, hard to say, but over the years, passing so much faster than they used to, he'd learned to temper his expectations, not wanting to be one of the bitter and disappointed, that vitriolic majority. He tended, for better or worse, to play it safe, more likely to take the known over the unknown, always seeking sanctuary and comfort in the ordinary, a glass of beer, a twi-night doubleheader, a good day's work, never wanting to push it. It was his greatest weakness, this lackluster acceptance, this giving in. But it was also, he felt, the one thing that kept him sane, that left him whole and impassive.

That's why he'd probably wind up back at Dead Letters. It

was what he knew and it's probably where he belonged, and sometimes that was enough. At least there was always Bunko. He'd already been on the phone with his buddy, and it didn't take much to see how thrilled Bunk was. Kid, this is a big day, he kept saying. I'm so fuckin' proud of ya, Jesus fuckin' Christ, you just don't know. But Eamon did know—you could hear it in his familiar boom, this warmth, a kind of tenderness. But he also knew that Bunk's mood had greatly improved since finding out Anal and the Two Puckers were being shipped off to the D.C. Bunker. Kid, he said delightedly, it was all your doing that done this.

It had been his doing, after all. There was even talk of a commendation or some such nonsense. Just give him a raise. Fuck the medals. First thing he'd probably do was take some personal time. Take a trip somewhere. Clear his head out. Hell, maybe he'd go see that fucked-up brother of his. Drive down to the south of Florida. He'd always wanted to charter a boat out of the Keys. Go hunting for marlin and tuna on that turquoise water.

It was hard to think of all these things in the bright bright sunshine. It was not a time to dwell, to rehash it all. It was the beginning of May, and the spring would always be a time of soft breezes and solid blue skies. It would always be so, no matter what, no matter what ugliness you found under the sun.

Printed in the United States
By Bookmasters